IDENTITY THEFT

IDENTITY THEFT

BASED (LOOSELY) ON TRUE EVENTS

JOHN G. HARTNESS

Charlotte, NC

FALSTAFF
BOOKS
WWW.FALSTAFFBOOKS.COM

For Addie and Bonnie Alexander, sisters in everything but blood.

CHAPTER 1

I probably should have just forgotten about the twenty-six dollars. That's what I thought as the three-hundred-pound man with a black widow's peak, four chins, and more prison tattoos than I have liver spots stuck my feet in a bucket of water. And no, I was not at some bizarre Eastern European nail salon for a mani-pedi.

Nope, I was in a warehouse near enough to Walt Disney World to smell the vomit from Space Mountain, and I was pretty sure my afternoon was about to go from unpleasant to downright painful. I was tied to a metal folding chair with zip ties, and not the little skinny ones that are such a pain in the butt on packaging. No, these were the industrial-strength, fasten-things-to-other-things-for-years-on-end kind of zip ties, the ones that are like a quarter inch wide and longer than my ex-husband's dick.

Wait, that's a pretty low bar. These things were long. And thick. Aaaannnnd now everything's a penis. Goddammit, I need to get laid. But now was neither the time nor the company for such as that.

But back to Andre, with the tattoos, the bucket of water, and surprisingly soft hands for a mobster and I assume torturer. To be fair, he hadn't actually tortured me yet, even though the water was a little colder than I would have preferred. I figured the torture was coming, though. How else would he find out what he wanted to know? Of course, I didn't *know* what

1

he wanted to know, whatever that was. So this was probably going to hurt. A lot.

"This will hurt a lot less if you just tell me what I want to know," Andre said, proving that we had a head start on developing that really simpatico torturer/torturee relationship that you read about in all the trendy psychological journals.

"Sure," I said brightly. I gave him my best "I'm a totally innocent middle-aged divorced woman with one kid in college, another in high school, and no idea how I'm going to come up with tuition for two in a couple of years" smile. It comes naturally. The expression, not so much the smiling. "What is it you want to know, exactly? I'll be happy to share."

He froze in place, a pair of jumper cables in one hand. By the expression on his face, this was not an answer he was expecting. It made sense, I guess. I bet most of the people he tied up and tortured weren't terribly forthcoming. They probably had a higher pain tolerance than me, though. Look, two kids proved a couple things to me. One, I can tolerate an exceptional amount of pain and smile when it's all over if I get something incredible out of it. Like my daughters, Jess and Kristen, who are both amazing. But it also taught me Thing Two, which is that pain really really sucks and I want to do everything in my power to avoid it.

I have spent a lot of the last sixteen years focusing on Thing Two. Pretty much every day since Kristen was born, as a matter of fact. My focus on Thing Two has saved me from a lot of things: yoga, spin class, water aerobics, running, cycling, and CrossFit. It has not saved me from my belly, boobs, and ass hanging onto the baby weight like it's a life preserver, nor has it turned me into some kind of badass Linda Hamilton type who does pull-ups on her bed frame in the insane asylum. So when Andre asked me what I knew, I just needed him to narrow the field a little, and I'd be happy to tell him everything.

"What do you know about our operation in Orlando? I don't want to hurt you, but I will if you try to hold anything back."

Well, shit. See, this was going to be a problem. Because I didn't know anything about their operation in Orlando. I didn't even know who "they" were, except for Andre, which probably wasn't even his name, but that's what I decided to call him because he looked a little like an Andre. Probably because of the wrestler. The one that was in *The Princess Bride*. I think his name was Andre.

Your mind goes funny places when you're tied to a chair with your feet in a bucket of water and a giant gangster standing in front of you with jumper cables in his hand and a determined look on his face. But no matter where my mind went, it didn't dig up any long-lost (or short-lost, for that matter) information on "they" and their "operation." Because I didn't know any. And that was going to get me electrocuted within sniffing distance of the most magical place on earth.

I laughed. It was one of those dinner party faux pas laughs, the kind you make when you accidentally flick a booger across the table and it lands in the hostess's soup course. It was one of those laughs that said "I'd really rather be on any other continent right now, and that includes Antarctica, and I don't even like penguins." I laughed, and said, "So, here's the thing, Andre. Can I call you Andre? I feel like we should be on a first name basis at this point, don't you?"

"My name is not Andre. It's Barry."

"Figures," I said. "But it fits the movie in my head a lot better if you're an Andre. Or a Gregor, like the Russian frenemy guy on *Arrow*. Don't judge me. You know one more scene of Stephen Amell on that salmon ladder and you'd think about switching teams. Unless you're already on that team. That's unfair of me, to make heterosexual my default position just because I happen to be straight. Mostly straight. I mean, sexuality is a continuum, right? Are you gay, Andre?"

Andre/Gregor stared at me in a way my paternal grandfather would have called "poleaxed." I'd never understood the expression before that very moment. But looking at Gregdre's face (see what I did there? Like Brangelina, or Bennifer, but way scarier, with more tattoos. Well maybe not. I think Angelina has gotten a lot of ink done in the past decade or so.) I understood exactly what the word poleaxed meant. Too bad I was probably going to die before I got to tell Grandpa Henry. Also too bad Grandpa Henry died fifteen years ago, but he and I are both pretty much over that by now.

"You are a very strange lady," Andor said (Definitely Gregdre. Andor sounds too much like the planet with the Ewoks from *Return of the Jedi*.).

"Oh, Gregdre," I said. "You have no idea."

Then my best friend drove through the side of the warehouse in my 2012 Prius, and I was so happy to see her I didn't even think about how much this trip was going to make my insurance go up. Well, I didn't think about it much, anyway.

CHAPTER 2

Three Days Earlier

I stared at the screen, mouth hanging open, as I felt my blood pressure rise. I closed my eyes, took three deep breaths, counted to ten, then counted to ten in French and Spanish, wished for a moment that I was fluent in either French or Spanish, and that I knew how to count to ten in more than three languages, because for at least the past three years, my rage has definitely been pegged at the "need to count to ten in at least six languages to not scream at people" point on the dial. Then I opened my eyes.

It was still there.

I was looking at my bank account online. Not a big thing. The kind of thing a lot of people do every day. Especially people like me, who have just barely clawed their way back into some semblance of financial…not security, so much as not complete catastrophe. Everything looked about right, but as I gave a quick look at my recent transactions, something caught my eye. It was a twenty-six-dollar charge from ChowSprint, a food delivery service.

No big deal, right? Everybody knows that delivery services are over-priced as hell, but in the middle of a pandemic, who wants to sit inside a restaurant with a whole bunch of plague-bearing assholes that you didn't want breathing in your air before they might be carrying the closest thing

4

we'll ever get to Stephen King's Captain Trips? Thanks for that, Steve, by the way. If the rest of your books come true, I'm road-tripping to Maine to kick your ass. Assuming I don't get eaten by a big fluffy St. Bernard or run over by a sentient car.

But I've never ordered from ChowSprint. I use FoodieRide, or Meal Locator, or I just dangle the keys in front of my sixteen-year-old daughter and tell her if she'll go in and pick up takeout, I'll let her drive. That last one saves me a lot on delivery charges and tips, but it costs me nearly as much in Xanax and vodka.

I clicked on the transaction just as my email dinged and the little red circle with a "1" in it popped up on my screen telling me I had new mail. This caused more of a dilemma than it should for any reasonable person, because I was torn between following up on this fraudulent charge and giving in to my ever-so-slightly OCD loathing for having unread notifications on my computer screen. Seriously, those little red bubbles make me twitchy. I once borrowed Jess, my oldest daughter's, phone and almost broke out in hives at the number of unread emails and ignored voice mails she had on there. I literally could barely dial the thing, my hands were shaking so hard.

When I was done with the call, I handed the phone back to her just as a thought struck me. "How many of those unheard voice mails are from me?"

"I don't know, Mom. I haven't listened to them." She might be twenty years old now, but she somehow has never lost the fourteen-year-old "duh" in her voice when she speaks to me. I've stopped wondering when she'll grow out of it and now wonder if she'll live to get her undergraduate degree.

So I was in a real conundrum. Do I chase down this ChowSprint thing, or do I check my email? I realized that I'd spent longer thinking about checking my email than it would have taken me to check, read, and respond to the email, so I clicked on the little postage stamp icon.

"Son of a bitch." Well, the point was moot, because checking my email directly led to me digging deeper into the mysterious charge. The email was a ChowSprint order confirmation sitting in my inbox smirking up at me like a smartassed housecat. Which I know good and well is redundant. I clicked on it, and the whole situation became clearer.

There was a ChowSprint delivery order for a pair of BobbyRay's Italian subs, no lettuce, no tomato, extra oil and vinegar, extra mayo on garlic parmesan loaf. Apparently the two most whitebread identity thieves in America had somehow hacked my debit card and ordered really awful subs with it. I mean, seriously. Extra mayo? That's like adding bland on top of your bland. *Now* I was offended. I mean, it's one thing to steal my identity, but to order shitty delivery with it?

No. This would not stand. I had to take action. So I did what any forty-seven-year-old woman in America does when something egregious happens—I posted it to my social media. Within seconds I had ten angry face emojis, a couple of caring hug emojis, and three seemingly inappropriate eggplant emojis. But I had done my duty to the world. I had shared my outrage with all eight hundred and twenty-three of my cyber-friends.

Now it was time to cancel my card and see what could be done about getting these little mayo-loving bastards brought to justice.

THREE HOURS LATER, my hands hurt, my bangs were plastered to my face with rage-sweat, I had circles under my armpits, wet lines under my boobs, a canceled debit card, and a margarita in a forty-four-ounce Big Gulp cup that I dug out from under the back seat of my car and gave a quick wash before deciding that half a pint of tequila would kill any germs still living in the cup and just threw a bendy straw and a buttload of booze in that bad boy.

I was sitting in a faux Adirondack plastic lawn chair on my back patio, trying to remember if it was supposed to be summer or fall, (I live in North Carolina, and it's often difficult to gauge the seasons. We basically have three weeks of Winter, then there's Getting On Towards Summer, Summer, Holy Shit It's Hot Summer, Oh Yeah It's Still Summer, Steamy Moldy Summer Because It Rains Every Goddamn Afternoon, Almost Not Summer Anymore, Fake Fall To Remind You Why You Keep Living, Don't Forget About Summer, Oh Hell No I'm Not Through With You Yet Bitch Summer, and then three weeks of Fall.) looking out at the small patch of dandelions and other assorted weeds that passed for my back yard, and trying to remember if I had any more tequila when my best friend Rhonda walked through my sliding glass door and out onto the patio.

Rhonda has a key. Most people give their neighbors a key to their house after they've lived next door to them for a few years, built up a rapport over conversation, wine, and backyard grilling. I gave Rhonda a key the day after we moved with the ominous and oh-so-prescient words, "Hi, I'm Lexi, I'm your new neighbor, and I have a problem with keys. As in I lock myself out of places. A lot. Usually in really embarrassing circumstances. So if you'd just hang onto this key and not ask too many questions about what I am or am not wearing when I come ask you for it, I'd really appreciate it."

I've met me. I long ago decided that the minor embarrassment of walking next door in my bathrobe (or maybe less) and asking for my spare key because I was just about to step into a bubble bath when I remembered that the latest issue of *Entertainment Weekly* should be in my mailbox and without thinking about the fact that I was wearing nothing but a bathrobe (or less) and a smile, I walked out to my mailbox only to realize when I got back to the porch blissfully unobserved that I had closed the door. Which locked automatically, because teenagers and remembering to lock doors are not things that exist together in nature. I may or may not have decided this after a pair of helpful policemen found me trying to climb through my own now-broken bedroom window while attempting to avoid broken glass, the stickers on the holly bushes beside my house, and the indignity of showing the entire neighborhood exactly how long it's been since my last Brazilian. I failed at avoiding literally all of those things.

So Rhonda has a key. And in the eight years we've been next-door neighbors, she's become my confidant, my wingwoman, my shoulder to cry on, my staunchest supporter, and the person designated to talk me out of my really terrible ideas. It's to the point that before I go home with someone from a bar, I am under strict instructions to text Rhonda his name, cell phone number, address, and a photo. Rhonda watches a lot of *Criminal Minds.* A. Lot.

Unfortunately, it's been a long time since I went to a bar, much less hooked up with anyone there, so I haven't had to avail myself of that particular service Rhonda has on offer. I have taken advantage of all the rest, numerous times before, during, and after my divorce. More before than during or after. You might think that odd, or possibly callous. One of these days I'll let you meet my ex, and then you can decide whether or not that assessment is valid.

"Day drinking on a Thursday? And we've moved on to the big-ass sippy cup already? What the hell, babe? Hold that thought. Whatever it is, I'm betting I'm gonna need some mental reinforcement of my own to listen to it, so what are we drinking?"

"I'm drinking a margarita. I'm also out of margarita mix and tequila, but you know where the liquor cabinet is, so go for it. Just stay out of the Absolut Orange, that's Jess's."

"Her shitty vodka is safe from me. I prefer my booze to taste like booze, not breakfast. You still got that bottle of Maker's I brought over for New Year's?"

"Unless you drank it," I replied. "I only drink clear liquor. It's got less calories."

"You know that's bullshit, right?" Rhonda asked.

I put one hand over my ear and shouted "Lalalalalalala!" I tried to put both hands over my ears, but my right was occupied with a massive cup of slushy alcoholic wonderment, so I ended up with one hand and a giant sippy cup of margarita pressed to my ears.

I heard the sliding glass door close, because Rhonda was raised in the South and the concept of "don't let the cold air out" is for more than just refrigerators. A moment later, she came back out and plopped down beside me with my big mixing bowl full of ice, a bottle of Maker's Mark, and a handful of straws.

"What in the hell are you doing?" I asked, leaning forward to watch as she set the bowl down on the patio between our chairs. She then deposited the whiskey bottle in the center of the bowl and twisted it around until it was buried in ice cubes. Then she proceeded to squeeze the ends of the straws, fitting one into another until she had an incredible alcohol conveyance system that allowed her to keep her Maker's on ice, sitting on the ground where it wouldn't freeze her, and still lean back in her chair and drink comfortably. It was like an alcoholic Rube Goldberg machine.

"Okay, spill," Rhonda said, leaning back in her chair and straightening out her long legs. She was in shorts, of course. Rhonda always wore shorts if she could help it. If I were 6'1" in bare feet and had legs like an Olympic cyclist, I would, too. I'm not, and I don't, so the only thing I was showing to the sun that day were my pudgy little feet and my arms.

"My identity was stolen," I said, feeling the scowl crawl back over my face. I dissolved it with the application of a huge slurp of margarita.

"Holy shit! Did they get into your bank account? Did they sign up for credit cards with your name? Did they order a whole bunch of dirty magazines and have them sent to your house without you knowing about it? Can I see them? Are there any good ones?" Rhonda leaned forward fast enough that she got her straw tangled up in her big red curls, and I

8

laughed at her. "Lexi! This is serious stuff! They could do some real damage to you! And did they send you dirty magazines? Because I've heard of people doing that."

"No, they didn't send me dirty magazines. Are there still dirty magazines? I thought everybody just looked at porn on the internet nowadays."

"Some people are pornography purists," Rhonda said with a haughty sniff.

"Anyway, Miss Purist," I continued. "No, it was nothing like that. They just hacked into some site where I had my debit card information stored and bought some stuff."

"Oh my god! What did they buy? Was it guns? Were they cartel people? Was it human trafficking? Did they use your card to buy a little virgin white girl? I hear that's what people do."

"Okay—one, I am blocking YouTube on your computer. Two, I'm pretty sure there's not enough money in my account to rent a well-used hooker, much less buy a virgin child. And three, no, it was nothing so dramatic. Damn, where do you think we are, on an episode of *NCIS*?"

"I wish. Can it be New Orleans, though? I have had a thing for Scott Bakula ever since *Quantum Leap*. So what did they buy?"

"Lunch."

"Huh?" Rhonda looked confused. Befuddled, even. Maybe downright confounded, if I was to put a finer point on it. Her big green eyes peered at me over the rims of her heart-shaped sunglasses and her eyebrows were stretching for her hairline like it was a life preserver and they were going down for the third time.

"They bought sub sandwiches from ChowSprint and had them delivered to Orlando."

"From Monroe? That'll be a hell of a delivery fee."

"I'm pretty sure they ordered from a BobbyRay's in Orlando," I said.

"Oh. Okay. What else?"

"What do you mean what else?"

"I mean what else did they buy with your stolen debit card information, or are you telling me you are sitting out here in the back yard in the middle of a weekday afternoon drinking a margarita the size of a small planet while your daughter is inside doing video-conferenced Trigonometry class because somebody ordered lunch with your money?"

"Ummm…" I paused, because Rhonda can be a little hard to follow when she gets on a roll, and sometimes I need to take a minute to

JOHN G. HARTNESS

untwangle her sentences. This was one of those times. Or maybe I was drunk. Could be both, I suppose. "The second one?"

"The one where they didn't steal nothing but a couple of sub sandwiches?"

"Yeah, that's the one. With extra mayo." I probably put a disproportionate amount of disdain into that bit, but I really don't like mayonnaise.

"Honey," Rhonda started, and I knew I was about to get a lecture. "Honey" is Southern for "dumbass," and whenever a Southern woman starts a sentence with "honey" and she's not a Waffle House waitress, you're probably about to be informed exactly to what degree you are a dumbass, and how much of your dumbassery everybody around you has now been exposed to, and she's going to use small words, and short sentences, and do everything in her power to make sure you understand her, which will be no small feat, since it is understood, with a single word at the very beginning of her sentence, that you are a dumbass and thus have difficulty understanding even the simplest of topics. In case you haven't figured it out, Southern is a complicated language with a lot of nuance. It's taken me thirty years to start to learn it all, and I'm constantly baffled that my daughters, both of whom were born here, innately understand things that still trip me up after all this time. I think it has something to do with overexposure to sweet tea through my breast milk.

"Honey," Rhonda said, looking at me with something akin to pity and something like fear that I would maybe accidentally stab myself to death with my own plastic straw by accident. "You look like you've run a marathon today. And not the newfangled ones where people train for months and then go drinking when they're done. No, more like the first one, where the dude died at the end of the race. Your hair is some kind of weird rat's nest, your makeup might as well not have happened at all—"

"That's because it didn't. I wasn't planning on seeing anybody but Kristen today, and I do not make a habit of getting made up for anyone whose first view of the world was from my vagina directed outward."

"Oh. Nevermind that bit, then. But that does not excuse the hair, the impressive underboob sweat you've got going on, or the day drinking. Especially not if you're telling me that your tragic and traumatic identity theft was what, twenty bucks?"

"Twenty-six. Delivery, remember. That shit's pricy."

"Okay, twenty-six dollars. And that was enough to make you devolve into this wreck of womanhood instead of the fine flower of femininity that you typically display?"

That last part was a shot. I'm about as much a fine flower of femininity as I am a rocket scientist. (I'm not, by the way. I'm a middle school music teacher. I have not the faintest idea about rocket science. But if you want somebody to teach your son or daughter the difference between a flute and a saxophone, I'm your girl.) "It wasn't the money. Okay, it was partially the money. But mostly it was the pain in the ass. The debit card still had Peter's name on it, too, so we had to have a conference call to get it canceled, despite the fact that he's not on the account anymore. Then I called the Orlando police, but they told me I'd have to call the local police, since the victim is here."

"But the crime was there," Rhonda said.

"Those are literally the exact words that came out of my mouth," I said, nodding. "That logic did not have an effect on their decision."

"And I'm gonna guess that the Monroe police department wasn't interested, because the bad guys are in Florida," she said.

"Nailed it," I agreed. "And the FBI didn't give a shit, because it wasn't enough money for them to be interested, despite it technically being a federal crime to use the internet to steal stuff across state lines. Oh, and when I called the company whose site I'm pretty sure got hacked, their customer service person either didn't care, or didn't understand what I was trying to tell him, because he kept offering me a refund and asking if he could bundle my cable, phone, and internet service."

"Did he work for the cable, phone, or internet company?"

"No."

"Okay, so that explains the disheveled appearance. What do you blame for the day drinking?"

"Well, despite the fact that I am a grown-ass woman who works for herself and can get drunk in the middle of the day if I feel like it without justifying it to anyone, let's see if I can come up with something. How about this—I have to wear a mask like Doogie Howser to go to the grocery store; there's a plague running rampant across the globe; the economy is in the shitter; my favorite sushi buffet has been closed for six months; I've put up with a couple years of apocalypse so far with not a zombie in sight; my ex is late with child support again; I've spent an entire summer in North Carolina having hot flashes; and some son of a bitch in Orlando used *my* debit card to have sub sandwiches delivered for lunch!"

"Okay, when you put it that way, maybe we should drink more."

I leaned back in my chair, a surprising amount of my rage dissipated after screaming at my best friend for just thirty seconds. "I agree."

I raised the straw to my lips and was just about to bestow upon myself another dose of agave-built bliss when I heard the sliding glass door open.

"Mom?" my daughter called.

"Yes, dear?"

"There are a couple of guys on the porch. They say they're with the FBI."

CHAPTER 3

T he two men now seated at my dining room table certainly looked like FBI agents. At least, they looked like what almost five decades of television has taught me FBI agents should look like. There was one that was bigger than the other, and the little one looked older than the big one by a good ten years. I liked the little one better. I'm not totally comfortable around people that are in that weird age between my oldest child and forty, because I'm never sure if I'm supposed to think of them as children or adults, and most thirty-year-olds don't consider themselves children anymore.

I don't either. Until I talk to a thirty-year-old, and then I'm pouring rum in my Metamucil and painting flames on my walker. So I focused my attention on the smaller agent, if that's what he really was, and not some covert operative for a shadowy government agency dedicated to the capture and torture of middle-aged divorcées. When I thought about it that way, I focused back on the young one, because if I'm going to be tortured by anyone, I wanted it to be the cuter of the pair.

The young agent introduced himself as Agent Kaplan and produced a badge and ID that supported his claim. I mostly believed him, but I've seen every season of *Supernatural* twice, so I know how easy it is to fake a badge and ID. But I couldn't think of any rock stars named Kaplan, so if he was faking, he was doing it wrong. He was tall, and I mean tall for a normal person, not tall compared to me. I'm barely five-three, so there are Muppets that are tall to me, but Agent Kaplan was taller than Rhonda, so I knew he was legitimately tall. When you spend your whole life seeing people's faces from underneath their chins, your perspective gets a little out of whack on things like that.

Agent Kaplan was built, too, with broad shoulders and arms that bulged in his suit jacket. He had short brown hair, cut in kind of a generic office-drone style, which did absolutely nothing for his features, which were a little too squared off for that haircut. He would have been a lot cuter with some length to it, to frame out his face better. But maybe cute isn't what federal agents look for in their haircuts. I don't know. I've never cut a federal agent's hair. Or anyone else's, for that matter. Not since the infamous Sneeze with Clippers incident of 2012. Kristen forgave me pretty much as soon as she got out of middle school, but it made for a rough couple of years. Lots of hats. Lots.

Agent Burns was the older agent, and he looked a little like a Burns. Not like Mr. Burns off *The Simpsons*, with a long pointy nose, bald head, and fringe of hair around the sides. Well, come to think of it, pretty much exactly like that. So he looked like Homer's boss on *The Simpsons*, but slightly less yellow. I almost asked him if he was okay, then realized that there was a bright yellow folder from Kristen's homework lying on the table in front of him. I got that out of the way, and he looked much less like he had a liver condition. I was relieved. Jaundice is no joke. I don't exactly know what it *is*, but it's no joke.

"Do you know why we're here, Mrs. Lieberman?" Agent Burns asked, and I really wanted to give him an answer he would like, just to hear if he'd say "Eeeeexcellent."

Unfortunately, I had no idea. "I have no idea," I said.

"Did you report a cybercrime this morning?" Agent Kaplan asked.

"Oh," I said. "Yes, yes, I did. I'm glad you're here." I popped up and walked over to my computer, only having to reach out to steady myself on the back of one armchair, and I grabbed all the printouts from my research into my identity theft. "Here's everything I have on the perp. You can see here they ordered subs, with extra mayo, super disgusting, to be delivered—"

"That's not why we're here," Agent Burns said, holding up a hand to stop me.

I froze. I don't like the whole "talk to the hand" thing. I really, really don't like it. I think it's very rude, and despite the fact that I have been accused of rambling a little now and then, I don't think it's a good thing that a sign of cutting someone off mid-sentence has become a part of our established nonverbal communication. I have told my girls more than once if they ever use that gesture with me, they had better be prepared to be missing at least one finger when they put their hand back down.

So it was with great restraint that I didn't snap Agent Burns' pinkie finger off and shove it in his ear, but rather just said "Oh," and walked back around to my seat. The fact that I wasn't sure exactly which of the two hands I saw in front of me was real and which hand was tequila-induced may also have impacted my decision.

"Are you drunk, Mrs. Lieberman?" Agent Kaplan asked.

"It's Miz," I corrected primly.

"Are you drunk, Ms. Lieberman?" He repeated the question, proving that trained interrogators are better at staying on point than teenaged girls. I could pretty much always throw my girls off by pointing out the window and shouting "Squirrel!" But Agent Kaplan was having none of it.

"What makes you think I'm drunk, Agent Kaplan?" I asked.

"You smell like a frat house on Sunday morning, you're barely able to sit up straight, and you just slurred the word 'what,'" he replied. Damn that investigative training. All of those were pretty good indicators that I was, in fact, drunk as a skunk. Mission accomplished.

"Yes, I am," I said. "I have been heinously violated, and..." I saw Rhonda put her hand over her mouth and was pretty sure that I had mispronounced "heinously" in a way that appealed to the twelve-year-old boy in her. I blinked twice, reducing the number of agents in my vision from four to two, and went on. "I have been the victim of a crime, my privacy has been violated, and I sought solace in the consumption of blender drinks. Is that a problem, Officer?"

"Agent," Agent Burns corrected.

"Sorry. Is that a problem, *Agent*?" I asked. Then a thought hit me. "Or were you asking because you'd like some? I'm sorry, I am being a *terrible* hostess. Please forgive me. My mother would roll over in her grave if she knew I treated guests in my home in such a fashion. Would y'all care for a drink? I'm all out of margaritas, but I have rum, vodka, bourbon—"

"You're out of bourbon," Rhonda corrected.

I turned to look at her and noticed for the first time that she wasn't all that steady in her seat, either. I also noticed that somehow between lounging in the patio chair beside me sipping Maker's through a straw and sitting at my dining room table across from a hunky FBI agent, somehow two of the buttons on Rhonda's blouse had come undone. Part of me was appalled at her forwardness, but a lot more of me wished I had thought of it. Of course, I was wearing a sweaty Dolly Parton t-shirt that passed the sniff test when I picked it up off the bedroom floor this morning, so there wasn't really a chance to unbutton anything, but still.

"My apologies, Agent Kaplan. It appears I am suddenly and unexpectedly out of bourbon," I said. "But the offer stands." I stood as well, then decided that was not my best idea and sat back down. As I did, I considered my rapid descent into Suzanne Sugarbaker the moment it was time to play hostess and decreed, internally, that it was time to get the hell out of the South. Up until the time I was in my twenties, the word "y'all" had never crossed my lips, and now here I was sounding like Melanie Hamilton swooning over Ashley Wilkes in her father's parlor. No, as soon as I was sober and Kristen finished high school, I was moving back to somewhere that understood that tea should be hot and bitter like my rage, and if I was really lucky, someplace with all four seasons, not just Summer and a very few weeks of Thank God It's Not Summer.

"No, ma'am, I do not want a drink. You did report an identity theft this morning?" The tiny part of me that was sober admired Agent Kaplan's effort. Here he was, sitting across the table from a drunken raving lunatic and a woman who seemed to be auditioning for a *Desperate Housewives* reboot, and he was determined to keep things on track. He was probably going to be an excellent agent once he finished puberty.

I tried to focus. I needed something unpleasant that would give me a spike of sobriety and help keep me from getting distracted thinking about anything else that might make part of Agent Kaplan's suit bulge. Then I caught sight of a photo on my mantle, of me, my two girls, and my ex, and that sobered me right up. It was one of those family photo shoots that churches and scout troops sell as fundraisers, and right as I parked the car, my husband told me that he was having an affair with his receptionist at work, had been doing so for six months, and wanted a divorce. Then I had to go into the family life center at the church on the corner and see all our neighbors, sit next to that weaselly prick and pretend to be a happy little family, all the while wishing I could rip his stupid mustache off his face, lip and all, and shove it down his throat.

Yep, looking at that photo and the walrus mustache that I hated for the whole time he wore it sobered me right up and allowed me to focus on the matter at hand. Which was not, contrary to Rhonda's behavior, jumping FBI agent bones in my dining room.

"Yes, Agent Kaplan, my identity was used to make a fraudulent purchase around lunchtime today in Florida. Since we are in North Carolina, that crosses state lines and I believe that makes it a federal wire fraud…thing." I was doing so good until I couldn't remember the word "case."

"Okay," Agent Burns said, pulling a small notebook out of his inside jacket pocket. I tried to see his gun while he did it, but either it was very small or maybe he only pulled it out when he intended to use it. "How many fraudulent charges were made?"

"One."

The two agents looked at each other. Apparently, the fact that there was only one charge made my case somehow less interesting. Agent Burns raised an eyebrow at me but kept his notebook in hand. "What was charged, and for how much?"

"Lunch. Sub sandwiches from BobbyRay's, delivered via ChowSprint."

The other eyebrow went up to match its friend. "And how much was the charge?"

"Twenty-six dollars."

"So you had one fraudulent charge on your debit card, for twenty-six dollars' worth of lunch delivery, and you called the Federal Bureau of Investigation?" Agent Kaplan's brushy hair would have been standing on end even if it was long enough to lay down. A flush started at his collar and started to creep up his neck.

"Um…yes?" It came out a little more of a question than I wanted it to. He was far less cute when he was angry.

"This is a little…smaller than the cases we are usually assigned. In fact, I think you told the operator that your entire financial life was in ruins and you were one hundred percent certain that the Russian mob was behind this whole thing," said Agent Burns, whose mouth was twitching like he was trying to hold back a grin. I didn't know if he was almost-laughing at my case or at his partner's growing anger, but I was really starting to like Kinda-Amused Fed better than Cute Angry Fed. Maybe looking like a cartoon villain wasn't so bad after all. And he looked old enough to have learned to put the toilet seat down. I had no such illusions about Agent Kaplan.

"Well, they could be," I protested. Okay, maybe I whined more than protested, but I definitely said it.

"We're going to leave now," said Agent Kaplan, standing up and moving very slowly and very stiffly, like if he bumped into anything, he would explode into a giant ball of rage and testosterone. Which would have been the most interesting thing to happen on that dining room table in, well, ever, if I'm being honest. My ex wasn't exactly what we would call imaginative. Or attentive. Or thoughtful. Or really considerate, charming, attractive, wealthy, intelligent, or talented, when I think about it. He was dependable, and when we got married, that was enough. I guess he saved all the other adjectives for his girlfriend. I got mustache burn on my thighs and late child support checks.

"Does this mean you aren't going to investigate my case?" I asked. I didn't get up. The longer I'd been sitting almost upright, the worse an idea being completely upright seemed, and I had absolutely zero faith in my ability to remain any degree of upright if I tried to stand at that moment.

Agent Kaplan whirled around, and his smaller partner put a hand on his elbow as if to say "I got this."

Then he actually did say, "I got this," which was kind of amazing, especially to drunk me. Drunk me is easily amazed. Drunk me also had a rapidly waning aversion to nebbishy middle-aged federal agents, and a rapidly shrinking attraction to young hunky ones.

"I got this, Kap. Why don't you wait in the car?" Agent Kaplan stalked out without saying anything else, which was probably the best outcome I could have hoped for. "Ms. Lieberman, we aren't going to investigate this case. We have a lot of things we have to investigate, and that means that sometimes legitimate crimes that are technically in our jurisdiction don't fit our threshold for dedicating resources to them. Your case unfortunately falls into that category. While I am sorry that your debit card was compromised, we cannot spend any manpower on a credit card fraud case that is less than fifty dollars."

"But what about the Russian mob thing?" Rhonda asked.

Agent Burns looked at her, almost surprised, like he'd maybe forgotten she was there. That would be a first—a man forgetting a six-foot redhead with her boobs falling out five feet from his nose. Even gay men loved Rhonda's boobs. Hell, I wanted to motorboat her most of the time, and I'm at least sixty percent straight.

"I'm sorry, I didn't catch your name." He held out a hand to Rhonda, and I was impressed by the amount of the sentence he directed to her face. Most men can't manage a word, but at least half his sentence included him looking her in the eye.

"I'm Rhonda," she said, holding out her hand. "Rhonda Mabry. I live next door. In the house with the jacuzzi."

Agent Burns just looked confused. "Um...that's nice. Mrs. Mabry—"

"Miss. I'm divorced. And available."

Now he looked downright uncomfortable, maybe even a little scared. I wondered if that's what a mouse looks like to a cat that's sitting there about to kill the aforementioned mouse. Because that's kind of how I felt —like Rhonda was the giant tabby getting ready to pounce all over Agent Burns and gobble him up, and all I could do was sit there and watch.

"Um...Miss Mabry, do you have any evidence that there is Russian mob involvement in this case? Was there something particularly Russian about the..." He looked down at his notebook. "Subs they ordered?"

"I don't know," Rhonda said, leaning forward. "Do Russians *really* like mayo?"

Agent Burns took three quick steps back. "No more than any other group of people, I believe. Thank you, Ms. Lieberman, Miss Mabry. If you have any further information about this case, please do not hesitate to call our main number, but at this time we do not feel that this is a matter for the FBI." With that, he scurried backward for the door, only bumping into one wall and stumbling over one end table on his way out. Pretty impressive, given that he never took his eyes off Rhonda the entire time. It was like he was a mongoose watching a cobra, so he could be ready to dodge if she struck at him. Then he was gone, and I heard the slap of cheap dress shoes on the sidewalk and a car start seconds later.

Rhonda leaned back in her chair and looked over at me. "Well, poop. Do you think the jacuzzi thing scared him off?"

CHAPTER 4

M om?" My daughter's voice floated down the stairs.
"Yes, dear?" I called back.
"Are you going to jail?"
"Not planning on it, sweetie."
"Okay."

The "okay" was not accompanied by the sound of a closing door, the universal sign that your teenager is through with you and has no interest in ever speaking to you again until either (A) you stop being the stupidest person in the world, which is probably never going to happen, or (B) they get hungry. Leaving her door open after yelling down the stairs to me, rather than at me, was my daughter's most eloquent way of saying, "I would like to discuss this further at your earliest convenience." I don't often get to have conversations with my daughter lately that are longer than a description of dinner or a condemnation of her wardrobe. Or a condemnation of *my* wardrobe, frankly.

"Honey, why don't you come down here, and I'll explain why there were federal agents in our dining room?" I called.

There was no response. This means nothing in the parlance of teenagers. With normal human beings, asking a question and receiving no response means that you probably have not been heard and should repeat yourself. That is a possible meaning when dealing with teenagers as well, but the least likely out of all possibilities. Much more likely are (A) they heard you and don't care because you're a moron, (B) they heard you and are pretending not to because you don't agree with their opinion/wardrobe/choice of friend/preferred video game platform/favorite flavor of Pop-Tart/desired college major and are thus a moron, or (C) they are formulating a response to explain to you the exact degree to which you are a moron.

This was none of those, which may be a first in the history of parent-teenager conversations. Instead, a few seconds later, I heard a crush of rhinoceri thundering down the stairs. Two things to note here. I am well aware that the plural of "rhinoceros" is, in fact, "rhinoceroi," but I like "rhinoceri" better. Also, my daughter weighs one hundred fifteen pounds when she's wearing combat boots, which is always. How in the world she manages to make the entire house shake on its foundation by walking down the stairs in a relatively controlled fashion is one of the world's great mysteries. Like how they get toothpaste in tubes in the first place, or exactly how motion-detecting toilets work. Have you ever wondered why sometimes they'll flush when you're just sitting there, minding your own business checking email or reading a John Grisham novel? And then sometimes, you can stand up off the toilet, dance the Charleston in the stall, and do three backflips without triggering the flush. Also, there is obviously a proximity sensor built into the manual button that triggers a flush when your hand gets close, startling you and making you really need to sit back down on the pot because you have to pee all over again. Just me? Okay.

Kristen came downstairs in a Fortnite t-shirt, a skirt short enough to be considered a belt on a normal human being, candy cane-striped leggings, and one purple and one red Doc Marten boot. Funny, she had another pair just like those upstairs… "Hi, Aunt Rhonda."

"Hey, Krissie-girl," Rhonda said.

"Wow, it smells like a frat party in here. What have you two been drinking?"

"Yes," Rhonda replied. "The answer to what we've been drinking is yes."

At the same time, I raised what I thought was a more pertinent question. "How do you know what a frat party smells like?"

For the record, my house had no odor of sweat socks, stale beer, rotted pizza, Axe body spray, or vomit. It did smell like cheap margarita mix, suntan lotion, and bourbon. I think that was much more like a sorority Spring Break back seat, but I was never in a sorority, and my college Spring Breaks were spent working at the university library, because that's how I partied back in 1993. God, it's a wonder I ever got laid enough to spawn once, much less twice.

"I was being symbolic, Mother." There it was—the "you're so stupid it hurts" tone. Good. I was starting to wonder if I was going to have to deal with body snatchers in addition to identity thieves. There's only so much one woman can handle.

Kris flopped down in that disjointed and yet boneless way of teenagers and reached for the plastic tumbler sitting in front of Rhonda. I had no idea when she'd gotten a cup or fixed a real human-sized drink. The last thing I remembered, she was drinking straight bourbon through a straw. "Can I have some?"

"Sure," Rhonda said.

I leaned over and snatched the cup from my daughter, setting it in front of my best friend. "No," I said. "Not until you're twenty-one."

"Good lord, Mother. It's not like it's the first time I've had booze."

"Okay, then. Not until you're thirty."

"Fine. Why was the FBI here? Were they really FBI? The young one was cute. Built like a brick—"

"They were here because I have been the victim of a heinous crime," I said, before I could find out if my daughter had any idea what a brick shithouse was.

"You mean when those dudes hacked your ChowSprint account to order shitty sub sandwiches?"

"Yes," I replied.

"Mom, I don't think that qualifies as something you call the FBI about."

"It was a crime committed across state lines using the internet. That's exactly what their cybercrimes division was created to handle," I said, using language I found on the FBI's website. I'm even kinda sure I got the name of the division right. Kinda.

"I'm pretty sure they were thinking more human trafficking and kiddie porn, not rescuing a middle-aged woman's credit rating from raving mayo addicts," Kris replied.

"You knew about the mayo?" Rhonda asked.

"Oh dear lord, Aunt Rhonda. She has screamed about the mayo all day," my daughter said. "You would think they ordered subs laced with arsenic the way she has bitched about the extra mayo."

"Mayonnaise is disgusting," I said. I could hear the irritating prim tone to my voice, and if it was irritating to me, it must have been incredibly grating to my daughter. Fine. That's what she gets for picking on me about the mayo.

"Well, what did they say?" Kristen asked.

"What did who say?" I replied.

"The FBI."

"About what?"

"About your heinous crime? And please tell me you didn't try to use the word 'heinous' when you talked to them. You kinda slur the 'h' away, and I'm almost totally sure the feds don't care about your butthole."

"Don't disappoint your mother, dear," Rhonda said.

I stared daggers at my daughter and my best friend as I thought back to whether or not I used the word heinous in my talk with the cops, and yup, sure did. Rhonda even snickered at me then, too. "Leave my butthole out of this," I said, adding to the list of phrases I never thought I would utter before I had children. "They…"

"They weren't impressed," Rhonda said.

"With your butthole or with the Case of the Purloined Hoagies?" Kris asked.

"Either," Rhonda replied, and the two of them dissolved into giggles.

"They weren't interested in the crime that had been committed, and I'm sure they had no opinion about my butthole," I said.

"Don't be so sure," Rhonda disagreed. "I'm pretty sure I saw Agent Bulgy checking you out."

"God, I hope not," Kristen said, mirroring my own thoughts.

"Hey!" I protested.

"Sorry, Mom, but you look like kind of a train wreck today. Usually you're like medium hot. Not so much I sweat bringing my boyfriends over to meet you, but enough that I know you're spank bank material for some of my geekier friends. But today you look like…well, you look like you've been sitting out in the sun drinking margaritas straight from the pitcher."

"You only know that because your window looks out onto the patio. Besides, the dishwasher was running, and I didn't have any clean cups. Because somebody has about six place settings' worth of dishes scattered around her bedroom."

"I know that because there's a big pale green spot on your shirt," Kristen said.

I looked down. Shit. She was right. There was a huge wet spot where something, probably margarita, had dripped on my shirt. And of course it was right on my boob. Now it looked like I had some kind of weird condition where I was either sweating in a weird place or lactating sideways. Neither of those are conducive to seducing federal agents. Which is not what I had any thoughts of doing. Really, I didn't. Not much, anyway.

"Okay, so yes. I was day drinking. But I'm an adult. I can do that. Especially on days that I have undergone severe emotional turmoil and personal tragedy."

"Mom, you got ripped off for less money than it costs to fill up your Prius."

"That is beside the point, young lady! It is a sense of violation that I hope you never have to endure. This is the type of thing that parents live through so that their children don't have to. The kind of thing that we suffer with to shield you from it. The kind of thing—"

Kristen leaned over to Rhonda and fake whispered, "Is this where *Battle Hymn of the Republic* should start to play under her monologue?"

Rhonda, being the good friend that she is, didn't miss a beat. "I was thinking maybe *America the Beautiful.*"

"Ooh, the Ray Charles version?"

"Totally the Ray Charles version."

They both looked at me as I sat there, my mouth hanging open. Kristen motioned with one hand. "Go ahead, Mom. I'm listening. Really, I am."

"No, you're not. You're drinking the last of Rhonda's booze."

Rhonda snatched her glass back. "Hey! Don't get between a menopausal woman and her liquor. That's a good way to get dead."

"Don't worry," Kris replied, wrinkling her nose. "What did you put in that, lighter fluid?"

"There wasn't much daiquiri mix."

"But there was obviously plenty of rum."

"Not really. So I might have added a little vodka to top it off."

"Oh good God," Kristen said. "I might be the one in high school, but you two totally drink like you're scrubbing the lines off the booze bottles in your parents' liquor cabinet."

Rhonda and I shared a look, then a shrug. "She's not wrong," Rhonda said.

"Speak for yourself. I had a margarita."

"An entire pitcher, made with an entire bottle of Patron, is not a margarita."

"It wasn't a very big bottle."

"Oh, then that's okay."

Kris put two fingers in her mouth and whistled loudly. Since there were no taxis nearby, she got our undivided attention. I also think a couple of neighborhood dogs went into convulsions. My kid can get *loud*. I wonder where she gets that from.

"Can we get back to the part where there are federal agents in our dining room?" my daughter asked.

"Oooh, yes, can we?" my neighbor purred.

"Oh, for Pete's sake, Rhonda," I said. I turned my focus to Jess. "Sweetie, nothing bad is going to happen. They misunderstood the report, so they were here to clear up a few things is all."

"Misunderstood like somebody told them this was a mob conspiracy and a matter of national security?" Dammit. I knew I should have plugged up the vent in her room. Little sneak could hear everything that was said in the dining room.

"Well, it might be," I protested. It wasn't much of a protest. Not even a rally, really. There were no clever slogans on signs, no good chants, not even any Neo-Nazis. Not then, anyway. Those would come later.

"Are they going to send you to Gitmo? I just need to know if I need to pack my big suitcase when I go stay at Dad's tonight, or if I'll have a home to come back to Monday night and I can just take my duffle."

Crap. I forgot that it was Peckerwood's weekend with Kris. He only gets one a month, because every other weekend is "too much" for his "new lifestyle." By that I assume that he means his favorite stripper might starve if she's deprived of his dollar bills two Saturdays in a month.

"You can pack the duffel," I said. "Wait, tonight? Monday? Why are you leaving tonight? Why won't you be back Sunday night? And what about school Monday?"

"Monday is Labor Day, and tomorrow is a teacher workday or something. Either way, there's no school, and Dad doesn't have to work, so I'm staying an extra couple days. You said okay to all this like a month ago."

I'm sure I did. But the request probably came from Peckerwood, not Kristen, so all I heard from his mouth was "Blah-Blah-Blah, I'm a cheating asshole."

"Oh, okay, then. You can pack your duffel, sweetheart. I promise I'm not going to Gitmo this weekend."

"She makes no such promises for Fall Break, though," Rhonda said.

"One week at a time, Aunt Rhonda. That's how we have to take the important things, like not going to a remote federal prison where nobody admits we exist. One week at a time." She threw her arms around my neck and gave me a kiss on the cheek. "I'm glad you're not going to Gitmo, Mom."

"No, you can't have the rest of my margarita," I replied.

"Worth a shot," she said, then turned and headed back up the stairs.

Rhonda watched her go and looked at me. "You know she just made off with the pitcher, right?"

"Yeah, but if she knows I know, then it'll mean I let her have booze. And that'll take all the fun out of stealing it."

"I'm not sure if you're an evil genius or a terrible influence."

I shrugged. "Like that cute kid on *Full House* said, 'Why can't it be both?'"

CHAPTER 5

Nicknames aside, I don't hate my ex-husband. We had ten fantastic years together, four mediocre years together, two really spectacularly shitty years together, and now we're on our fourth year apart and I no longer want to pop his eyeballs like grapes every time I see him. I'm still adjusting to this, as it's something of a new feeling, and I'm not sure how I like it. I'd gotten accustomed to having him as the most hated figure in my life, and without him filling that role, I've had to pay more attention to politics to find someone truly deserving of my loathing. Fortunately, there are always plenty of options.

So no, I don't hate my ex. I don't *like* him very much, either, and while I don't wish him any harm, I wouldn't shed a tear if he were suddenly offered a transfer to his company's main office in Bora Bora. Since he's a distribution manager for a company that makes bubble wrap, I don't think there's much chance of that, but a girl can dream.

For the record, I did not fall in love with a man that wanted to make a living in the material safety and handling industry. I fell in love with a man who was going to take Broadway by storm, who was going to spend three years in New York honing his on-stage chops before moving to LA and getting into television, probably as a supporting actor or a character actor, but that could be lucrative and consistent work. At least, that's what he told me when we were getting high on the roof of the university's theatre building and screwing like rabbits under a moonlit sky.

In reality, I married a man who was an extra in three feature films, all of which lost millions of dollars. He also appeared in one made-for-tv movie as an "office drone." That was literally how he appeared in the credits: "Office Drone." That was his crowning achievement as an actor. Well, that or playing perhaps the world's oldest Mercutio in a community theatre production of *Romeo & Juliet*. But we agreed not to speak of that production after he split his tights during the Tybalt fight during a performance and his codpiece flopped out for all the world to see. It was perhaps the funniest production of *Romeo & Juliet* in history, as Tybalt tried to duel a Mercutio with two swords flapping in the breeze, one considerably shorter than the other.

I didn't mind him not being a big-time actor; it's not like I was fulfilling my college dream of playing first chair flute in a major symphony. I was teaching middle school music and raising two daughters and loving it. I still love it. Most of the time. I love my students, let's put it that way. I even like my principal. My assistant principal, superintendent, and at least eighty percent of the parents I have to deal with...yeah, that's another story. But the point is that I was happy with our life, and Peter wasn't.

Yeah, his name's Peter. Not Pete, but Peter. And zero sense of humor about any name jokes, especially when Little Peter made his stage debut. Because the number of "Peter's peter" or "Peter's pecker picked a peck of pickled peppers" cracks that I had to choke down was somewhere in the neighborhood of the gross national product of Belize. That's a bigger number than you might think, given the size of Belize.

But anyway, Peter is a humorless little man with an obnoxious mustache, a more obnoxious midlife crisis convertible, and an even more (and it's possible, though difficult) obnoxious twenty-something wife with bleached blonde hair and an IQ roughly equivalent to her cup size (more a comment on the massive nature of one of those things than the minuscule nature of the other. You guess which is which). And now he was standing on my front stoop, because the only way he was ever setting foot back inside that house is if he broke in, smirking about my identity theft trauma.

"So some smartass kid hacked your debit card and bought lunch with it. So what? He probably looked you up online and plugged in your street address, just hoping that your house number would be your PIN. It's not anymore, is it? Because I told you about that. You've got to be more security conscious. The next time it might be something serious, not just a few bucks' worth of subs." Kristen was taking her own sweet time making it down the stairs, forcing me to stand at the door with a hangover and talk to my ex-husband. If I'd known I had raised her to be such a vindictive bitch, I wouldn't have given her the dregs of my margarita. It was mostly melted ice, anyway.

"No, Pete, my PIN number is very secure, not that it's any business of yours. How did you hear about this in the first place?" See what I did there? I called him Pete. It's petty little crap, but it brought a little joy into my afternoon.

"Evelyn told me. You two are still friends on Facebook, remember?"

Ugh. That bitch. Evelyn is Peter's older sister, and she thinks he's just as much a doucherocket as I do, but every once in a while, she'll be overcome by this strange fit of familial loyalty and tell Peter anything that I've posted to social media that could be the least bit amusing to him or embarrassing to me, usually with a concentration on the latter. Then I'll message her and chew her out, she'll apologize and beg me not to cut her out of my life, and I'll re-friend her. Rhonda calls her my carcinoma, because every time I deal with her, she says I cut off a piece of my nose to spite my face. I don't really think the metaphor holds up, but it's easier to just let it lie than argue about it. Anyway, this must be one of those times that Evelyn liked her brother more than usual, because she ratted me out. Again.

"Remind me to murder your sister the next time I see her," I muttered, then turned back into the house. "Kristen! Hurry your ass up, or I'm going to strangle your father and spend the rest of my life in prison! Then you'll have to live with Aunt Rhonda, because I left you to her in my will!"

I wasn't *that* close to strangling Peter. He was being relatively undouchey, and given the tender state of my skull, I was particularly sensitive to such things. After Rhonda left, I stopped drinking, mostly because I was out of tequila, and that was several hours ago, so I was sober, and regretting pretty much every decision I'd made since I decided to wear my medium cute underwear today instead of my super-frumpy "home" underwear.

"Well, have you called your bank, at least?" Okay, now he was getting douchey.

"Of course I called my bank, Peter. They cancelled my debit card and are sending me a new one. It should be here in two days."

"Are you okay for cash? It's a holiday weekend, so the mail might be screwed up. Here, take this, just so I know you're not going to starve while we're off having fun." He reached into his pocket and pulled out a folded stack of twenties. I looked at it for a minute, really wanting to tell him where he could stick his cash, but he did have a point. I didn't have any access to my bank account until Tuesday at best, and the one credit card I had that wasn't maxed out would have been hard pressed to pay for my identity thieves' sub sandwiches.

So I took the money. "Thanks. I appreciate it."

"Don't worry about it. I'll just take it out of next month's child support. Not that she's a child anymore." He let that last part trail off like I wasn't supposed to hear it, a tactic he'd mastered when we were married that I no longer had to live with.

"I'll take it off of last month's when you get around to paying that," I said, and turned to go back inside. I heard the porch creak and whirled back to see him standing there with his foot in the air. "Freeze. You can wait for her in the car. You are not coming into this house."

"Oh, come on, Lexi. Don't be like that. This was my house, too."

"*Was* is the operative word, Peter," I said, and swung the door closed in his face. I'm pretty sure I didn't hit him in the nose with it. Not a hundred percent, but pretty sure. Okay, kinda sure.

"Real mature, Mom," Kristen said as she bounded down the stairs.

"I revert to my inner middle schooler where your father is concerned. Say hello to Vanna for me."

"Her name is Meredith."

"Whatever. Miss September."

"Mom." The disapproval was heavy in her voice, and I could tell by the look on her face that she thought she was being the mature one. She probably was.

"I'm sorry, sweetie. You have fun with your father and his trollop."

"Try not to get alcohol poisoning while I'm away."

"I'm pretty sure there's not enough booze left in the house after your Aunt Rhonda got into the rum." And the bourbon. And the vodka.

She gave me a hug and a kiss, and she was gone. A few seconds later I heard Peckerwood's convertible roar to life in a gas-guzzling, compensatory proclamation of virility and insecurity, and then I was alone.

Alone. Independent. All on my own for four and a half glorious days. I could order pizza with all the pineapple on it I wanted, and nobody could judge me for it. Except the delivery guy, and I didn't really care what he thought.

Alone. No need for anything but ratty t-shirts, sweatpants, and braless wonderment. No kid needing my help on homework, asking me when dinner would be ready, or asking to borrow the car. Nobody to yell at about music too loud, or data overage on her cell phone, or using up all the bandwidth on the home wifi. I was completely on my own for the next ninety-six hours.

I hated it.

I wandered from the front door into the den, looked over at the couch half-covered with Kristen's schoolbooks. Of course she didn't take any homework to her dad's; no way would she have time for school with whatever fun stuff Peter had planned to further reinforce his position as the "fun parent." I picked up and folded the fleece blanket she liked to bundle up in on the couch, no matter the season. It was teal, pink, purple, and blue in a swirly pattern, a threadbare fleece that Jess had bought her for Christmas the first year she'd had a part-time job. My oldest had been so proud of having her own money to buy gifts for me and her sister. She got me a new toaster, one with slots big enough for bagels, that I still use four years later.

I moved her books into a neat stack on the coffee table and sat down to watch Netflix. Then I got back up immediately, because the most twenty-first century thing ever is to sit on the couch and binge Netflix, and I was not going to be that cliché single woman. Also, the mere idea of watching the gigantic screen of our television with my hangover made me start bleeding from the ears.

I cleared off the dining room table, noticing that neither of the FBI agents had left a card so I could get in touch with them if there were any new developments in the case. Must have been an oversight. Or maybe they were afraid of Rhonda. I emptied the dishwasher, put all the blender bits and booze cups into a new load, and started the machine. Then I looked in the fridge, realizing with some irony that if I wanted anything other than a turkey sandwich for dinner that I was going to have to order delivery, and swore that under no circumstances would I get subs. And certainly no mayo.

Then I sat down at my desk and opened up the email confirmation from ChowSprint again. The blind, incoherent rage I felt upon the initial theft was gone, replaced by a cold, completely coherent anger that burned deep in my soul. The delivery address stared at me like a neon sign that said "THIEVES LIVE HERE."

I opened up Google Maps and looked at the house where my purloined sandwiches had been delivered. That's how I had come to think of them—*my* sandwiches. Even though I'd never had them, didn't order them, and if you put one in front of me as a random meal, I would refuse to eat them. I paid for them, so they were mine. And they were delivered to this unassuming ranch home on an unassuming street in an unassuming neighborhood in a suburb of Orlando, Florida.

There was nothing out of the ordinary about the house. It was a white stucco home with slightly Spanish influences in the architecture, a neatly manicured lawn, and some low shrubs out front. It looked like every other house on the street. There was a burgundy SUV parked out front, and the two-car garage was closed. I assumed that the garage was a junk room, like any normal person would have.

It looked perfectly normal and unprepossessing. Just like you would want your home to look if you were a secret Russian identity theft/human trafficking/drug running operation. I knew what I had to do. The authorities obviously weren't going to do anything about this blatant threat to not only my credit score, but our national security. So I was going to have to.

I picked up my cell from the dining room table and tapped the screen. "Rhonda, it's Lexi. Are you off work Monday? Good. Pack a bag. We're going to Florida."

CHAPTER 6

I t's a testament to our friendship that Rhonda was at my house twenty minutes later with a rolling overnight bag, a purse the size of Manhattan, a huge floppy sun hat, one of those rollup makeup bag things that you know is going to unroll to hold an entire Sephora, a soft-sided blue cooler with wheels, a bright orange Camelbak with the straw wedged in her mouth like some kind of demented Huntress S. Thompson, and white-framed sunglasses with lenses the size of dinner plates. She wore a pair of white shorts that would make Daisy Duke self-conscious, the most adorable little white flip-flops, and a red sleeveless top with a plunging neckline that showed off her tanned midriff and her sparkling bellybutton ring.

"When did you get your bellybutton pierced? And did you just have all this packed? Is this like your suburban zombie apocalypse bug out bag? Bags?"

"I didn't. You know I hate needles," she said, creating a pile of luggage behind my silver Prius. "It's fake, see?" She plucked the ring off her tummy, and I could see that it was just a little loop of wire with a faux sapphire hanging from it that she could pinch onto the skin at her navel. "You wanna try it? It'll clip to other places, too, if you know what I mean."

I froze with my hand in midair. "I think I'll pass. We're close, but I don't think we need to share...belly button lint."

"Your loss," she said, reaffixing the ring to her belly.

I focused on the rest of her gear to drive my mind firmly away from thinking about wherever else she may have affixed that dangly little blue heart. There are some things you just don't want to know about even your best friend. "What's in that Camelbak?"

I had a good reason to ask. Ever since she read the first Tucker Max book, Rhonda has wanted to go somewhere with booze in a backpack drink dispenser. I've so far managed to talk her out of doing it on charity bike rides, church whitewater rafting trips, neighborhood hikes (although that one was probably a mistake, because after five minutes walking alongside the balding and spherical president of our HOA, I wanted to mainline vodka myself), and PTA meetings (also probably a mistake, because there has never been a PTA meeting that wouldn't be improved with alcohol). I was fairly certain that this trip was going to see the debut of the Rhonda Mabry Vodka and Tang Dispersal Device, which was really going to need a better name, or at least something that could be made into a decent acronym, if it was going to catch on.

Yeah, Vodka and Tang. It's a real thing. At least in Rhonda's world, which means it's a real thing in my world. Her logic is that since vodka is alcohol, and there are no organic elements in Tang, that a mixture of vodka and Tang could be left in a container indefinitely and remain safe to drink. Because there's nothing to spoil, and the alcohol would keep mold from developing. It's an as yet untested theory, because no amount of vodka has ever remained outside of a bottle in Rhonda's vicinity long enough for any ingredient to spoil or grow mold. I would never say my best friend has a drinking problem. I can't, because I've seen her drink a shitload over the years, and she's never seemed to have any problem getting it down.

"Fight club," Rhonda replied. When I looked at her in confusion, she grinned and said, "We don't talk about what's in the Camelbak. Now where's your shit? Are you ready to go? You're not ready. Why aren't you ready? This whole road trip was your idea. How can I be ready before you?"

"You can be ready before me because you were probably packing from the moment you left my house, when I had a daughter to ship off to my ex's, an ex to deal with, emotional trauma from dealing with my ex to sublimate, and a plan of action to develop. You just had to depend on my worse instincts to prevail and me to decide to go after these idiots on my own, which, let's face it, was a foregone conclusion. Thus, you're ready before me. Now throw your crap in the trunk and come help me pack."

"Trunk," she said with a snort. "Just open the back seat. You know your trunk won't hold my makeup bag."

She was right. I love my Prius, but it is not exactly the pinnacle of on-the-go storage. That's okay, I never needed it to be. Peckerwood got his convertible to go along with the divorce papers, and I got the Prius. It was as much a celebration of the fact that I was never going to have to lug around another car seat as it was any grand proclamation of my independence, but it sure didn't hurt my feelings to go to the dealership and find out that my credit score had gone up forty points just by getting a divorce. I always knew there was something holding my credit rating down, I just never realized it was Peter.

I popped the locks, left Rhonda to stow her gear however she saw fit, and headed back inside. I had a lot of packing to finish, and if we were going to be out of the Carolinas by midnight, I needed to haul some serious booty.

Five minutes later, Rhonda walked up to my bedroom to find me sitting on the floor surrounded by piles of clothing with my head in my hands. "What. The. Hell. Is this shit?" she asked from the threshold. That's as far as she could get without struggling to find a clear space to put her feet, since there was a stack of blue jeans on the floor in front of her, then a stack of capri pants, then a stack of folded sweatpants.

"I can't decide what to take with me," I moaned without looking up.

"We're going on a road trip to beat the shit out of a couple of teenaged assholes who ripped you off for twenty-six dollars. Or maybe we're going to expose a massive Russian mob human trafficking slash drug running operation. One of those. But I'm pretty sure this doesn't require Bob Mackie to help you select a wardrobe. Hell, this doesn't even call for Tim Gunn, unless you would be more productive by having a middle-aged queen standing here telling you to 'make it work.'"

"Couldn't hurt."

"Get up. Now." I got up. I didn't have a choice. I knew Rhonda's "drill sergeant" voice when I heard it. She'd never been a drill sergeant. As far as I knew, she'd never even seen one in real life. Rhonda's exposure to drill sergeants had, to my knowledge, been limited to multiple watchings of *Full Metal Jacket* as part of her duties as President of the North Carolina chapter of the Vincent D'Onofrio Fan Club. Yes, there is such a thing. Yes, Rhonda is really the President. And yes, she takes her position very seriously. But her work with the VD'OFC has given her certain perks, and one of them is enough viewings of the classic war movie to be able to channel R. Lee Erney at will. Which she did now.

"Now get yourself five pairs of underwear and put them in that suitcase."

I grabbed the required number of panties and turned to put them in the small rolling bag I had open on the bed. I had to put them down to remove Sir Grumbles, my cat, who was rolling around in the empty suitcase making sure there was a sufficient amount of cat hair in there before I put any clothes in.

When I set my clothes down on the bed, Rhonda immediately picked up the stack and started to cluck disapprovingly. "Oh, sweetie," she said. "I know it's been a while, but you do remember that there's this thing called sex, right? And people *have* it? And one of the ways people get it is by letting other people that they want to have sex with see them in their underwear?"

"I've heard of this mythical beast with two backs, yes," I said. "But that's not what we're going to Florida for. I want to yell at these idiots, and maybe slap them around a little, not bang them. Besides, aren't we pretty sure this was done by a couple of kids? That's just gross."

"One, we aren't going to sleep with the people who stole your credit card info. Unless they're old enough and super-cute. Then all bets are off. But we aren't going to get to Florida tonight, and we aren't going to be *just* looking for your identity thieves. That means you need something to go to a bar in when we get to Charleston tonight, and something to go out in tomorrow night after we've dealt with your little identity thieves once and for all. And both of those somethings need to at least give you the potential to take your clothes off in front of someone other than me, and trust me, you do not want these pink cotton things with yellow daisies on them to be what you are showing off to someone who you want to plow your most fertile garden."

"Leaving aside your atrocious metaphor, and ignoring the fact that my garden is thankfully no longer fertile, you have a point." I pulled three pair of comfortable panties out of her hands and put them in the suitcase, then looked over the pile of "special" underwear and grabbed a pair of those. Then I carefully navigated the minefield of clothing to squeeze past Rhonda at the door. "Excuse me."

"Where are you going?" she asked my back.

"Kristen's room. She's been raiding my underwear drawer again, and we're going to have a talk about who exactly she's wearing my black lace thong for when we all get home Monday night." I entered my daughter's bedroom, studiously ignored the devastation within, and kicked enough books, bags, sweaters, and shoes out of the way to get to her dresser. I reclaimed the black thong I was looking for, along with the matching bra, and nabbed a red bra and panty set I didn't recognize while I was at it. I wasn't sure if it was mine or Kristen's, but if it was mine, it needed to go on this trip, and if it was hers, then she was grounded forever. I returned to my room and dropped them in the suitcase, then picked up Grumbles and dropped him on top of a pile of jeans, where he promptly rolled over and began to writhe happily atop the clean laundry. Little shit.

"Do I need to walk you through the rest of this packing process, or can I go downstairs and play Fruit Ninja until you're done?" Rhonda asked.

"I'll be down in five minutes," I said. "And Fruit Ninja? Aren't you like the only person in the world who still plays that?"

"Sweetie, that was my euphemism for looking at porn. So I'm going to go play Fruit Ninja on your couch until either you're done packing or I go blind." With that, she turned and flounced down the hall, her red hair bouncing along like something out of a Jessica Rabbit cosplay.

I looked over at the cat, who was now sitting on my favorite t-shirt licking his crotch. "Grumbles, if I could do that, I'd never leave home." But I can't, and there was vengeance to be had, so I finished packing the rest of my clothes, left everything else scattered across my bedroom floor for the cat to wallow on for the weekend, and went downstairs, clumping heavily so Rhonda could hear me coming and stop whatever she was euphemisming before I came around the corner.

"Let's go," I said. "It's time to get our Thelma and Louise on!"

Rhonda looked askance at me. "Ummm...they both died. Pick somebody else to emulate."

"Butch and Sundance?"

"Both guys. And died at the end."

"Bonnie and Clyde?"

"Closer. At least one was a female. But still died at the end."

"Yoda and Obi-wan?"

"Okay, now you're just screwing with me."

"Do that, I would not," I said in a scratchy voice, then led the way out to the Prius to hunt down some hardened criminals. And maybe a hookup. But mostly criminals. Who we would not be hooking up with, no matter how cute they were. Unless they apologized first. And were of age. And really cute.

CHAPTER 7

T he sun was low in the sky as my house shrank in the rearview mirror. The detour through Charleston would add an hour to our total driving time, but it meant that I could stay in one of my favorite cities for the night. Not to mention that Rhonda had enough hotel frequent traveler points from her company credit card that we booked a place right downtown that promised a rooftop pool and walking distance to several bars. I had a sneaking suspicion that me hooking up was one of my neighbor's ulterior motives for going on this trip with me. Her hooking up was another, but that's one of Rhonda's ulterior motives for all sorts of things, like going to the grocery store, checking the mail, getting gas, going to the post office. You name it, she's scoped it for boy-meat, as she calls it.

I admire Rhonda's openness about sex and her desire for it. She has thrown off the yoke of Puritanical bullshit, as she calls it, and goes after whatever she wants, whenever she wants it. She spent fifteen years with a husband who wasn't nearly as interested in her body as he was with the box scores in the morning paper, and for her fortieth birthday, she gave herself a divorce. Since then, she's been a take-no-prisoners woman on a mission to make up for every night of passion she missed out on in the last ten frigid years of her marriage.

And she's done a pretty good job of catching up. Trust me, I've heard way more of the gory details than I ever wanted to. I know more about the ass freckles of the local lawn guys, pool boys, roofers, postal workers, UPS drivers, dog walkers, and pizza delivery drivers than I ever thought I wanted to know. Sometimes Rhonda accuses me of having sex vicariously through her. I usually respond that I don't have time to get laid myself because I'm always listening to her stories about getting laid.

I envy her a lot of the time. She has a freedom to her that I've never mastered. I blame my kids for it, but it's totally not their fault. Jess has invited me to conference with literally every professor she's had that is remotely cute and possibly available, and Kristen signed up for volleyball at school last year just because she thought the coach might be into me. She was, but I had to remind my daughter that I'm mostly straight and not interested in women that are spectacularly more fit than me. Now if she ended up with a smoking hot Home Ec teacher with a baking fetish, we could talk.

I knew as I pointed the car toward Charlotte and I-77 South that I had at best four hours before Rhonda was going to be dragging me into a nightclub with more makeup on than I felt comfortable with and my boobs pushed up to my chin in the sexiest bra I had in my suitcase. And I made sure to pack some reasonably sexy ones, not just because Rhonda was watching, but because she is not above cutting the straps on anything she finds not acceptably enticing and forcing me to walk into a bar with the girls swinging free. I love her, but I did that once, and once was enough. The last time I spent an evening that conscious of my nipples, I had a kid attached to one.

I leaned down to flip on the radio, and Rhonda swatted my hand away. "Oh no, honey. We are not kicking off our revenge road trip with NPR. I love me some Diane Rehm, but this journey is going to begin in the only way one can—with Steve Perry." Then she grabbed the sync cable out of the console and plugged in her phone. Seconds later, the opening licks of "Don't Stop Believing" filled the car.

"Just for the record," I said between verses, "Diane Rehm retired."

"Whatever. Just sing along and put the hammer down on this hybrid, girl!"

So I did, feeling the little electric engine whine higher and watching my hometown shrink behind us. We were heading off on an adventure, a journey with no expectations, except a couple of days of way too much drinking, staying up way too late in hotel rooms talking trash with my best friend, and slapping the face of the pimple-covered shithead who stole my twenty-six dollars.

I might have underestimated the dangers inherent in two middle-aged women alone in a strange town with no kids to rein them in. Or maybe I discounted the possibility that anyone sophisticated enough to crack a secure website for financial information might actually be a real criminal and not just some asshole kid. Either way, my life was about to change, and if not for the better, at least for the more terrifying.

FOUR HOURS LATER, we pulled up into the valet line of the Charleston Marriott, and Rhonda was out the door before I got the car in park. She moved faster than a white girl on free pumpkin spice latte day, with the words "gottapeegottapeegottaPEE" going rapid-fire under her breath. I'd offered to stop half an hour before, but she said she could hold it. I offered again just north of town, but she said she was fine, despite her voice being half an octave higher the second time I mentioned it. Now she was squeaking like a ceiling fan at a funeral home and hauling ass for the lobby restroom, leaving me to deal with the valet and bellhop.

"Need a hand with your luggage, ma'am?" the young man asked, and before I snapped at him not to call me "ma'am," I noticed that he was, at his very best, my oldest daughter's age. I decided not to traumatize the polite Southern boy who hadn't even voted in his first Presidential election yet, and just said, "Yes, please. I don't think my friend is going to be a whole lot of help."

He laughed and blushed a little. It was precious, the little flush on his freckled cheeks. He looked at the car and said, "I probably won't need a cart. I can—"

I cut him off. "Son, you are looking at two middle-aged divorced women on a weekend getaway without their children. I know you are thinking to yourself, 'how much luggage could two people take?' and probably something like 'it's not like that car can hold much.' But let me promise you…" I look at his nametag. "Stefan, this is not your normal excursion. This car is not your normal Prius. When it comes to a woman's luggage, this thing becomes the Tardis of hybrid subcompacts. When you start taking bags out of that trunk, it's going to look like a clown car just puked on your sidewalk. So please, for your own sake, get a cart."

He looked at me, the corner of his mouth twitching. "You're funny. You—"

"Remember, Stefan, before you say I remind you of your favorite aunt, teacher, or neighbor, that you work for tips," I cautioned.

He stood there brain-locked for a second, then recovered. "You and your friend should check out Wet Willie's on Market. They have great blender drinks."

"Good save, son." I patted his cheek as I walked by and handed him the keys. "Good save. The room is under Mabry."

I walked into the lobby, an opulent faux-antebellum affair that might have been thirty years old at the most. It looked like the props department from *North and South* just deposited all their set dressing there when they finished filming. A beautiful young Black woman with a colorful head scarf was checking Rhonda in when I walked up beside her.

"Everything come out alright?" I asked, proving that men are not the only ones who can remain perpetually middle schoolers.

"Oh sweet baby Jesus I thought I was going to pee all over my shoes. Good lord, why didn't I make you stop in Columbia?"

"Or Summerville?" I asked. "Or North Charleston? Or any of the other literally fifty places we could have stopped since you first mentioned you needed a little bit of a potty break?"

"If we get home on Monday and that's the worst mistake I've made on this trip, then I haven't been trying hard enough. Now did you get Junior to take care of our bags?" She handed me a key card.

"I did. I also told him if he got them up to the room before we made it there, you'd show him your boobs."

The girl behind the counter laughed, a musical sound that echoed off all the white marble in the lobby. "Oh, that's delightful! Stefan has probably carried the whole cart up to your room by now!"

"Oh, honey, that's sweet," Rhonda said. "But no man that young wants to see boobs as old as mine."

"Ma'am, I hate to argue with a customer, but you must have forgotten what men say about breasts," the girl, whose name tag read "N'Lyra," said. "If you've seen one pair..."

In unison the three of us finished the line. "You want to see them all!" Then we laughed, and N'Lyra slid a couple of yellow squares of paper across the counter to us.

"These are good for a complimentary breakfast. They're supposed to

41

be reserved for a wedding party, but some of them didn't show up. You made me laugh, so I hope you enjoy it."

"Thank you, N'Lyra," I said, slipping the breakfast tickets into my purse alongside the room key. "I'm sure we will. Come on, Rhonda, let's get changed and see what kind of trouble we can get into tonight."

RHONDA DIDN'T SHOW Stefan her boobs. Mostly because I told her that I never said anything of the sort to the poor boy, and we didn't want to terrify the child by her just ripping her shirt off like she was working the pole right there in the hotel room. And when I say "hotel room," I really should be saying something like "mega-luxury suite," because there were two bedrooms, each with their own bathroom, a kitchenette, a living room with a fold-out sofa, and a separate dining area with a table for six.

"Good Lord, Rhonda, how many points do you have?" I asked as I walked back into the living room from putting my bags in my room. I slipped out of my shoes, and the carpet felt like I was walking on clouds, it was so plush. I plopped down on the couch next to Rhonda and picked up the remote.

She was tapping away at her phone. "I don't know. A couple million."

"Even after this?"

"Oh yeah. I've got our room in Orlando covered already, too. My whole team travels on my company card, and my company card is linked to my Marriott account. I don't just get points when I travel, I get points when *any* of them travel."

I didn't know exactly what Rhonda did for a living, but I knew she managed something like thirty people all over the East coast, and all of them were on the road a lot. "How do you make sure they stay at Marriotts? You don't have millions of points at every hotel chain, do you?"

"No. This is our main one because they're everywhere, and the points are easy to redeem. They stay at Marriotts because I tell them to, and I take good care of them with the higher-ups, and I make sure that their mileage checks and other perks are never late. You take care of your people, and they'll take care of you."

That was the most I'd ever heard Rhonda sound like a manager, and I was honestly impressed. The Rhonda I spent time with was Party Rhonda, or Beat Up My Ex Rhonda, or Flirt with the UPS Guy Rhonda, or Bad Influence on My Children Rhonda. This was Damn Good Boss Rhonda, which spoke to there being a Good at Her Job Rhonda and a Smart as a Whip Rhonda tucked away in there somewhere. This weekend was turning out to be a revelation, and we hadn't even made it to Florida yet.

"So where to first? Strip club? Dive bar? Biker bar?" There was Gonna Get Me In So Much Trouble Rhonda. That's the one I thought I was taking a trip with. Good to see she hadn't gotten left behind in North Carolina.

"Let's get something to eat first. If I'm going to hang with you all night, I'm going to need to keep my strength up." I said.

"Okay, but we'd better make sure they have a full bar. Because if you're gonna hang with me, you're going to need to get your courage up, too."

Oh, how right she was.

CHAPTER 8

Our night started off at TGIFriday's and ended up in the drunk tank, and if that don't sound like the first line of a country song, I've never ridden topless in the back of a pickup truck down the main drag of Myrtle Beach with a beer in one hand and a bottle of Cuervo in the other. Shut up, I was eighteen, drunk, and perky, so I could get away with that shit. I try that today and my nipples will be pointing all cockeyed and down at the ground like they're looking for their contact lenses.

I ordered the triple appetizer plate with wings, potato skins, and cheese sticks, and Rhonda got some kind of garlic chicken thing that left me wondering if she knew something about the vampire population of Charleston, because by the time we split some kind of melted chocolate orgasm cake thing for dessert, my wingwoman smelled like an Italian kitchen. Or maybe an Italian brothel. Hell, coulda been both for all I know. I've never been to Italy. Not even Little Italy. Although I did sleep with a dude in a canoe once, but that's as close as I've ever been to Venice.

After Friday's, with our bellies full of grease, chocolate, and a pitcher of strawberry daiquiri, I called us a Lyft, and we headed downtown to party. I left my car in the hotel parking lot, because I've been out drinking with Rhonda before, and I know that trying to drive after a couple hours on the town with her is a good way to find out exactly how good a Prius is at climbing a tree. I've never tried to climb a tree with a Prius, but I expect it would be about like a hippopotamus trying to ride a skateboard —hilarious to watch but dangerous for everybody involved. So that's why we were standing in the parking lot of a chain restaurant in Charleston, South Carolina, waiting for a woman named Fran in a Subaru to come whisk us away for the adventure of a lifetime. Or at least a few hours of harmless groping and drinking for free with rednecks at a bar. I knew which one my money was on.

At just the appointed time, a silver love child of an SUV and a station wagon pulled up, and after a quick check to make sure that the driver was indeed Fran and not some random axe murderer, we got in the back seat. Rhonda immediately fished a twenty out of her bra and leaned forward between the two front seats.

"Fran, honey, I know you're getting paid to take us to the address my friend put in, but here's an extra twenty bucks to make us regret every decision we've made for the last decade and drop us off at someplace skeevy, loud, and crawling with men," Rhonda said.

Fran was a twenty-something woman who looked like somebody scared the shit out of a toothpick and then slapped eyeglasses on it, so I had little faith in her knowing any place like what Rhonda described. But this wallflower flicked out her hand and snatched that twenty out of the air like she was catching beads on Bourbon Street and gave us a grin full of unnaturally white sparkling teeth. "I know just the place. It's a little ways out from downtown, but the drinks are cheap. The music sucks, but it's loud, and the men are all drunk, stupid, employed, and nearsighted."

Rhonda leaned back, a Cheshire Cat grin on her face. "It's so nice to find somebody who gets me. Let's roll, Frannie!"

I slammed back into the seat giggling as all four cylinders of that Subaru worked overtime, whipping a U-turn out of Friday's and heading north toward the bright yellow lights of North Charleston, which Pat Conroy once accurately described as smelling like the asshole of an elephant. That man had a way with words. Fran bobbed, weaved, turned, spun, and somehow navigated the narrow streets until I couldn't have told you if we were in Charleston or Kansas. We turned down a side street, more an alley than anything, between two warehouses that looked like they'd last shipped or made anything in the Carter administration, and finally pulled into a parking lot that materialized out of nowhere. She pulled up to a tattered burgundy awning out front of a nondescript building and dropped the Subaru into park.

"Here y'all go," she said, turning to look at us with a business card in her hand. "I don't know if you can get data out here on your phone, so you might not be able to get Lyft to work. If you can't, call me and I'll come get you and take you back to wherever y'all are staying."

I took the card, thinking to myself that there was no way in hell I wouldn't get full internet on my phone in the middle of a civilized city, completely disregarding the fact that I was in South Carolina, which should have rolled the clock back twenty years on my definition of "civilized."

"Thank you, Fran," I said, reaching for the door handle.

"Y'all carrying?" she asked as I had one foot out of the car.

I looked back at her. "Carrying what?"

"A gun. You got your concealed carry, don't you?" By the look in her eyes, she wasn't joking.

"Ummm...no," I said, wondering if I needed to specify "unlikely to get shot up in the next four hours" in our description of the perfect watering hole.

"Oh," Fran said, a little crease appearing between her eyebrows. "Well, it'll probably be fine. Ain't been no real trouble out here in a few months. I reckon y'all'll be okay. Have fun!" She put the car in drive, and I finished getting out of the back seat, closing it just before she pulled out of arm's reach.

I looked over at Rhonda, who grinned at me in the way that can only be fueled by daiquiris. "You sure about this, Rhonda?"

"Girlfriend, I ain't never been sure about nothing in my life except that men suck and we only keep them around to get shit down off the top of the refrigerator and open jars of pickles. Now let's go get our drink on and shake our asses a little bit!" Then she strutted past me, already well on her way to the ass-shaking part of her evening.

The bar was every bit as sketchy inside as the tattered awning, unlabeled metal door, and blinking neon sign proclaiming it as "Dixie's Joint" were outside. We were met with a blast of hot air and loud Kenny Chesney as soon as Rhonda opened the door, and I could see just enough past her shoulder to know that there was dancing happening, but it was all of the "line" variety. I immediately began digging in my purse for my phone, because Mama don't line dance, but stopped in my tracks when Rhonda hit a wall.

Not a literal wall, just a slab of humanity that may as well have been a wall. He was big. Not just normal big, but the kind of big that says "I was thrown out of the pro wrestling industry for unnecessary roughness." He was not quite the width of the door, but close, and so tall he literally blocked all the light coming from the buzzing fluorescent overhead. There was a leather vest hanging open over his KISS t-shirt, and I swear his chest was so massive that Gene Simmons' tongue in the picture was life-sized. He had a bald head roughly the size of a beach ball, with thick red muttonchops sideburns and a bulbous nose.

He smiled down at Rhonda. "Welcome to Dixie's. Y'all are lucky. It's Ladies' Night, so y'all get in free. I just need to make sure you don't have any weapons, so if you'll hand over your purses for inspection, y'all can head on in."

Rhonda looked up at him, after she took a step back so she could actually see his face, and smiled. "Honey," she said in an accent that sounded like something right out of *Gone with the Wind*. "I didn't bring a pocketbook, and I'm sure you'll agree there's nowhere in this dress I could hide a weapon. But I did bring a pair of thirty-eights, and believe me, they're loaded." She hefted her breasts for emphasis, and it was all I could do not to fall over laughing. For one thing, Rhonda hasn't been a thirty-eight since before she *turned* thirty-eight, not that I expected Bubba the Bouncer to be able to see that.

For another, I knew full damn well she had a little razor tucked into her bra, just in case of emergencies, she said. I wondered what kind of emergency would necessitate her slicing her nipple off, but decided it was safer not to ask. Instead, I just held out my purse for the giant to paw through. "Here you go. I'm carrying the ID for both of us tonight."

"Oh, you won't need ID," he said absently, then froze as he realized that he'd just told two women who were admittedly well past the legal drinking age that they both *looked* well past the legal drinking age, and this might put a damper on our willingness to drink in his establishment. He looked back and forth between Rhonda and me, his eyes huge. "I mean, we don't card unless somebody looks really young."

He probably saw from the scowl on Rhonda's face that this wasn't exactly the most helpful response, and tried to correct himself again. "I mean—"

I decided to save him from himself. "We get it, sweetie. We aren't twenty-one anymore. And I don't have a gun in my purse. So unless you're really interested in what brand of makeup and tampons I use, can I have my purse back?" He handed it back to me like it was radioactive, and I breezed past him and Rhonda.

Rhonda followed, and we made it all of ten feet past him when she started to crack up. "That. Was. Hilarious!"

"I have long since learned that the word 'tampon' is all it takes for almost any heterosexual man to lose interest in any purse, glove compartment, suitcase, or conversation. This was very useful when I was still married. Good to see it still works." I looked around the... I guess you'd call it a "club," but if it was a club, I wasn't sure I wanted to be a member.

There was sawdust on the floor, but I'm pretty sure I could still see a couple of bloodstains through it. The dance floor was half a dozen sheets of plywood out in the middle of the room with about a dozen rednecks in cowboy boots, trucker hats, and NASCAR t-shirts spinning, twirling, and clapping off the beat to mediocre country music. There was one guy out there, too, and he looked like he couldn't decide whether to scratch his watch or wind his ass, he was so lost in what he was supposed to be doing. But about every sixth beat, he'd turn in the wrong direction and bump right into one of the women, who'd turn him around and shove him the right way, usually with a smack on his ass. So he was getting some kind of action, even if it was a little hapless.

The bar was...underwhelming, to say the least. It was a cinderblock wall with what looked like just loose boards laying on top of it, and I'm pretty sure I could see the top of a couple Igloo coolers open below the level of the bar. There were shelves made of milk crates holding an assortment of bottom-shelf liquors, and one lonely bottle of Absolut sitting by itself on the top "shelf." I reckoned that was what passed for good liquor in this joint.

The bartender was *much* more impressive, being a shirtless guy in his twenties with a six-pack, a glistening, muscular chest, and long flowing hair. He looked like Fabio from a distance, until we got close enough for him to lean forward onto the bar and smile at us before saying in a thick Southern accent, "Howdy, ladies. What'll it be?"

It was the smile that did it. I try not to be too superficial, really I don't. I can deal with a lot. Except my ex's porn stache, but there's a lot of backstory going on there that doesn't involve his facial hair. But if I have one thing that squicks me out, one thing that will send me running for the bathroom on a blind date speed-dialing the emergency bailout contact in my phone faster than even an admission to being a Libertarian, it's bad teeth.

I cannot abide looking at somebody with bad teeth. Not crooked teeth. That doesn't bother me. I mean, I have friends from England, and they're fine. But yellow teeth, black teeth, missing teeth, or just...gross teeth? That's my trigger. And Meth Mouth Fabio behind the bar was about to give me some serious heebie-jeebies. He grinned, and it was like there was a little miniature black and yellow picket fence winking at me, with about half the stakes hammered in crooked. My first thought upon seeing his smile was that he might should have spent a little less time in the gym doing the clean and jerk and more time in the bathroom cleaning his nasty mouth.

Rhonda, knowing my aversion to all things dentally foul, grabbed my elbow before I could spin around and head for the door, and hissed in my ear, "We don't have a ride, so you might as well have a drink while we call Fran for an extract."

"Make that extract ASAP, or whatever they say in those military movies," I hissed back, and slipped onto a bar stool, pulling out my phone and staring down at it. I'd sit there, and I'd drink, but if anybody was looking that bartender in the face, it was not going to be me. I'd managed to go years without barfing onto the floor of a sleazy underground bar in South Carolina, and I was trying hard to keep my streak alive.

"We'll have two shots of Absolut with Stella back, please," Rhonda said.

"Oh, we ain't got Stella," MM Fabio said. Now that I knew what his teeth looked like, he even sounded less hot. An ability to visualize is both a blessing and a curse. A blessing when I'm having some "alone time" with an Alexandra Christian novel and a bottle of Malbach, and a curse when there's a jagged-toothed monster five feet from the top of my head.

"Okay, whatever pilsner you have will be fine," Rhonda said.

"I don't know what a pilsner is. We got liquor, and we got beer."

"Absolut and Bud Light," Rhonda said, and I could almost hear her beer-snob soul shatter into pieces and rain down upon the sawdusty floor.

She slipped onto the stool next to me, and I glanced over at her. "Okay," she said. "It might not have started out great, but this place can't possibly get any worse, can it?"

I knew we were screwed the moment she said it.

CHAPTER 9

Not only did my phone not have data, I didn't even have signal on the damn thing. I handed Fran's business card to Rhonda and said, "You try to call her."

"Where in the hell do you think I've got a cell phone in this dress?" she asked.

I looked again. It was pretty damn tight, and I couldn't *see* any bulges, but Rhonda has always been a master of secreting important things on her person where Indiana Jones couldn't have found them. Not that either one of us would have stopped Harrison Ford from looking. Even Old Harrison was hot as hell.

"I have faith in you. Now make the damn call." She gave me a dirty look, then reached into her top, under her left boob, and fiddled around in there for a second before coming out with her cell phone. I swear, that woman is part kangaroo.

"Did you have the surgeon put in a pocket when he did your boobs last year?" I asked.

"No, but that woulda been a good idea. Get 'em adjustable, so if I need to carry stuff I could swap out to smaller implant and use the leftover space to hide my weed or something."

"You haven't smoked weed since the 90s," I said.

"I have a dream of legalization," Rhonda replied.

"If it's legal, you won't need to hide it."

"Do not fuck with my titty pocket fantasy, Lexi! It's a good fantasy, one that won't get screwed up by male clothing designers, so give me just these five seconds to dream of pockets built into my fake boobs."

She closed her eyes, and I watched her count to five. Well, not really. I was actually staring at her chest, trying to figure out where that phone had come from. Her boobs looked exactly the same as they did before she pulled an iPhone out of them, and it wasn't one of the little tiny phones, either. That thing had a screen big enough that neither one of us needed our reading glasses to dial it. Yes, we have both reached the point in life where true convenience is measured in whether or not we have to spend five minutes hunting around for our spectacles before doing something.

Rhonda let out a long calming breath and looked down at her phone. She held it out to me with a grimace. "I can't get a signal, either."

I turned to Meth Mouth Fabio and, keeping my eyes firmly affixed to the planks that passed for a bar top, asked, "Can I use your telephone? It's a local call."

"My phone don't work here, sorry," he said, and I caught just enough of a whiff of his breath to know that his teeth weren't the only thing rotten going on in that boy. He needed to see a doctor. Or a mortician. Or maybe a goddamn veterinarian, because his breath smelled like a dog fart trapped in a hot minivan in the parking lot of a Costco on a July afternoon.

"Well, how do people get home if they get too drunk?" Rhonda asked, and out of the corner of my eye, I saw her jerk back a little, like she got a zap of static electricity. She must have looked at his teeth again. Braver woman than me.

"There's a couple taxis that start showing up around midnight. They make a loop through the parking lot and pick up anybody that looks like they're ready to go home."

I looked at my phone. It was nine-fifteen. This was gonna be a long three hours. "We're gonna need another half-dozen shots and probably a six-pack of beer. Hell, just give me the bottle and two highball glasses."

"Bottle's a hundred bucks, and we got shot glasses and beer glasses." Nothing in his voice sounded like it was unusual for someone to drink an entire bottle of Absolut in his presence. I looked at the red Solo cup in my hand, what passed for a "beer glass" in this divest of dive bars, and then looked at the clear plastic "shot glass" sitting next to it. "Just gimme some extra cups."

He handed over the bottle and half a dozen red plastic beacons of redneck style, and me and Rhonda wove through the crowd headed for a table in the back corner of the room. I was feeling the serious need to have my back to a wall, and with the daiquiris from Friday's and the shot and beer I'd knocked back since getting to this shithole, I figured sitting down would be the safest move for me. Rhonda had a six-pack of Bud Light in her hands and her best "don't fuck with me" look on her face, but it turns out that the kind of walk and grimace that will part crowds on busy city streets like you're Moses parting the Red Sea does nothing to dissuade the one drunk son of a bitch brave enough to line dance in public in South Carolina on a Friday night.

But no. The yokel apparently decided that flailing around to the pounding beat of big hat country music was less likely to get him laid, or at least a handy in the parking lot, than chatting up a pair of middle-aged women with a shitton of booze and push-up bras that were working overtime.

"Hey ladies, y'all are looking mighty fine tonight," he said as he stopped in front of our table. I tried to ignore him, hoping he'd go away, and just poured myself a healthy slug of vodka into a cup and downed it. Oof. That was rough. I did it a couple more times and prayed that Dionysius would come bless me with a sunken stupor sooner rather than later. Tex was not dissuaded by my aggressive attempts at ignoring him. He grabbed a chair and spun it around, sitting backward on it and ostentatiously adjusting himself. I looked, I'll admit it. And by what I could see, he didn't need a whole lot of adjusting, because there wasn't a whole lot *to* adjust, if you get my meaning.

I'm saying he had a little dick. Or at least that he wasn't showing off anything impressive at the moment. Who knows? Maybe his really is a grower. If so, and it grew into something impressive, it would be the only remarkable thing going on with this dude. He was maybe thirty-five, about two hundred pounds, and normal height, I guess. I was sitting down, and I'm not what you'd call tall anyway, plus I'd been drinking for several hours and was more focused on getting more alcohol into my system than establishing this douchebag's precise measurements. He wore a blue checked cowboy shirt, with honest to Jesus pearl snaps on the pockets and the little embroidery that looks kinda like the back pockets of a pair of Jordache jeans, with a bolo tie and a ten-gallon cowboy hat that engulfed his five-gallon head.

Now let's be clear, we were in South Carolina. Not Texas. Not even Oklahoma, Mexico, or even goddamned Calgary. There were no cattle ranches anywhere close by, and I did not remember seeing a horse tied up to the hitching post out front of the saloon when we ambled in. Or did we mosey? I'm not sure I know the difference between an amble and a mosey. I think amble is a little faster, and probably shakes your ass more. Maybe Rhonda ambled and I moseyed. Yeah, that's probably it. So this guy wasn't even a rhinestone cowboy, unless he had a piercing I couldn't see, because there wasn't a single rhinestone anywhere in sight.

"Howdy, pardner," I said, leaning forward to put my elbows on the table and give him a clear shot at my cleavage. What can I say? I was bored, and if flirting with this moron kept me occupied for the next couple hours until the taxis started to run, it would be worth showing a little skin here and there.

"Where y'all ladies from?" he asked. "I don't reckon I've seen y'all before, and I'm sure I'd remember anybody as pretty as you two." Nice of him to make sure his flirting was spread evenly between us. No point in making one of us jealous about who got to not sleep with him first.

"We're just passing through," Rhonda said. "When does this place start to show some action? It's pretty boring so far." She waved a hand at the four women line dancing, now managing pretty well without Tex screwing up their moves. Past them were a couple of pool tables occupied by fat men with trucker hats, and a dart board where another pair of husky boys threw pointy things and passed bills back and forth between them.

"Action?" Tex said. "What kind of action y'all looking for?" I didn't know somebody could make something sound like a leer, but he managed. I was impressed. Skeeved out, too, but impressed. "My name's Henry, by the way. Like Doc Holliday."

"I'm Lex—"

"Lexus," Rhonda said, cutting me off. "Like the luxury machine she is. I'm Esthere. Like nothing."

"Nothing I've ever seen before, that's for sure," Tex said. I reckon I should call him Henry, since I knew his name now and he was about as Texan as I was a luxury car.

Henry wasn't a bad-looking guy, more silly-looking than anything. It just looked like he was trying too hard, with the big hat, and the pearl snaps, and the boots. He even had a pair of jingly silver spurs on his feet, for God's sake. But if you stripped away all the stupid trimmings, he was all right. He had pretty brown eyes, and a decent face, and he was medium build. He didn't look like he spent every day in a gym, but he wasn't some couch potato, either. Outside of his outfit, the only thing he really had going against him was a mustache that was obviously a source of great pride, since it was huge and waxed into such perfect shape that I swear he spent more time waxing his mustache than most guys spend waxing their cars. And for once that's not a euphemism for anything.

"So what kind of action y'all looking for? Dancing? You wanna play a little strip pool? You wanna go out back and ride on the bull?" Henry asked, and I swear the way his hand twitched I thought he was gonna reach up and twirl his mustache. If he did that, I was going to start walking west 'til I reached a cell tower, and I didn't give a good goddamn how long it took.

Rhonda laughed out loud. "Damn, son! We just met. How about you at least let me get through a couple of these beers before you go talking about me riding anything of yours?"

Henry looked confused, then he blushed bright pink. It was so cute I forgot how irritated I was at his suggestion that we go out back and screw within a minute of meeting us. "No!" he protested. "That ain't what I meant. There's a mechanical bull out back, and if you can last eight seconds on it, you get a free beer. If you last a minute, you drink free the whole night."

We'd already spent a hundred bucks on a twenty-dollar bottle of vodka, but when I saw the light in Rhonda's eye, I knew we were not getting away from this place until she had wrapped her thighs around some faux leather and given it her absolute damnedest effort to get us some free alcohol. Never mind that we had more booze on the table in front of us than two women of our stature could drink without a trip to the emergency room.

I'd seen that look on Rhonda's face before. She had sale fever, and nothing was going to stand in the way of her getting a bargain. This was the kind of madness that leads women to fistfights over plastic colanders at Black Friday sales, causes yuppie women with Escalades to run Camrys off the road hauling ass to Krispy Kreme when the two-for-one dozen glazed deal is on, and has led to bloodshed in toy store parking lots over the last Tickle Me Wherever doll that somebody abso-damn-lutely had to have that Christmas.

She stood up, raised the Absolut bottle over her head like Lady Liberty's torch, and said, "Henry, my boy, take me to that bull. Mama wants to riiiiiiide!"

CHAPTER 10

The last time I saw something as decrepit as the mechanical bull out back of Dixie's Joint, it was up on blocks behind my high school boyfriend's cousin's trailer. That was a 1954 Chevy pickup truck with a pup tent in the back that had an old mattress in it that me and Billy Ray used to fool around on when we didn't feel like going to the dance after football games. Which was pretty much every Friday night it wasn't too cold to get naked in a tent in the middle of the woods. Which was pretty much every Friday night, on account of living in the South and us being horny teenagers who had our own ways of keeping each other warm.

Even now, more years later than I will admit in the company of anyone who doesn't have access to my birth records, I'm pretty sure taking a ride in that truck down I-85 with no headlights at a hundred miles per hour would be safer than getting within ten feet of that fake bull. It was big. Bigger than those things always look on TV, and while the ones in movies always looked like they were made out of brown leather so it at least vaguely resembled cowhide, this thing was made out of that special kind of gray metal that you know only comes from one place, so it was obviously constructed of scrap from the Navy yard, with a blanket and what looked like a bath mat tied across it to make some kind of rudimentary saddle.

An eight-ball gear shift stuck up out from where the "bull's" shoulders would be, I reckon to be used as a saddle horn, and there were a couple of puddles of various fluids underneath the machine that I really hoped were hydraulic fluid and oil, because if they weren't, then we'd stumbled on a den of White trash Satanists, and we were about to be sacrificed to their Dark Lord and Master. I hoped they appreciated that I was wearing my good underwear when they murdered us both.

"What. The. *Fuck*. Is that?" Rhonda asked, stopping cold two steps out the door.

"That is Hornicus Prime," Tex said, gesturing at the bull like he could have possibly been talking about anything else. He didn't just say the name of the contraption, he *proclaimed* that shit, like it was something he was proud to be associated with. The city of Charleston was spiraling downward in my estimation like Taco Bell down a toilet thirty minutes after you eat it.

Now, Hornicus wasn't just ugly. It didn't just look like a torture device built out of surplus military parts. It was an ugly torture device built out of surplus military parts with its own goddamn *light show*. Because as soon as Tex waved at it, the damn thing started to spin around, buck up and down and front to back, with smoke spewing out of one end and little jets of flame shooting out the other. Four spotlights came on and swooped around the crowd. (Yes, there was a crowd. There were about thirty people out back of this joint, more than were inside by a wide margin. I wondered why for about a minute and a half before I noticed that at least three of every four people out here had cigarettes in their hands.) Then the spotlights changed colors and strobed around until they finally settled back on Hornicus, bathing the fake bull in a deep red light that made the smoke coming out of its butt look downright menacing.

"Did that thing just breathe fire?" Rhonda asked.

"Or was it shitting fire?" I asked. "I can't really tell which end is the front."

"The gear shift is on the front, Lex," Rhonda said, suddenly an expert on the physiognomy of homemade mechanical bulls. It did make sense, though.

"Oh," I replied. I looked at Tex. "Did that thing just breathe fire?"

"Hell yeah, it did!" Tex let out a whoop and yanked his hat off and slapped his thigh with it. This exposed an impressive combover that wrecked every charitable thought I'd had about his appearance. I mean, bald can be sexy. Really short hair can be sexy. Long hair can be sexy. Shit, even a skullet can be sexy, if you're Hulk Hogan. Scratch that. Hulk Hogan couldn't pull that look off, either. So it's long hair, short hair, or bald. But a combover? A combover says you aren't willing to accept what the mirror is telling you. A combover is your mind deluding you into thinking that if you tell the same lie loud enough, and often enough, then it'll become true. And that shit only works for politicians.

So Combover Tex was not only excited that Hornicus Prime breathed fire, but he seemed...proud? "Henry," I said. "Did you...build that thing?" I gestured in the general vicinity of Hornicus. I didn't point directly at it because I was afraid that it might somehow see me pointing and take offense. And I did not need a mechanical bull that shits fire coming to life and deciding it was pissed off at me. But the fact that I considered the possibility reminded me that I was well on my way to being absolutely shitfaced, so I needed to get my happy (not really all that happy) drunk (and getting drunker by the second) ass to a chair post haste.

"I did indeed. You are looking at the proud creator, designer, fabricator, and integrator of the greatest technological marvel of the Lowcountry, Hornicus Prime."

"That's...something," I said, pushing past Tex as he took a bow. I weaved through the completely open area in front of me and collapsed into a chair after setting my vodka down on the table. I tried twice to put my cups next to it, but the table kept moving and I decided to just put the damn things on the ground. I could drink from the bottle anyhow. I was a grown-ass woman, and if I wanted to drink right out of the bottle, wasn't anybody gonna tell me not to.

"Sweetie, how much of that did you...oh shit," Rhonda said, looking at the level of liquid in the bottle. She waved frantically at Henry, who came high-stepping over like his ass was on fire. Or like his spurs made him take extra-big steps to not get stuck in the dirt floor of the patio. "Henry, sweetie, Lex is gonna need some water. A lot of it."

"I don't need water, I got vodka," I said, reprising the theme of many of my college weekends. "Henry's cute. You should probably have sex with him," I told Rhonda, reprising the morality of many of my college weekends.

"The jury's still out on whether or not Henry's getting lucky, darling. Right now, let's get some water in you so I don't end up holding your hair back in an hour." Henry got back with another stack of Solo cups and a pitcher of ice water that didn't look like it had too many things floating in it. He poured me a cup full, and I knocked it back like it was vodka. I should probably have been more concerned that I was now comparing my water drinking to my vodka drinking and not the other way around, but I wasn't concerned about very much anymore. On the plus side, the decor of the bar was way more awesome now that it was all kinda fuzzy.

"So what do you say, little lady?" Henry said, smiling that oily smile at Rhonda again. Well, really, he was smiling at her boobs. I'm not sure Henry could have told you what color Rhonda's eyes were if you put a gun to his head, but he could give you a detailed description of the little bit of lace peeking up over the top of her dress. "You ready to mount up on Ol' Hornicus?"

I tried not to laugh. I didn't try very hard, but I did try. I failed miserably, but I did make at least a token effort. "That sounds like the world's worst name for a penis I've ever heard," I said.

"If that's the worst one you've ever heard, I can give you the numbers of some guys I've dated," Rhonda said. She turned back to Henry. "I would, sweetie, really I would, but one of us needs to sit here and make sure Lex doesn't fall right out of her chair, and if I go ride Hornicus, and you operate the controls, there's nobody left to watch her. And you know, you never leave anyone behind." She saluted as she misquoted the Navy SEALs. Or maybe she was just misquoting some movie about Navy SEALs. I've never asked a SEAL if that's really a thing. But it was a good sentiment regardless.

"Oh, you ain't got to worry about her falling. Dixie had all her chairs equipped with five-point harnesses a couple years ago after one real drunk dude fell over and got himself a concussion. If you look on the back of her chair, you'll see the seat belts." Rhonda got up, and I heard a *click*.

"Son of a bitch," she said. "That's maybe the smartest thing I've seen since glow-in-the-dark condoms."

"What's so smart about that?" I asked.

"It lets the guys who ain't got nothing going on at an orgy sword fight each other and make lightsaber noises without anybody thinking it's weird," she replied. She said this with a straight face. My best friend, who I have lived next door to for many years and who I knew was a little wild but apparently had no real concept of the depths (or maybe heights) of her depravity, just talked in a completely normal tone of voice about men making lightsaber sounds and slapping peckers with other men to keep themselves amused between bouts of sex at an orgy. There was apparently a lot more going on in my subdivision than I was getting invited to.

"Sweetie, I'm going to reach around you now. I promise I'm not feeling you up, I'm just putting your seatbelt on so you don't get hurt," Rhonda said, throwing the straps over my shoulder.

"That's okay," I said. "You can feel me up. Best offer I've had all night."

She buckled me into my seat, without feeling me up, and I was only a tiny bit disappointed. She did look really good in that dress, so I wouldn't have minded if she'd copped a feel or two. Maybe later. I knew where she was spending the night, after all. That is, assuming Henry didn't get lucky. I was pretty sure Henry wasn't getting lucky. Not unless he had a pair of clippers somewhere close by. If we could do something about the combover situation, he might stand a chance.

"Okay, Henry," Rhonda said, downing another beer after she clicked my final restraint in place and poured me another cup of water. "Let's get riding!"

With that, Rhonda strode across the dirt like a gladiator into the arena, her dress in place of armor, and up to the block set up to help people onto Hornicus' back. There were blue pads laying on the floor all around the mechanical bull, which I reckon was all the help the proprietors thought anybody would need getting down. Rhonda put one foot up on the step, or tried to. The problem was, her dress, as I mentioned before, was *really* tight. Like, she couldn't really lift her leg more than six inches tight. Not without tearing something, at any rate.

She tried a couple times, then looked at Hornicus, looked back at Henry, then looked at me. I didn't know what she was looking for, so I decided on generic encouragement and hollered "WHOO! You go, girl! Ride that thing like it's a quarterback!" Then I gave her a double thumbs up and my very best "you got this" grin.

A look crossed over Rhonda's face just then. It was a look I've seen many times, and it usually results in us getting thrown out of any place with linen tablecloths. It has also at times ended up with my daughters banned from various social and religious organizations for ours and the surrounding counties. It's Rhonda's "fuck it" face, and when she puts it on, shit is about to get *real*.

Well, shit got real, all right. Because Rhonda, with the unmitigated gall of someone who doesn't live here and will never see any of these assholes again, just yanked her damn dress all the way up to her waist, stepped up on that mounting block, and straddled Hornicus Prime with nothing on her bottom half but a bright red thong and a pair of her very best "fuck me" heels.

At that exact moment, the thought running through my head was, "Damn. Rhonda's been working out."

CHAPTER 11

Now I don't know if you've ever been in a shithole redneck bar in South Carolina when a woman hikes her skirt all the way up to glory and straddles a mechanical bull named Hornicus Prime, but if you have, then you probably need therapy. I'm pretty damn sure I do, and not just for what I saw in the mosh pit at Lollapalooza that one time. When Rhonda literally showed her ass on the back patio of Dixie's, I was pretty sure we were not making it out of that place with our virtue intact. Then I remembered exactly who I was talking about, and that "virtue" was not a word frequently applied to either of us, and decided that I'd settle for getting out without a felony conviction or a course of penicillin.

The first thing that happened was that Tex, or Henry, or whatever the hell we're calling him, leaned forward to get a better look, snapping off the joystick that apparently controlled the movement on the giant mechanical bull Rhonda was currently straddling. Then he slammed his hand down on the desk in front of him in his excitement, which I learned later led to him crushing the speed control knob. So what was supposed to be a slow, sexy ride on a mechanical bull to get Rhonda some free beers and maybe get Tex Henry a little action in the bar men's room later, turned into a whirling dervish of steel, fake boobs, and fire.

Hornicus had been gently undulating back and forth like one of those soothing water and sand sculptures that your stoner uncle had when you were a kid. But when Tex got his first look at Rhonda's jiggling butt cheeks and he beat the shit out of the controls, Hornicus's pace, which had been roughly in time with a Sarah McLachlan album, cranked all the way up to full on Rob Zombie in about a half a second.

That bull started slamming back and forth and up and down and spinning round and round like it was the newest vomit comet at an amusement park, something designed by a sadistic meth addict with a vertigo fetish. Rhonda bent over at the waist until her ass was higher than her head, then slammed back so hard I was pretty sure her butthole was jammed up somewhere about her kidneys. She gave up on any semblance of rodeo style, gave up on making a show out of holding on with only one hand, and latched onto the gear shift saddle horn like it was the last life jacket on the Titanic.

I stood up, remembering about halfway through the motion that I was buckled into my chair for safety, and sat back down. Hard. Chair and all. There was a loud *crack* from my ass area, and since I wasn't in pain, I thought the chair was probably in danger of—*THUD*.

Falling apart beneath me. I sat down even harder this time, because I was flat on my back in the dirt with my legs splayed out in the air above me and my underpants and indignity on display for anyone who might have been looking. My only saving grace was that Rhonda's ass was more interesting than my crotch, so she drew most of the attention. There have been times in my life when I would be offended about another women getting more eyeballs on her ass than I was getting on my accidental panty flash, but they're rare, and none have ever happened when I was on my back in the dirt on the back patio of a shithole bar in South Carolina while I was strapped to a now-broken chair.

I clapped my knees together, trying to salvage some iota of gentility from the situation, and took stock of my situation. Everything hurt like a son of a bitch, so I was pretty sure I wasn't paralyzed. The fall had shocked me pretty much sober, so I could operate complex machinery like the buckle on the seatbelt holding me to the chair, which I immediately released. I stood up, wincing and swearing that if I lived through this trip, I was finally going to unwrap that Pilates DVD I'd bought and give some serious consideration to working out. Then I took a deep breath and turned my attention to the greater problem—Rhonda and the Runaway Hornicus.

I've got to give it to both of them—they were persistent as all hell. Despite getting slammed up and down and back around so much she had to feel about like she was gonna crap a watermelon any second, Rhonda refused to simply let go of the gear shift and fall to the padded floor. And Hornicus, despite looking like a Rube Goldberg version of a shitty Transformers knockoff, just kept on keeping on, spinning and jumping, and twirling and humping in ways I hadn't seen since the first time I went to a gay bar in the nineties. Tex Henry was one hundred percent useless, leaning over the controller like he was, just staring at Rhonda's ass. There were three men gathered around the bull, making a loose circle about ten feet away, but they didn't look inclined to help in any way. I think they were just hoping to see a titty pop out.

As Hornicus spun her around, Rhonda saw that I was free of my bargain basement bondage gear and hollered, "Lexi, get me the fuck off this thing!"

"Just let go, dumbass!" I yelled back. "There's pads on the floor!"

"I can't," Rhonda yelled. "My thong's hooked on the saddle horn!"

I almost asked her exactly how she managed that one, but I've been in some situations where my underwear has ended up in unfortunate places, and it's almost always better not to know. I'm sure given enough time and enough security camera and cell phone video angles, we could figure out at what point in the bull ride from hell Rhonda's underwear had gotten looped over the gear shift, but I couldn't see anything helpful coming from that knowledge. It's like how sausage gets made, or how porn gets made—the less you know about it, the more you can enjoy your life.

"Okay! I'll get you off!" I shouted. Then I froze as every eye in the bar swung in my direction. "Oh, screw all y'all! That ain't what I meant!" I ran (okay, stumbled quickly) over to Tex Henry and said, "Shut it down!"

"I can't!"

"The hell you mean you can't?"

"I grabbed my joystick too hard, and it snapped off!"

"I did not come over here to talk about your dick, Henry."

"It wasn't a euphemism (that's how you know Tex was a whole lot more sober than me. I couldn't have said the word 'euphemism' right then if you put a gun to my head and spotted me the first two syllables), dammit. The controller's broke!"

"Goddammit," I muttered. *Okay*, I thought, *What does Kristen tell you to do when the computer messes up?* I don't know much of shit about technology, but that's why I had kids, so they can change my diapers when I'm old, and so they can keep track of new shit for me. If there was one thing I'd learned raising my girls, it's that when something seems irrevocably

63

fucked, unplug it and plug it back in. I scanned the far walls, looking for anything that might fit the bill, then finally saw a plug snaking its way up between two blue wrestling mats and going into a socket about ten feet from where Rhonda and Hornicus were gyrating in separate but painfully intersecting orbits.

I ran (okay, stumbled again) in the direction of the socket, only to be caught by a pair of strong arms around my waist. "Where you going, little lady?" came a boozy voice in my ear.

I spun around and looked up into a face that only a mother could love, and then only if she was really astigmatic and maybe had a cataract or two. This particular pinnacle of Lowcountry style wore a greasy blue work shirt with "Peter" in a white oval on his chest, open to reveal an even greasier tank top that managed to, with a great deal of effort, contain his impressive belly, and a pair of jeans that might have started life as blue, but there wasn't any clean fabric visible for comparison. He smiled down at me with a grin that made Meth Mouth Fabio the Bartender look like an ad for proper oral hygiene, and his yellowed picket fence teeth didn't even have the courtesy to be lodged in a handsome face. No, Peter looked a lot like a bulldog chewing on a wasp's nest, all weird lumpy spots and red splotches.

"I gotta go," I gasped, trying to get out of his grip without touching him and trying to tell him to let me go without drawing a breath from his airspace. The stench of cat piss rolled off him like fog off a lake, only more putrid, and my eyes started to water after the third second in contact with him.

"Nah, stick around. We can dance, baby." He grinned at me and leaned in like he was going to kiss me, and that's the point where I'd had enough. My resolve to get out of the night without any major drama was long since shattered, so now I just tossed any plans to make it out of Charleston without a criminal record in the shitter after them, and I kneed Peter the Stank Monster square in the balls.

He let go of me, and I immediately went against every self-defense class I'd ever taken. Instead of doing the smart thing and getting as far away from my larger attacker as possible, I decided I'd watched enough Rhonda Rousey matches on YouTube to be a goddamn MMA expert, and I slammed my elbow into ol' Peter's nose. I heard a *crunch* from the middle of his face, and blood literally *fountained* from his nose. Have you ever been watching when somebody turns on one of those big fountains? There's a little splut, then a bigger splat, then a good-sized splash, then shit just *gushes* everywhere. Peter's face was like that, only with snot and blood.

I didn't stick around to watch the fruits of my labor. Not much, anyway. I turned back to the main problem at hand—my best friend had her ass hanging out on the back of a fire breathing mechanical bull and her panties were tangled up in the bull's non-euphemistic gearshift. I marched the rest of the way over to the plug and yanked it out of the wall. A whine of slowing motors ground to silence, and as I turned to watch, Hornicus made one last revolution, snorted out one last gout of fire from his nose, and fell still.

Rhonda reached down to her crotch, and after a moment or two of tugging, pulled her hand away and slid backward, falling to her butt on the blue wrestling mats surrounding the mechanical bull. I staggered over to her and pulled her up. I'm not sure which one of us was the least steady on our feet, but we each needed a hand on Hornicus to stay upright.

"I think I gotta puke," Rhonda whispered.

"Can you puke and run at the same time?" I asked.

"Probably not. Why?"

"Because I kicked that dude over yonder in the balls and broke his nose, so I think I might be going to jail," I said.

"Well, I just flashed my ass to half of Charleston, so I'm probably gonna be your cellmate," she said.

One of Rhonda's trio of admirers stepped up to us, applauding with every step. "Damn, girl, you sure do have a nice ass," he said. He was a white-haired man with a close-cropped white beard. He looked Rhonda up and down, then licked his lips. "How about you let me smack it for twenty dollars?"

Rhonda raised one eyebrow at him and asked, "How about I get the first shot?" Then she punched the old man in the nose, dropping him flat with one punch. "There," she said to me as she grabbed my hand and started pulling me toward the door. "Now we'll *definitely* be cellmates."

CHAPTER 12

Rhonda blew Tex Henry a kiss as we stumbled for the door, making a brief stop by our table to pick up her last three beers, and we slammed back into the main body of the bar. A pair of burly cops were just crossing the floor, and as we passed them, Rhonda leaned in and said, "Be careful, there's some dude with spurs talking about knowing karate and a chick just rode the mechanical bull butt nekkid. It's crazy out there, man." The cop's eyes got big, and he hurried out onto the patio as we booked it for the front door. We woulda made it, too, if it hadn't been for the jealous wife and the twelve-gauge.

Now I have never been the kind to fool around with another woman's man. I've barely been the kind to fool around with an unattached man, and have historically been so clueless about men's attention that they have to lay on the ground in front of me with a boner that I can fall on for me to actually get laid. So I have absolutely zero experience with jealous wives or girlfriends. I don't know them when I see them; I don't know how to deal with them; and I definitely cannot tell the difference between one who wants to yell and scream at me and one who wants to shoot me.

So when a wild-eyed woman in a housecoat, slippers, curlers, and face cream burst in the front door looking like something off the *Carol Burnett Show* holding a shotgun, I froze in my tracks. My mind could not compute for a moment exactly what I was seeing, so I didn't register the threat. Then she pointed the scattergun at the ceiling and pulled the trig-ger. The shotgun barked like thunder, and the threat was abso-damn-lutely registered.

"Where's that harlot that's screwing my Henry?" she hollered as she racked the slide. I was impressed with how she handled the shotgun. Peckerwood took me out dove hunting one time in some kind of weird attempt to get me interested in the outdoors, or maybe to prove to me that he really went hunting on his hunting trips, or maybe just because he thought he could murder me in the woods and call it a hunting accident like when Dick Cheney shot that dude in the face with a shotgun, only the dude didn't die, so maybe Peckerwood thought better of it at the last minute and just decided we should sit out in the woods all day, and I should have to pee in the woods and learn the hard way that not every plant in the forest is an acceptable substitute for toilet paper. The point is, I had handled a pump shotgun before, and it wasn't near as easy as she made it look. There was a little catch thingy that made the slide release, and if you didn't flick that, you weren't doing nothing, but she didn't have any trouble, just jacked another shell and pointed the gun out over every-body's head.

"Where is she?" the she-devil markswoman bellowed again, and I took a moment to really consider her outfit. She was little. Not just skinny, but *little*. She was maybe five feet tall and a hundred pounds, which made her handling that gun even more impressive. She had flaming red hair and at least ten percent of her body weight was in her boobs, which made some significant lumps in her fuzzy terrycloth housecoat. It was a nice pale pink, a subdued color that wasn't near as red as the little bits of her face I could see around the green crusty facial mask she was wearing. The slip-pers matched, which was nice, and there was a little marabou poof on the toes that matched the hem of her robe. All in all, it was a pretty nice ensemble if you're going to run out of the house in the middle of the night and wave a gun around in a redneck bar. She did lose points for the curlers obviously coming from two or three different sets, but not many. Nobody can keep up with all those damn things, so there's always one or two random curlers anytime you do your whole head.

"Now, Clarice, we done talked about you coming in here waving that gun around." Meth Mouth Fabio the bartender was already around the bar with his hands held out to his sides, a placating tone in his voice. He was moving slow and keeping his voice low and even, like he was talking to some kind of wild animal. From the looks of things, this was not his first rodeo with Clarice the Spurned Avenger.

"Lowry, you can kiss every inch of my country ass, and you know it. Now get the hell out of my way before I fill you full of lead. I done told Willis at the door that I ain't gonna shoot nobody in the bar. I'll wait 'til we get to the parking lot, so you don't have to bust out any extra sawdust before Saturday night."

"Well, that's mighty considerate of you, Clarice, but didn't you see the police car out front? We can't be having you waving a gun around in here tonight. Might not look good to the boys in blue, who are out back talking to Henry right now."

There was a lot to unpack in that sentence, most of it for me centered around the implication that there were some nights he didn't give a shit if The Real Housewives of Redneckia came into the bar armed to the teeth, but the only part Clarice heard was that Henry was out back. When she heard that name, her eyes went wide and she started forward, straight for me and Rhonda.

We stepped aside with haste, and She stomped past us, only to slow after a few more steps and turn around, almost like she was in slow motion, bringing the barrel of the shotgun down as she rotated, until she was facing me and Rhonda and the gun was pointed right between us. "You look awful familiar," she said to Rhonda. "Have I seen you some-where before?"

"I've often been told I look like a taller Susan Sarandon," Rhonda said. Now those words *had* been said before, but I'm not sure they'd ever been said by anybody other than Rhonda herself. And maybe me, the fourth or fifth time she asked me, depending on how many margaritas I'd had on a given night.

Clarice the Gun Girl looked puzzled by this, as if it kinda made sense, but kinda didn't, which was pretty good for Rhonda, since kinda making sense was pretty much her high water mark. She let the barrel of the shotgun keep drifting downward and turned back to head outside. We had just started moving toward our escape again when the patio door slammed open hard enough to hit the wall. I spun around as a woman I vaguely remembered from being outside during Ms. Rhonda's wild ride came busting through the door.

She'd stuck in my head because of the truly impressive level of white trash fashion sense she was employing, and believe me, that bar was set pretty high in Dixie's. She didn't just have on Daisy Dukes, she had on Daisy Dukes with the button undone and the top rolled down enough so that we could see more than enough of her rebel flag underpants to know that she definitely had it going on down South. Or maybe that she wanted the South to rise again. Or some kind of dick joke. I don't know, I was real drunk.

A Playboy bunny belly ring glittered just above her panties, and below her tied-off Whitesnake t-shirt with the collar cut out and a rip artfully sliced in the neck to plunge the whole thing down between the valley of her boobs that managed to be both massive and completely immobile, even as she jumped up and down and pointed at us. "Clarice! That's her! That's the whore right there!"

I leaned over to Rhonda. "She talking about you or me?"

"Pretty sure I'm the one that was on a mechanical bull with my ass in the breeze. That's pretty high on the whore-o-meter."

"Good point. Why don't her boobs move when she jumps like that?"

"Either her bra's too tight or she got shitty implants."

I chuckled. "This is where I'd find that picture of the little kid saying 'why not both?' if this was on Facebook."

Rhonda snorted, then tried to act serious as Clarice swung back around and marched in our direction, leading with the shotgun. This was the first time I'd ever had a gun pointed at me, and even though it technically wasn't pointed *at* me, with a twelve-gauge you don't have to be all that precise, so I'm counting it. I didn't know how one was supposed to respond to this, but I did learn that having that much adrenaline coursing through your system right after half a bottle of vodka made it so that something else ran through your system real fast.

"I gotta pee," I said.

"I think we've got more important shit to deal with right now," Rhonda replied.

"I think you don't know how bad I gotta pee," I replied. I held up a hand to Clarice, who was now just a few steps away with blood in her eye. "I'm sorry," I said. "I've really gotta go tinkle. Can I run to the ladies' real quick? I'll come right back and then we can deal with why you want to murder my best friend."

Clarice looked at me all kinds of confused, then took in my crossed legs and the little wiggle that had come over me while I said my peace. "Alright, go on. But hurry right back. I don't want this shit to drag on all night. I've still got three or four steps to my beauty regimen and two episodes of *Dr. Phil* on the DVR, and I've gotta work in the morning."

"I'll bring her right back, I promise," I said. I grabbed Rhonda's wrist and gave it a tug, but she didn't come with me. I looked back, and Clarice had the shotgun pointed square at Rhonda's chest. "What's the matter? I told you I've gotta go!"

"You can go. She ain't going nowhere, though."

I blinked a few times trying to make sense out of the situation. This was another woman. A woman in her thirties, so a little younger than us, but a grown-ass woman nonetheless. How did she not understand what was going on? "I can't go to the bathroom *alone*," I said. "I'm in an unfamiliar bar, far from home, and I've gotta pee. How in the world am I going to get my business done looking at unfamiliar walls if I ain't got anybody to talk to? Be reasonable. I said I'd bring her right back."

Clarice swung the shotgun over in my general direction, and that's when Rhonda struck. She moved faster than a damn cobra, just taking two steps forward and grabbing the barrel of the gun. She yanked it out of the other woman's hands and flung it off behind her before she laid into Clarice with a slap that sounded like, well, like somebody slapping the ever-loving piss out of somebody else.

Clarice stared at her for a second, then went into full-on Tasmanian devil mode. She sprang at Rhonda, knocking her to the floor, and straddled her on the way down. She sat on Rhonda's tummy and started raining down slaps like she was Rocky working a speed bag. Well, if Rocky hit like a girl and only connected with about every third slap. I'd never seen somebody be two feet away from another person and miss trying to hit them so often.

Rhonda lay there and took if for about seven seconds, which was six more than I expected her to, before she reached up and backhanded the snot out of the raging Clarice. The other woman froze, straddled across my best friend on the floor of a dive bar, housecoat hanging open all the way to Glory, one curler hanging loose with hair stuck all up in her green face crap, and just gawked at Rhonda. "You hit me!"

"Bitch, you tackled me and slapped me like eleventy-seven times!" Rhonda snapped back. "Now if you don't want to make out, get the hell off me. And if you do want to make out, wash your damn face and buy me a drink first. But either way, get the hell off me!" Rhonda reached up to shove Clarice off her, hopefully so we could run like hell for the door before things went even more sideways, when the patio door slammed open again and Mr. Even More Sideways came busting in.

"Freeze!" yelled the cop Rhonda had sent outside after Tex Henry. He had his gun drawn and a "don't fuck with me" look on his face. "Everybody in here is going to jail 'til we can sort this shit out!"

I suddenly realized two things. One, that I didn't have to pee anymore. And two, that spending a night in jail with wet legs was going to *suck*.

CHAPTER 13

J ail wasn't as bad as I expected it to be. I didn't have to worry about dropping any soap, because I didn't stay long enough to take a shower, and I didn't have anybody try to make me their bitch or take all my cigarettes out in the yard, because it turns out they don't do any yard time at the city drunk tank, and certainly not between one and seven in the morning. I did have a moment of deep embarrassment when I had to pee in a much more exposed situation than I've been accustomed to since college (there were a few bonfires out in the woods that saw me pissing on moss-covered logs), and it didn't smell particularly good, but once the big metal door slammed shut and I saw that Clarice was in the cell across the hall, I relaxed a little bit.

I still didn't feel completely safe, but I thought that the five other women in the cell with me were a lot less likely to try to kill me or Rhonda than the woman who was pretty sure that Rhonda riding her husband's mechanical bull's gearshift was a euphemism instead of the bizarre reality that it was. I sat next to Rhonda on a hard metal bench attached to the wall. "Is this the Big House?" I asked in a whisper.

"I'm pretty sure this is a Child's Medium, at best," Rhonda replied. One of the other women, a thick-shouldered woman with short hair and tattoos, snorted. I looked over at her, and she gave me a wink. I clutched at Rhonda's arm, and the woman winked at Rhonda, too. I'm not opposed to the idea of sleeping with another woman. God knows it can't be any worse than my ex-husband, but I don't think of jail as a pickup spot. But what do I know? This was my first time in jail. Maybe it's where all the bad girls go looking for romance. When I got out, I decided to call my cousin Lucy and ask. She's a court reporter down in Gaston County, so she's my expert on anything having to do with the judicial system. If anybody knows the level of hookups that usually go on in a drunk tank, it'll be Lucy.

We passed an otherwise uneventful night in the drunk tank, our fitful sleep sitting up leaning on each other's shoulders interrupted by the clanking of cell doors, intermittent vomiting from our cell and others, and one fistfight over the superiority of the Clemson Tigers over the South Carolina Gamecocks. I, for one, was happy to see that some things remained constant, and college football was just as divisive among convicts as it was among people on the outside.

I was just about to the point where I was ready to figure out how to arrange enough privacy to pee again when a pair of men in the spectacularly unflattering multiple brown tones of the Charleston Police Department came into the hall and opened the cell door. One of them was a big wall of humanity with the kind of belly that let you know he had not seen his pecker without a mirror since the last time South Carolina had a Democrat for a governor. He had a big round head with his brown hair cropped close to his skull, and a tight beard on his moon face that kinda made it look like his head was a basketball that somebody had just dropped onto his shoulders, avoiding the need for a neck altogether. His partner was the Jack Spratt to his...Mrs. Spratt, I guess. He was a skinny little shriveled-up man with a stringy gray goatee, one of those narrow mustaches that you can't tell if he trims it to look like that or if it just grows funny, and a no-shit swooped back pompadour hairstyle that would not have been out of place in a James Dean movie. There was more hair product on his head than in the entire women's drunk tank, and that's not even taking into account the damage we'd all done to our 'dos over the course of the evening.

"Do you think he changes the oil in his car, or just rubs his head on the engine block?" Rhonda whispered to me. I snorted, as did half the women in the cell. Pompadour turned red all the way to the tips of his ears, because Rhonda's whisper has sometimes been heard three houses over. She is not known as the subtle one in our neighborhood.

"Let's go, ladies," Big Boy said, while his partner just stood there, kinda quivering. I wondered if this was a Barney Fife kind of situation, where Pompadour only had one bullet for his gun, and he had to keep it in his shirt pocket. I kinda hoped so, because I figured I could hide behind my tattooed new girlfriend if he started trying to shoot Rhonda. "Y'all stop at the front desk, pick up your shit, and pay the fine. Lurinda, you go first and show 'em what to do."

Tattoos stepped to the cell door and patted Big Boy on the cheek. "Will do, Clyde. You say hey to your mama for me, okay."

"Yes, ma'am. I'll see you Wednesday night for choir practice. Don't forget you got the solo next Sunday."

Tattoos, now apparently Lurinda, smiled up at the mountainous choirboy cop and said, "I'll be there. Long as happy hour don't run late." Then she walked out the door, leading a bunch of staggering drunk and hungover women like she was the Pied Piper of Bad Decisions, a title I usually gave to Rhonda.

Rhonda, of course, stopped in front of Pompadour and gave him a peck on the cheek. "Thank you so much for your hospitality, Deputy. I *do* hope we can do this again next time I'm in town." I put a hand in the small of her back and shoved her down the hall away from the vibrating guard before he either shot her or exploded. Either way was going to lead to me covered in bodily fluids, none of them sexy, and I was not in the mood for that. I just wanted to get a cab back to our hotel, take about fourteen showers, and sleep for twelve hours.

Then we could continue our quest for justice against the sons of bitches who stole my identity. The sense of righteous fury that started this whole trip began to bubble up again as I realized that I had now spent more time in jail than the nefarious criminal masterminds who perpetrated a federal crime upon me.

But of course there was one more stop before we could leave. A stern woman with biceps the size of my thighs and a bosom that probably had its own zip code handed us both a big clear zip-loc bag with our possessions, and I was surprised to see my bottle of vodka still in there. There was even a line on the side where they marked the level. Not only was I surprised they gave it back to me, but I was stunned they didn't drink any of it. I was also horrified to see how low down on the side of the bottle that line was, and I offered a silent apology to my liver for the pain I had inflicted upon it. My liver was resolutely not speaking to me.

After we got our stuff, we were herded down a narrow hallway, through a cheap wooden door, and into a small wood-paneled room with a very bored-looking man sitting behind a big desk. There were four other people sitting behind tables on either side of him, and one woman over in a corner typing everything. On the desk in front of him was a nameplate that declared him "Hon. Eustace P. Rutherford, IV," because of course he was.

We all formed up in two raggedy lines, and Judge Eustace P. Rutherford, IV, slammed a gavel down onto his desk. "Order!" he yelled, which seemed excessive since nobody was talking, but we all kept right on not talking, and he went on.

"Y'all are all here on various counts of drunk and disorderly, disturbing the peace, public intoxication, stealing a police car...again, Lurinda?"

"I can't help it, Judge. It's my Tourette's acting up," Lurinda replied. I was pretty sure that wasn't how Tourette's worked, but since I'm no expert and I didn't want Lurinda to kill me right there in the courtroom, I kept my mouth shut.

"Whatever. Okay, when I read your name, if you want to plead guilty, say so, and then you can go over to Errol over yonder and pay your fine. If you want to plead not guilty, then you can sit down and wait until we're through with everybody else and then you can have your trial. Mr. Bigham, the Assistant District Attorney, will serve as the prosecution, and Ms. Tellerson from the public defender's office will provide your defense if you do not have an attorney. If you request a jury trial, you will likely be remanded back into custody until we can get that bullshit settled. Now, I've been running this courtroom for sixteen years, and there has only been one jury trial in all that time. That man could have paid a forty-dollar fine and gone home, but because he had to drag everything out and make things difficult, he served thirty days at the county work camp in addition to his forty-dollar fine. Keep that in mind as you contemplate your decision. Irene, who's first?"

"Terri Jo Allen, drunk and disorderly," a woman in a very nice cream blouse said from her table.

"Ms. Allen, how do you plead?" the judge asked.

"Guilty, your honor."

"Seventy-five dollar fine. Don't do it again. Go pay Errol and get on home." The judge turned to the rest of us. "See how easy that was? Let's keep it like that."

The next five women were pretty much like that. One or two charges, fines ranging from fifty to a hundred dollars, and they were out the door. I noticed that Errol even had him one of them little credit card swipers so people could pay fines by debit card. Lurinda was the big winner, getting a hundred and fifty dollar fine on account of it being her sixth offense.

Finally, there was nobody left but me and Rhonda. I wasn't sure how two women with the last names of Lieberman and Mabry ended up at the end alphabetically, but I didn't really care. I'd gotten thirsty along about the third guilty plea and started sipping vodka to pass the time.

"Alexis Lieberman and Rhonda Mabry," the woman called.

"Here," I said. Rhonda elbowed me. "What? I don't know what I'm supposed to say. I ain't never been arrested before."

"Now ladies, y'all are probably wondering why I kept you 'til last," Judge Rutherford said, leaning forward and steepling his fingers. "It's because of the varied nature of the charges against you, which are among the most…diverse I've ever seen come out of just one night of drinking."

"Well, Your Honor," Rhonda said. "We are truly exceptional drinkers."

"Apparently, Ms. Mabry," the little judge replied. "The charges against both of you include public intoxication, drunk and disorderly, simple assault, public nuisance, destruction of private property, destruction of *public* property, resisting arrest, and assaulting a police officer."

I thought about it as he went down the list, and while I was pretty sure we hadn't done any real damage to the police car, which made destruction of public property a stretch, all the others were pretty solid.

He turned to Rhonda. "Ms. Mabry, your charges further include, lewd and lascivious behavior, public nudity, simulated copulation in a public place, and bestiality."

"Now that last one's pure bullshit, Your Honor," Rhonda said. "Hornicus Prime is not a real animal, so even if I did hump his gearshift, there wasn't no bestiality involved."

To his credit, Judge Eustace P. Rutherford, IV, did not bat so much as an eyelash at Rhonda's statement, just picked up a red pen from his desk and drew a short line on the piece of paper he was holding. "Fair enough. No bestiality."

"Thank you."

Then he looked at me. "Mrs. Lieberman, you are charged with all of the above, and a further charge of public urination is added to your bill."

"I didn't mean to pee, Your Honor, but I've never had a gun pointed at me when I was shitface drunk before," I said.

Judge Rutherford just sighed. "How do y'all plead?"

"Can we plea bargain?" Rhonda asked. "Isn't this the part where we offer to roll over on our supplier and you give us immunity or something?"

"Ms. Mabry, this is not *Law & Order*. If anything, it is much more like *The Benny Hill Show*. So no, I will not be granting you immunity in exchange for information on your supplier. For one thing, you don't have a supplier. You bought your alcohol in the bar where you were arrested, and you didn't have any drugs on you when you were brought in."

"Well, of course not, Your Honor," Rhonda said. "We don't do drugs. Except in states where marijuana is legal, because let me tell you, them little THC gummy bears will do you all kinds of righteous. Have you tried those? Probably not, huh?"

"No, I have not tried—stop. Just. Stop. Talking." He put his hands on the sides of his head, and I knew it was over. I've been with Rhonda when she's returned things that were on clearance that couldn't be returned, when she argued that she should be allowed to use an expired two-for-one coupon, and when she'd talked her way out of about eighty-seven speeding tickets. Whenever her mark puts his hands on the side of his head, he might as well just walk away. Because he's done.

"Mrs. Lieberman, Ms. Mabry, if you will both plead guilty, pay a fine, and promise to never set foot in the city of Charleston again, I promise to make the fine very reasonable." Oh, it was truly over now. That kind of minor concession is like blood in the water to an experienced Karen like my friend Rhonda. I hoped she never turned her powers to evil, because she would truly be the kind of force that assistant managers talked about in hushed whispers.

"Two hundred dollars apiece and we'll stay out of Charleston for two years," she countered.

"Two hundred and fifty, and I retire in four years, so stay gone until then."

"One-fifty and we'll steer clear of the city for five," Rhonda said.

Judge Rutherford slammed the gavel down and said, "Sold! Go pay Errol and get the hell out of my courtroom."

I had just opened my pocketbook to pay Errol when the judge cleared his throat. "Mrs. Lieberman?" he asked.

"Yes, Your Honor?"

"Could I trouble you for a slash of that vodka? It has been a very long week this morning."

I walked over to the desk and set the bottle down. "Keep it, Your

Honor. You deserve it." And that's how we kept from going to prison in South Carolina.

CHAPTER 14

Twenty-four hours later, we were back on the road to Florida, rehydrated, scrubbed free of the top three layers of flesh, and with brand new criminal records and the fingerprint ink to prove it. That stuff is harder to get off than…well, me, if I forget to take my Adderall. Some things require a certain amount of focus, no matter how much fun they are.

But we were headed south once again, with TLC on the radio and the windows down, butchering the rap parts and trying to remember if it was a political statement or a fashion statement that Left Eye wore a condom as an eyepatch. We finally decided that it could be both. I picked up I-95 South right outside of town and managed to keep Rhonda from detouring us into Savannah for lunch despite her protests that she knew the perfect little spot down on the riverwalk with two-for-one piña coladas and calamari that didn't feel like you were chewing on an inner tube even a little bit.

I managed to put her off by convincing her that eleven in the morning was too early to start drinking except in Las Vegas, New Orleans, or divorce court, and we were in none of those places. We were on a mission for justice and righteousness and twenty-six dollars and the vanquishing of mayonnaise-lovers everywhere.

Jacksonville, Florida, had none of the inherent charm or day-drinking potential of Savannah, so we were able to get in and out of a Ruby Tuesday's with minimal damage to our schedule. We needed to make it to Orlando tonight, because we'd lost an entire day's worth of travel recuperating in Charleston, and I had justice to mete out. I also at some point needed to look up what it meant to "mete" something, justice or otherwise, and if there was any special equipment I was going to have to go get before I could mete the shit out of the bastards who stole my identity.

I'd been keeping a careful eye on all my credit cards since the theft, and there had been no suspicious activity. There'd been no activity at all, since the first thing I did was to cancel all my cards. Now that meant I was paying for everything with the cash my ex-husband gave me and my sixteen-year-old daughter's emergency Visa card, which was glitter purple with a picture of the K-Pop band BTS on it. That got me a couple weird looks at Ruby Tuesday's, but if that was the worst thing that came out of the day, I'd take it.

An hour detour for lunch, half an hour detour getting turned around getting back on the interstate after lunch, two stops to pee, one stop at a liquor store big enough to have its own billboards, and another stop to pee had the sun setting on us as we finally rolled into Orlando.

I also had a fleeting hope that if I just drove straight to our hotel, Rhonda would be tired from being cooped up in the car all day and decide we could live on room service or maybe eat in the hotel restaurant, which would cut down the chance of me learning what the Orlando jail looked like by at least fifty percent. I might have been paranoid, given the fact that I'd been out drinking with Rhonda hundreds of times without going to jail, but since I hadn't been out drinking with her *since* getting arrested, I didn't know if we had turned a corner in our alcoholic adventures such that no night would be complete if it didn't end up with a massive tattooed lesbian choirgirl winking at me in a drunk tank. And I didn't really want to find out. I only brought a couple pair of what I would consider "prison appropriate" underpants, and I thought I might need to save at least one for the ride home.

My hopes were dashed when as soon as she walked into our room, she dropped the handle of her rolling bag, sprinted into the bathroom, and yelled out, "I have got to pee like a racehorse, but as soon as I shake the dew off this lily, you'd better be out of your travel clothes and into something that's more push up than strap down, because I haven't had a drink in thirty-six hours, and I think my liver is starting to think I forgot about it!"

I tried my best to ignore not only the sound of Rhonda peeing, which was a lot like if the entirety of Niagara Falls were moving into the hotel bathroom, and the fact that she was peeing with the door open. Again. "Privacy" and "modesty" are two words my best friend has never been well acquainted with. Kinda like "sobriety" and "whisper."

I tossed my bag up onto the weird little settee thing on the wall by the dresser. What the hell is that thing, anyway? It's too wide to be a chair, too shallow to be a couch, too low to be a table, and pretty much only useful for putting your suitcase on so you don't have to drag the foldy thing out of the closet. I stretched, pushing on my lower back to see if I could get it to pop, and heard more snapping and crackling from my spine than I did from my breakfast cereal. Getting old is not for wimps, y'all.

Then I peeled off what had started the day as a cute scoop-necked burgundy t-shirt and ended it a wadded mass of sweaty cotton that looked like it was good for nothing but maybe checking the oil in my car or cleaning up cat puke, and I dropped it in a shapeless heap on the floor. If it somehow miraculously dried out before we were ready to leave in the morning, or I miraculously started to give a shit, I'd fold it up neatly then. If not, then it's a good thing I stole it from Jess's room.

Once the sweaty shirt was gone, I reached around behind myself and popped loose the two clasps binding me into the Byzantine torture device that was my brassiere, and I let the girls free. The sigh of relief I let out was almost as loud as Rhonda's, and sparked a concerned query from the potty.

"Sweetie, are you alright? If I knew you needed to go that bad, I coulda let you go first. Or at least made sure you had toilet paper so you could pee in the sink or something."

"I'm fine," I replied. "I didn't pee. I just took my bra off."

"Oh, that makes sense. Why the hell did you wear a bra to sit in the damn car all day? It's not like I give a shit if you're flopping around a little."

"For one thing, I knew we were going to get out of the car for lunch, and it was easier just to have it on than try to put it on in the car."

"God, that's the truth," Rhonda said. "I remember high school. That sucked."

"And for another, I didn't want to worry about getting a black eye if we hit a rough patch of road. Your new store-bought boobs might not move much, but one bump and mine are bouncing around like somebody knocked over a whole rack of basketballs. Bring me a hand towel out of there, please?"

Rhonda came out of the bathroom and tossed me a small rectangle of white terry cloth, which I promptly used to mop up all the underboob sweat that had been making a break for my waistline since I unleashed the girls. There are a lot of things my mama taught me about being a woman—how to make biscuits from scratch, how to change my own tires and my own oil (which came in handy more than once in my marriage to Peckerwood, whose mama had not bothered to teach him those particular life skills), not to mix the red clothes with the white clothes in the laundry, how many Motrin you can take when your cramps are bad without completely shutting down your liver (Mama was a nurse; she knew things), and that I could be anything in the world I wanted to be when I grew up.

My mama did not teach me about underboob sweat. That one I had to learn on my own, and it was a lesson that started right after I finished nursing Jess and things started moving south. Not for the winter, but just moving south. I was at a summer family reunion when I first realized that my perky ladies were now laying much flatter against my ribcage than they used to, and the side effects on my clothing that were…unexpected, to say the least.

I think I was at my first cousin once removed Marcia Annette's house on the lake (which was really a cleared-out spot in the woods with an old Airstream trailer hooked up to the septic tank), and I had just finished changing Jess when I happened to look in the mirror. I saw in horror that even though I had managed to make it through a Fourth of July hot dog picnic without chili, mustard, or ketchup coming anywhere near my new top, there were these two perfect smiley faces on my chest, outlined in the darker pink of sweat-stained cotton. Except these were mutant smiley faces, on account of having only one eye apiece, but you get the picture.

I hadn't even noticed I was sweating, which is the worst thing about boobsweat. It's insidious. You can have half a cup of water tucked up behind the Hoover Dam of your underwire and not even know it until you move wrong, or the absorption rate of your bra suddenly changes, or the phases of the moon shift, or Uranus comes into prominence or some other stupid damn thing, and then all of a sudden it looks like a demented graffiti artist has painted an outline of half your hooter on your shirt.

The rest of that afternoon was spent sitting in uncomfortable folding chairs with vinyl netting cutting patterns into the backs of my thighs so I could stay bent over enough to hide the rings of Saturn on my chest, or with a baby pressed up tight to my chest if I was standing. I got home and immediately called Rhonda to ask her what I was supposed to do about this new and embarrassing development.

"Well, darling," she said. "There's only two ways to deal with the underboob sweat. Baby powder all over your tits or never wear a white shirt again."

I chose both. But all that meant was that I had a cascade of talcum powder coating the front of my abdomen as the gallon of boobsweat I'd had trapped in my bra all afternoon all came pouring out at once. At least until Rhonda threw me a towel.

"Jesus, child," she said. "Your boobs sweat more than a whore in church. Are you sure your titties aren't getting out and hooking up with somebody on the side? They look awful guilty over there."

I looked down. I didn't think my boobs looked particularly guilty, but then I guess I didn't know what guilty breasts looked like. Wait a minute, I *totally* knew what guilty boobs looked like, and they were right there across the room. I looked from my chest to Rhonda's, and back again. They looked nothing alike, except that there were boobs involved.

"Nope," I said. "I have examined the evidence, and I have found my breasts not guilty on all charges."

"Well put a shirt on and let's get your acquitted titties out to a bar and see if we can get 'em brought up on some all new charges!" Rhonda said, peeling out of her "road clothes" and changing into what I was starting to think of less as her "party" clothes and more her "get arrested" clothes.

I looked back down at my chest, now much cleaner and drier to the detriment of that poor hand towel. "Well girls, let's go see if we can keep Aunt Rhonda out of trouble." As I opened my suitcase and started looking for an outfit for the night, I only gave me about a one in three chance of success. I overestimated my chances by a long shot.

CHAPTER 15

Orlando is not considered a haven for adult nightlife. It has plenty of bars, sure, but when you stack it up to places like New Orleans, Las Vegas, New York, or even Cleveland, it kinda gets left in the dust as far as places for grownups to go out and do grownup things. And don't think I mentioned Cleveland as a joke. Those people managed to get their entire *river* to catch fire—they know how to throw down.

Given Orlando's more family-friendly bent than some destinations, and given that we had already spent fifty percent of our nights on this trip in jail, I started the night with high hopes for avoiding incarceration. It was also pretty important that I not get banned from another tourist city —I still had kids at home, and we were eventually going to have to vacation *somewhere*. My hopes were bolstered when Rhonda plugged Del Frisco's into the Lyft app, because even she wouldn't be able to find a mechanical bull in a classy steakhouse with white linen tablecloths.

And then she saw the neon beacon of silliness and regression to adolescence that was the sign for Slim & Slam's, a combination arcade/sports bar with franchises all over the country. The idea was that you have a meal, perhaps watching some flavor of sports on one of the nine thousand televisions in the main dining area, then after you've consumed enough random grease and fried whatever, you head into the arcade area where you wander around with your drinks and either fail horribly at games you sucked at as a child, or you try brand new games that you can fail horribly at. I've never seen the appeal, but as soon as Rhonda saw it, she started bouncing in her seat like a toddler with a bladder problem.

"Driver, sweetie, we gotta make a change of plans," she said from behind the driver's seat.

"I'm sorry, ma'am, they get really pissed if I don't follow the route. They're tracking my phone, so if I change things up, I get charged back," the driver replied. He was a nice-looking Black man with a trim goatee and shaved head. He looked a lot like Mike Colter, the actor who played Luke Cage, only without being a musclebound giant. And not bulletproof. Although I had no proof he wasn't bulletproof, and no real way to test that theory, since I didn't have a gun. Mostly because I don't own a gun, and they scare me. I'm not the most coordinated of humans, and I like my toes right where they are—attached.

"I've got that covered, sweetie," Rhonda said, holding a twenty-dollar bill out between the front seats. "The whole ride was supposed to cost like ten bucks, so this should more than make up for it, right?"

The last time I saw a bill disappear that fast (before the *last* time Rhonda bribed a Lyft driver) there was a thong and a lot of baby oil involved, and I was at Swinging Richard's, an all-male "revue" for a co-worker's bachelorette party. I spent the rest of the night wondering where that twenty went, because one minute Patty from HR was holding it out between her teeth as she leaned precariously close to the neon purple banana hammock that was precariously close to my nose, and the next it was gone, with no evidence where it went. This bill was much less worrisome in its departure, as the driver just folded it up and stuffed it into his shirt pocket. But that memory led my mind down all sorts of precarious paths, including wondering what the driver would look like in a neon purple banana hammock, and I realized I needed either a lot of alcohol or a detox center immediately.

"Okay, ma'am. Where to?"

"Slim & Slam's," Rhonda replied, looking over at me with a grin. "I feel a need to beat your ass at air hockey, girlfriend!"

"You just want to lean far enough over the air hockey table that you can pretend your boob accidentally fell out, despite the five minutes of work it takes you to get those things to move anywhere," I said.

"That too, but I'm still going to kick your ass."

She would, too. While I spent my college years pursuing a degree in art history with a minor in photography that left me qualified to talk about exactly why my darkroom skills were useless in a Photoshop world, Rhonda had spent hers as the toast of every house on fraternity row. She was known as the anchor of every beer pong team, the woman voted Most Likely to Outdrink the Football Team, and the undisputed champion of any game that could be played in a bar on a table, including pool, shuffleboard, foosball, air hockey, and a few things she told me about that I'm pretty sure weren't competitive games so much as new chapters in the Kama Sutra. I learned early in our friendship to never bet anything I didn't want to lose against Rhonda in a bar contest. The only thing I had even the slightest edge in was darts, because since her boob job she said her arms didn't move the same way and her aim was off.

"Okay, you can kick my ass, but I have got to get something to eat first. That Ruby Tuesday's lunch wasn't just mediocre, it was a long time ago, too," I said.

The car pulled up in front of the garish entrance, which was modeled after a 1980s arcade, except with slightly less of a feeling of desperation and a little less acne. Just a little. I felt a zit rising on my nose as we approached, but convinced myself it was just a hallucination. It wasn't. I was going to wake up in the morning with a carbuncle that would terrify Snow White's wicked stepmother, but if I was lucky, that would be the only crappy souvenir I woke up with. And I know I'm mixing up my fairy tales, but maybe Snow White had a wicked stepmother, too.

I pulled open the door to the bar and literally took a step back from the wall of noise that slammed into my face. It was like Pac-Man was banging Duran Duran in the middle of a basketball court, with all the bleeps, bloops, squeaks, screams, twangs, and tones. There were enough flashing lights to make me wonder if someone had preemptively called the cops on us, and as Rhonda shoved me through this portal to digital hell, a scream of joy erupted from one corner of the bar and a three-hundred-pound man leapt up onto a table that was never intended to endure such abuse, yanked his shirt up over his head and led the drunken revelers surrounding him in a cacophonous spelling of "Jets" that guaranteed I would forever more be a Giants fan.

"We gotta get out of here," I said. "Let's just take a Lyft straight to jail. That has to be safer than this."

"Come on, chickenshit," Rhonda said, her hand planted firmly in the small of my back. I stopped walking, and she dropped her hand to my butt cheek and gave me a sharp pinch.

"Ow!" I said. "That's my ass!"

"Yeah, and I'll take my hand off it if you'll put it in motion. I'm way too sober for this shit."

Now that was something we could agree on, and I staggered against the waves of noise to the hostess stand, where a twenty-something girl with a child's medium t-shirt stretched over her not childish or medium torso grinned at us from under a pair of pigtails in a shade of pink that reminded me of my senior prom lipstick.

"Welcome to Slim & Slam's! Where food and drink meet fun and games!" She grinned the perfect smile of expensive orthodonture, and said, "My name is Pippi. Would you like a table, or would you prefer to sit at the bar?"

Pippi. Of course her name was Pippi. "Table, please," I said. "One without the shirtless male centerpiece if you have it."

"Or if not, can we at least pick our own centerpiece?" Rhonda asked. "The bartender looks like he'd set off a decor nicely." She pointed over to a dark-skinned young man with wavy hair, a dimpled chin, and arms straight out of a comic book. I had to agree, he was pretty.

"Oh, that's Rafiq," Pippi replied. "I...don't think he plays for our team, if you get what I mean."

"Oh, honey," Rhonda replied with a laugh. "By the time you get to be my age, you understand that 'too pretty to be straight' is totally a thing. I don't want to take him home; I just want to look at him for a while. And maybe eat sushi off his abs."

Pippi looked confused. "I...don't think we have sushi on the menu..."

"It's okay, sweetie," I cut in to try and save the child from any more of Rhonda's influence. "We'll just take a table."

She led us to the far side of the restaurant, along the opposite wall as the Jets fans, for which I was grateful. Of course, this put us directly under a row of massive TVs, but looking around, there wasn't a seat in the place that wasn't flickering in the light of at least four sporting events. I'd barely hung my purse over the back of my chair when a pair of ebony legs appeared in my field of view. I looked up, and up, and up some more and finally the legs ended in a young woman with a smile at least as expensive as Pippi's, but whose shirt fit slightly better. At least I couldn't see all her extraneous piercings through the fabric.

"Hi, welcome to Slim and Slam's, where—"

"Tequila, STAT," Rhonda cut her off. "Patron. Four shots. Keep the lime and salt bullshit for the JV team." She turned to me. "What are you drinking?"

"Those are for you?"

"Honey, we walked in here thirty seconds ago. In that time, I've seen a man with boobs bigger than mine jump up on a table topless, found out the hot bartender is gay, and been upstaged in hotness by the hostess *and* the waitress, neither of whom are likely coming home with me, either, so yes, all four of those shots are for me. I suggest you get a few of your own to keep up, because this is shaping up to be one of those low self-esteem drinking nights."

I looked up at the waitress, who was standing frozen with her eyes wide. "It's okay, honey. I've seen this movie before. What's your name?"

"Talia."

"Talia, you go ahead and bring my friend her shots, and a glass of water, along with a strawberry margarita, double Patron, for me. Then you find some reasonably good-looking member of your wait staff to come flirt with my friend here."

Talia seemed to come back to life now that she had some direction. "Got it. Booze and flirting. I can make that happen." She turned, took two steps away, then came back with a question on her face.

I held up a hand. "Boy or girl doesn't matter. Rhonda's heterosexual but panflirtatious. She's not going to hook up with anybody tonight, but a few batted eyelashes will go a long way toward me not holding her hair back six hours from now."

Talia raised an eyebrow. "She's starting off with four shots of tequila, and you think it's gonna take her six hours to puke? I don't see it."

I laughed and waved her on. "Sweetie, we are middle-aged divorcees five hundred miles from home. This is not our first rodeo. She'll be going strong until you make last call, or I'll burn my Spanx." Talia walked off laughing, and our night of fun and games, almost derailed before it began, was back on track and about to be fueled by the finest nectar of the agave cactus known to man—Patron Silver.

CHAPTER 16

An hour later, with the fire of multiple doses of fine tequila swirling around our bellies in a mix of deep-fried appetizers, wings, and more ranch dressing than could possibly be healthy, Rhonda and I contemplated a move to the game room. The football fans had gotten quiet and dejected, and the table dancer had put his shirt back on, because apparently the Jets were doing what the Jets do, which was snatch defeat from the jaws of victory. I looked out across the wasteland of chicken bones, scraps of potato skins, mozzarella stick crumbs, and an untouched mound of celery sticks. I reached out idly for one of the green spears, only to have my hand slapped by my dearest friend.

"Leave those alone; they're nasty," Rhonda said.

"It's celery," I replied. "They're like eating crunchy air. Besides, they're better for me than literally anything else I've eaten tonight."

"Darling," Rhonda said, leaning forward onto one elbow like she was about to impart a secret of the universe to me. I knew what was about to come out of her mouth was most likely bullshit, because I have spent a great deal of time around Drunk Rhonda, and Drunk Rhonda is more full of shit than Sober Rhonda, and Sober Rhonda is more full of shit than a used car salesman on the last day of the month who is five cars shy of his quota and sees the sun setting fast on both his Salesman of the Month parking spot and his job. "If we wanted to go through life eating celery when there are other options, like literally any other food options in the world, we would have stayed married, because our ex-husbands were both so goddamn bland they made celery look interesting."

I put the celery down, waved Talia back over, and said, "Sweetie, I need two more shots of Patron, another strawberry margarita in a sippy cup, and our check. It is time to get our Skee-Ball on!" Talia, Rhonda, and I all high-fived, and moments later, with a couple of embarrassing questions about my purple K-Pop emblazoned credit card behind me, we were off to the game room.

If I thought the assault of my senses when we entered the restaurant was bad, the game room took that shit to a whole new level. It was louder, brighter, flashier, and except for the fact that there were no topless fat men dancing on tables—at the moment—it was even trashier than the sports bar part of the joint. The big difference for Rhonda and me was that this time we were drunk, so instead of being horrified at the spectacle before us, it triggered a deep-seated reflex built into every Southerner. I call it the "hey y'all, watch this" reflex. It has been the cause of more head-shakings, ass-whoopings, arrests, marriages, divorces, pregnancies, and excommunications than almost any other impulse in human history, and mine was triggered like a seizure by the ringing bells and the flashing lights of the Slim & Slam's game room.

"Let's go win some shit!" I yelled, flinging my arms wide and nearly dumping strawberry margarita all over a man who was unknowingly walking in the splash zone. He ducked, and I gave him an apologetic look. "Sorry."

"Not a problem, cutie," he said. "You here with anybody?" He was almost handsome. He had so much going for him—no visible missing teeth, both eyes able to focus on me at the same time, good chin, nice build, decently dressed in a button-down shirt and clean blue jeans. He was right there on the verge of cute, except for one thing—he had a mustache. I hate mustaches. I hated them even before Peckerwood grew one, but now I have an almost visceral reaction to seeing one. I kinda want to punch every face I see with a mustache attached. I don't have a problem with beards, or even goatees, but I see a mustache, and I just automatically move the wearer into the "dickhead" category in my mind, and there's nothing he can do to get out of it. Except shave.

"Yeah," I said, my voice cold. "Her." I pointed at Rhonda, except she was closer than I expected her to be, and I was drunk, or maybe she was wobbling toward me a little, but either way, what I had intended to turn into me gesturing to her turned into me poking her right in the boob with my index finger.

"Hey!" she said, turning back from where she was depositing her empty shot glasses on a nearby tray. She looked down to where my finger was buried up to the first knuckle in her breast, then up at me, then back down at my finger, then back up at me. "You just gonna leave that there all night, or what?"

I poked it a little, marveling at the realistic give to it. "It moves," I said.

"Of course it moves, it's my boob," Rhonda replied.

"I know, but I've never felt a fake one before."

"I find that offensive. I paid good damn money for them, so they're as real as the invoice."

"Well, if I'm not supposed to call them fake, what should I call them?" I asked.

"I don't really give a shit what you call them as long as you'll quit poking me in the tit in the middle of the video arcade."

I looked around. In addition to Mr. Almost Cute Except I Have a Mustache, we'd now drawn the attention of a bartender, a pair of teenagers walking by holding hands, and a woman with a pink mohawk who was giving us both an appraising smile. I put my hand down. "Sorry."

"Don't worry about it. You can feel my boobs all you want later, but right now, I have a serious air hockey itch, and you're gonna scratch it. So come on!" She grabbed my hand and pulled me deeper into the arcade, leaving our audience gaping behind us, but as we passed, I could have sworn I heard the mohawk woman say, "I bet that ain't the only itch she's getting scratched," under her breath.

There was an open air hockey table, so after a couple minutes' worth of fumbling around with figuring out how to pay for stuff (you have to take your real money and load it onto a little card so it's not real money anymore, and that way you either have to leave the joint with money left on your card, which of course you can't possibly be allowed to turn back into real money, or you end up trying to put exactly the right amount of money on your card for the amount of stuff you want to play, which is made all the more difficult by the fact that you've been drinking for six hours, but of course you can't pay for drinks with the stupid little card, you have to use real money for that, but this is all shit I figured out later when I got back to the motel and realized that I had thirteen dollars left on a card for a restaurant five hundred miles from home), we got our game on.

Or, Rhonda did, anyway. I suck at air hockey. Always have. There's just something about leaning over a table trying to keep track of a sliding puck that has been hard for me. Probably because I'm always worried somebody's looking at my ass. Then I start worrying if my ass is particularly fat that day. Or particularly flat. Or if it just looks lumpy in the pants I've got on. And before I know it, whoever I'm playing has scored like fourteen points, and I need to make an appointment with my therapist and my yoga instructor.

"You suck at this game," Rhonda observed after beating me like a drum for the third game in a row. "Let's try one of the driving games."

"Rhonda, I have driven a couple hundred miles a day for the last two days. The last damn thing I want to do is drive more."

"But this will be fun driving, not the old lady driving you've been doing."

"Old lady driving?" I raised an eyebrow. "Are you trying to say I drive like an old woman?"

"I'm trying to say my great-grandma drove faster, and she never had anything but a horse and buggy to work with," Rhonda shot back.

"Oh, it is on now, bitch," I said. "Let's go!" I marched over to the wall of driving, riding, skiing, dancing, and other games, and slid into a car right before a couple of college kids who looked like they were on a date could sit down. I felt like Kathy Bates in *Fried Green Tomatoes*. It was all I could do not to yell "Towanda!" at the top of my lungs. But I knew they wouldn't have any idea what I was talking about, and I didn't have time to spend seventy-two hours on an involuntary hold in a psych ward. I had tequila to drink, Rhonda's ass to kick, and identity thieves to hunt down and bring to justice. I had a mission. I was like drunk Batwoman. Without the spandex. That's a privilege, not a right.

"You ready to get your ass kicked?" I said, turning to my right so I could look at Rhonda. Except...Rhonda wasn't sitting in the car to my right. Mr. Almost Cute Except I Have a Mustache was sitting there grinning at me. I looked up, and Rhonda leaned down and stuck her head in the imaginary car window.

"I'm going to play pool with this couple of college boys. Maybe they can teach me the game?" She put on her best "dumb blonde" expression, which was pretty good given that Rhonda was neither dumb nor blond.

"Try not to teach them anything that's going to get you pregnant," I replied.

"Darling, if I get pregnant, you better get ready for the end times, because it's gonna be another miracle birth. My baby factory is closed permanently, and I've got the scar to show for it."

"Well then, don't get crabs," I said. "There's only one bed in the hotel room, and I don't want your cooties. Literally."

"You just drive and talk to the nice man in the car next to you. Let me worry about my coochie."

"I said cooties."

"Po-tay-to, po-tah-to." She leaned in, gave me a kiss on the cheek that I just *knew* left red lipstick glowing on the side of my face, and bounced off after a pair of young Adonises (Adoni? Adonoi?). I looked over at MACEIHAM (Mr. Almost Cute Except I Have a Mustache) and said, "Hey there. I'm Lexi."

He stretched out a hand across the gulf between the cars. "I'm Harrison. Good to meet you."

Harrison? Seriously? Who *does* that to a kid? I hoped to all fuck that he was rich, because otherwise his life in middle school was nothing but one long string of wedgies and bloody noses. "Good to meet you, Harry."

"Harrison," he corrected. *Oooookay. So the mustache isn't the only thing he has in common with Peckerwood. Good to know.*

"Sorry," I said. "Harrison."

"I don't mean to be a douche," he said. "It's just...middle school was rough, and the rhymes they came up with for Harry made me never want to be called that again."

I couldn't think of anything all that bad that rhymed with "Harry," but I was never really one that got a lot of stupid rhyming names made with my name. When your last name is Lieberman, the assholes tend to go straight for the low-hanging anti-Semitic fruit and ignore your first name. But I figured since it was his recurring puberty nightmare, it wasn't for me to judge. "What's your middle name?" I asked. "Is that any better?"

"Wainwright," he replied with a rueful smile.

"Yeah," I said. "That's not gonna be any better, is it?" I was starting to like this dude, even with that caterpillar on his lip.

"Not in the least," said Harrison Wainwright Mustache. "How about we race and the loser has to tell the winner the worst nickname they ever got stuck with?" He gave me a grin, and I suppressed a shudder.

That was some serious motivation, because the worst nickname I ever got stuck with involved a beach trip with the church youth group in the summer after I really launched into puberty but before I really understood about personal grooming. Let's just say that no girl wants to ever be called "Sasquatch," and having that turn into "Sas-crotch" almost instantly was even worse. There was no way I wanted to share that story with Harrison Wainwright Mustache, no matter how many margaritas I had running through my system.

And of course that thought made me realize *exactly* how many margaritas I had running very rapidly through my system. I now had two motivations. I had to win this race, and I had to pee.

CHAPTER 17

Thirty minutes and four rematches later, I had finally beaten Harrison Wainwright Mustache at Grand Prix Drivesalot or whatever the hell that racing game was called, released the floodgates on my poor abused bladder, and was now perched on a barstool across from HWM (Harrison Wainwright Mustache) laughing at his middle school nicknames and trying to remember if I'd done as Rhonda instructed and put on sexy underpants, because the chances that someone other than me and my roommate would see them was increasing with every sip of strawberry margarita I put in my system.

"Okay, now you show me yours," HWM said, his eyes crinkling in a smile over the rim of his beer mug. He had nice eyes, and if I watched him smile with his eyes, I didn't have to look at that fungal growth on his upper lip. I swear to God, sometimes I thought I could see the thing moving independently of the rest of his face, like it had a mind of its own or something.

"Excuse me?" I asked, faux-affront all over my face. I reached up and clutched where my pearls would be if I was wearing any, and used the motion to draw attention to my chest instead. I put on my very best Southern accent and said, "Why Harrison, I am shocked at the very suggestion! A lady never shows off such things on the first date."

"Yeah, well, ladies don't drink frozen margaritas like they're convenience store slushies, either. So give it up, cutie. What's your worst nickname?" He smiled broadly enough for me to see it even under his 'stache, and I knew I was trapped.

My mind raced as I tried frantically to come up with something that didn't involve a veritable forest of pubic hair or any other embarrassing crotchal incidents from my youth, and I drew a complete blank. I couldn't think of a single embarrassing nickname except for Sas-crotch, and I knew full well there had been dozens. I mean, I went to public school in the 80s, for god's sake, back when the cruelty of children was unbounded by anti-bullying programs, and as long as no bones were broken and there wasn't too much blood pouring from a wound, a parent's typical response to any injury, emotional or physical, was "walk it off" or "rub some dirt on it and go."

Resigned to my doom and to extending my celibate streak for one more night, I opened my mouth to tell HWM the saga of my unruly pubes, my first high-cut bikini, and the savagery that were seventh-grade Baptist girls on a church trip to Myrtle Beach, when out of the blue came my savior and my albatross, the yin to my yang, the dill to my pickle —Rhonda.

I didn't *know* it was Rhonda when I heard yelling and saw security converging on one corner of the game room from all the entrances and exits, but let's face it, I knew it was Rhonda. "I think we'd better go make sure my best friend isn't about to get arrested," I said, pointing in the general direction of the kerfuffle.

HWM raised an eyebrow, and for the first time I noticed that his eyebrows were almost as bushy as his mustache. I glanced down at his wrists, all of his arms that were visible under his dress shirt, and the hair there was thick and wiry. Hmmmm. I flashed to an image of me running my fingernails through his dark man-pelt and decided that if Rhonda got me arrested before I could sleep with this paragon of virility, I was going to drown her in a holding cell toilet.

"Does your friend get arrested in bars often?" he asked, putting a pair of twenties down on the bar and following me as I started to push my way through the growing crowd.

"Only once since we left home Friday afternoon," I replied.

"It's...Sunday night," HMW said.

"So you understand my concern," I called back over my shoulder. I elbowed a five-foot-tall coed in sweatpants with "JUICY" written on the butt, and she staggered out of my way to make a hole in the last row of spectators before the main event.

"Oh shit," I said, my eyes going wide at the sight before me. It was Rhonda, all right. It was Rhonda, holding a leather belt doubled over and standing behind a row of mechanical horses all sharing a communal set of video screens. Glaring at her from five feet away was a woman in her early thirties with a shirt that started life as white, but now had the distinctive pink hue of strawberry daiquiri covering a wide swath of the front. Between the pair of them, with his back pressed to one of the horses, was a cute man about the same age as Daiquiri Girl, who was rubbing his ass with one hand and holding up his jeans with the other one.

"What the fuck?" HMW said as he caught up to me. "Is she...holding that dude's belt?"

"Oh yeah," I replied.

"Is he...rubbing his ass?" HMW asked.

"That's what one usually does when somebody whales on you with a leather belt. You also might eat standing up for the next couple of days," I said.

"How do you know she hit him on the ass with a belt?"

I looked up at HMW and patted his cheek. "Oh, you sweet summer child. You act like this is the first time I've found my best friend about to throw down with some hussy in a bar because she yanked the hussy's boyfriend's belt off and beat him on the ass with it in front of God and everybody. The only difference is this time 'Whoop, There It Is' isn't playing over the loudspeakers. And we're not at a wedding reception."

HMW looked down at me, saw that I was one hundred percent sincere, and said, "You might be the hottest woman I've met in a year, but your friend is batshit crazy."

"You ain't seen nothing yet," I replied. "She ain't even started with her Jackie Chan impersonation, where she beats the hell out of somebody with anything in the room that ain't nailed down, including small children. And thank you. I think you're pretty sexy your damn self. But that mustache has got to *go*."

Rhonda threw her arms out to the sides and turned her face to the sky, drawing in a huge breath to let out her patented "I'm from Union County, North Carolina, and I will kick your ass so hard you'll be wearing your sphincter for a necklace" war cry, but a bouncer stepped in and planted a massive dinner plate-sized hand in the middle of her chest.

"Ma'am—"

Rhonda turned her formerly-heavenward gaze upon the massive

chunk of humanity in what appeared to be a girl's medium black t-shirt and said, "Son, did you buy my last two drinks?"

The bouncer, who was almost certainly a man who had his shit together in most barroom, or in this case game room, altercations, looked at Rhonda with the puzzled gaze of a bulldog that's just caught a Subaru. "Excuse me?"

"Are you deaf, son?" Rhonda was apparently well into ass-whooping mode, because her volume and cadence had veered sharply into Foghorn Leghorn territory. "I SAID, did you buy my last two drinks?"

"Well...no."

"Then you had best remove your grimy paw from my décolletage before I rip your arm off and shove it so far up your ass you can pick your nose from the inside."

The bouncer stepped back, which had the side effect of removing his hand from Rhonda's chest. In all fairness to the large man in the itty-bitty shirt, he'd placed his hand at the top of Rhonda's chest, about as far from anyplace inappropriate as he could. The problem was, all of Rhonda's inappropriate was pushed about as far up as it could go without her nipples getting caught in her hoop earrings, so he may well have inter-acted with more boob than he'd meant to. Either way, he stepped back from the obviously insane woman in front of him, and that left Rhonda an opening.

"Alright, you hussy," she started, and any hope I'd had about getting to go somewhere nice, private, and stocked with enough safety razors to massacre that goddamned mustache, went out the window when I heard where on the "oh shit" continuum her pronunciation of "hussy" landed.

Now in a normal setting, the word "hussy" probably doesn't come up every day. Rhonda and I do not live in a normal setting. We currently live in a world just peeking out of its foxholes after a year ravaged by pandemic, rioting, insurrection, conspiracy theory, videoconferencing, and a serious lack of pants. We have masks that match our sweatpants for when we "go out" to the mailbox, and we know entirely too much about the interior of our co-workers' dining rooms. So we have spent many, many afternoons sitting in our cul-de-sac on folding lawn chairs emptying pitcher after pitcher of margaritas and commenting on the behavior of the twenty-something stripper who moved in on the other side of Rhonda right at the start of quarantine.

Tigra (pronounced "tee-gra") is a dark-skinned beauty with tits that bounce spectacularly and an ass that doesn't wobble even the tiniest bit, so we hated her from the moment she first moved in. The steady stream of good-looking men leaving her house in the morning driving expensive cars added to our loathing. Then she had the absolute audacity to come meet us and be intelligent. Bitch.

She let us know early on that she's working her way through her MBA by stripping at the most expensive club in town, and that she likes to party and have a good time, but she'll make sure that none of her guests block our driveways in case we need to go to work in the morning. I'm at least thirteen percent certain that she didn't mean for that to make us sound like the boring middle-aged plebeians we are, so instead of slamming the door in her face, I gave her the name of my weed guy and welcomed her to the neighborhood. What? Good suppliers are hard to find in the 'burbs, and my guy delivers. He's all queer as a golf helmet, so I knew he wasn't going to be giving Tigra any special discounts.

The addition of Tigra to the neighborhood had two major effects on my life with Rhonda. First, the number of times the word "hussy" was used by either or both of us in a week increased by something like eight million percent. Second, we moved our afternoon drink-and-snarks to my back yard so we wouldn't be interrupted by the younger, perkier model of ourselves.

All that to say, that in a normal, slightly catty conversation, the word "hussy" has an "s" sound in the middle of it. Say it with me—huh-see. Huh-see. Hussy. Got it? Now, when the speaker is drunk, or pissed, or particularly judgmental, or any combination of the three, there is a transformation wherein the "s" sound becomes a "z." Huh-zee. Huh-zee. Hussy. If the person making the declaration of hussidom happens to be in the vicinity of the person being declared a hussy when the transition is made from "huh-see" to "huh-zee," then shit is about to get real. Really real, y'all.

Rhonda was deep enough in her alcoholism and her self-righteous fury that the poor woman whose boyfriend she assaulted with his own belt, who was simply trying to defend her property from an unanticipated sexual assault, although, in all fairness to Rhonda, with the pants he was wearing, what did he expect? I mean, he was totally asking for it going around in those...cargo shorts. Okay, the role-reversal falls a little flat when cargo shorts are involved, but you see where I was going with that. Anyway, the poor woman who was about to figuratively get her ass beat by the woman who out of nowhere showed up drunk as a skunk and literally beat her date's ass had been deemed a "hussy" by my best friend, and there was not an "s" to be found anywhere in that declaration.

Nope. Rhonda was tits-deep in double-z hussidom and about to throw down. I had to think of something fast, or it was back to the hoosegow for me and I would never see my twenty-six-dollars-worth of justice. So I did what any self-respecting wingwoman would do.

No, not head for the exit. I'm not that self-respecting. No, I leapt in between the two erstwhile combatants and shouted, "WAITAGOD-DAMMINUTE!" The bar fell silent. Even the pinball machines stopped their beeping and blooping. The only sound was a lone skee-ball rolling down the ramp and the seams of Rhonda's dress straining to hold everything in place after the addition of a fuckton of appetizers and a *metric* fuckton of booze.

"There is only one way to settle this. Like our ancestors did. With Bar Olympics!" The crowd erupted, the bouncer breathed a sigh of relief, five percent of the rage went out of Rhonda's eyes, and the hussy's boyfriend stopped rubbing his beleaguered ass for three seconds. HWM (Harrison Wainwright Mustache) looked at me, his bushy eyebrows raised, and I said, "Fuck off. My ancestors were Irish. There were totally Bar Olympics in my heritage."

CHAPTER 18

If you didn't go to college, or somehow managed to avoid joining a fraternity or sorority in your time there, or banging a fraternity boy or sorority girl and thus being dragged to their parties, or have never been associated with any of the tens of thousands of former fraternity boys and sorority girls who continue to live their very best life on the cornhole courts of meat market bars all across this great nation, then I suppose there is an infinitesimal chance that you are unfamiliar with the concept of Bar Olympics.

Bar Olympics is a way men have settled scores, proven their superiority, and dropped the panties of young women of questionable moral fiber —and even more questionable taste in men—for decades. Perhaps even centuries, but despite my implied geriatricity by my teenage daughter, I haven't been alive for centuries, so I don't know. The basic premise is this: two teams of drunkards compete in events designed to make them even more inebriated, each team hoping against hope that the opposing team is either more drunk or less dexterous than they are, so they can lay claim to that most masculine of prizes…bragging rights. You can't spend bragging rights. You can't eat them, drink them, or screw them, and yet every man I've ever known is more obsessed with the acquisition of bragging rights than he is with seeing every pair of breasts on the planet between the ages of eighteen and eighty. Usually if there are women, gay men, or other reasonable creatures involved in setting the terms of the wager, the losing team has to pay the winning team's bar tab. The boyfriend Rhonda had spanked was a big boy, and I did not relish the thought of paying for their booze.

Now, when I chose Bar Olympics as the method of settling Rhonda's conflict with the anonymous hussy, whose name was Sandra and who actually seemed like a very nice young lady, but she was younger than us, prettier than us, and if her shoes were anything to go by (and they always are), richer than us, and thus, a hussy, it was not with any worry about actually winning. It was more focused on being allowed to leave the bar without assault charges being pressed against my best friend, and maybe, just maybe, having HWM (Harrison Wainwright Mustache) pressed against me a little later.

That said, now that the gauntlet had been thrown and picked up, I was damn sure going to try to win. "How many people y'all got for your team?" I asked the hussy.

She looked around and started counting heads with a finger, letting me know to what degree she held home field advantage in this contest. I stopped her before she got too far gone and said, "We've got three. So pick one other shmuck to be your pivot man, and let's get this show on the road."

Rhonda tried to look me in the eye, but I could tell she was abjectly drunk and not sure which one of the men she was seeing was the real one, so she was splitting time between looking both of us in the eye. "Who's the third? Mustache boy over there? Jesus Christ, Lexi. You could just screw him. You don't have to let him on our Olympic team, too."

"Okay, one, whether or not I screw him is undecided as yet, and none of your business anyhow. And two, we need at least three events so we don't have a tie, and I'm not twenty-one anymore. I can't do flip cup, beer pong, *and* quarters all in a row."

I heard somebody behind me snicker when I said "twenty-one" and turned to freeze a frat boy in his tracks. "One word, Kappa-boy, and I'll wear your balls for earrings." I held up my fingernails in a claw-like gesture, which had the desired effect, because Junior Dickbiscuit kept his opinions on how long it had been since I was twenty-anything to his damned self, but also showed me that at some point in this adventure I had absolutely wrecked my nails. When I got home, I was heading straight to Walmart for a mani-pedi.

I turned my attention back to my teammates. "Now, I issued the challenge, so tradition dictates that they get to name the events."

"They'll pick beer pong," Rhonda said, although it sounded a lot more like "day lick beepug." I knew what she meant. That's how best friends are.

"Yeah, somebody always picks beer pong. If they go that route, you're our anchor, Rhonda." I looked at HWM and said, "If there's a wing race, that one's on you. We filled up on apps before we hit the game room, and if I try to stuff another chicken wing in my body, either my stomach or my dress is going to rupture, and we don't want either of those things to happen."

"He wouldn't mind if your dress ruptured," Rhonda slurred. It took me a second to translate "Hewoont minif yore drash rapture" into something applicable to the situation, but I got there eventually. Our best friend telepathy was pretty strong, but enough tequila will short out any kind of brainwaves.

Harrison just shrugged, and I couldn't tell if it was because he agreed with her, or because he had no damn idea what Rhonda was saying, but then I caught his eyes roaming all over my dress like he was looking for structural flaws and figured he agreed with her. That was nice. It felt good to have somebody look at me like a sex object again and not just a purveyor of food and washer of underpants.

"Whatever, Rhonda, focus. I'm good at flip cup, and I crush at quarters, but if we've got to do the one where you stack cups, I'm screwed," I said.

"I'm really good at that," HWM said. "I'm a structural engineer by trade."

"Oh," I said, a little surprised. I thought all structural engineers were math nerds who couldn't get dates. I pretty much thought all engineers were math nerds who couldn't get dates. But I guess there are a bunch of engineers out there, so some of them would have to be hot math nerds. Like unicorns of the engineering world. "Cool. Then that one's yours."

"What if it's that or eat wings?" he asked.

"Oh, then you're eating wings," I said without a second's hesitation. "I'll puke if I put one more thing in my mouth tonight."

I didn't realize how that sounded until Rhonda giggled and said, "Sorry, dude," to HWM, then I turned redder than Rhonda's hair. Sometimes I hate my best friend. I turned to the hussy and her BWSA (Boyfriend With Sore Ass) and put a hand on my hip. "What events do y'all choose?"

Hussy finally decided on their third team member, a cute little brunette with her hair in pigtails and a sorority t-shirt on. Sigma Sigma Sigma. I knew those bitches from back in my day. The running joke on campus was "Tri-Sigma, because everybody else has!" They responded by disparaging the honor and virtue of our house, the venerable Chi Omega, with a similarly vile chant.

"Chi-ho, Chi-ho, it's off to bed we go!
With an S-A-E on top of me,
Chi-ho, Chi-ho, Chi-ho!"

I was dating a member of Sigma Alpha Epsilon my sophomore year, so it was all the more galling for its truth. I *was* going off to bed with an SAE on top of me, and not for nearly long enough. The whole situation became untenable, and one night I found myself egging the Tri-Sig house at four in the morning. Which wouldn't have been quite as big a deal if I hadn't thrown most of the eggs through open windows. Look, it was summer, and it's not my fault they didn't have screens in their windows. If they'd made their boyfriends work even a little bit to plow their fertile crescents, they wouldn't have woken up with egg in their beds.

So here I was, twenty-something years later, and yes, I know exactly twenty-how many years later but that is not relevant to this story nor is it something I wish to dwell on, especially not as I am recounting my adventures in middle-aged Bar Olympics. But Little Miss Tri-Sig was way too adorable to hate, until she opened her mouth and said, "This should be fun! I bet you've all been doing Bar Olympics since before I was born!"

She was right, of course, but that is *not* something to say to a woman in her late forties standing in the middle of a crowded bar. Especially not with her potential hookup if she can convince him to shave before she bangs him standing right next to her. Pigtail hussy was going *down*.

"What. Are. The. Events?" I growled, my eyes locked with Pigtails. OH (Original Hussy) cleared her throat and said, "As the challenged party, we choose Cup Stack, The Three-Mile Island Challenge, and for the finale, Beer Pong!" She held her arms up over her head and jumped up and down, showing off to everyone in the bar exactly how tight and perky her little body was. If I jumped up and down like that, I'd give myself two black eyes and find my picture on nip slip sites for the rest of my life. OH just bounced a little bit in her tank top and drew lustful glances from most of the men and about half the women in the bar. "Cup stack is first," OH announced. "Who's up?"

I looked at a grinning HWM and a cross-eyed Rhonda, and said, "Hold her up. I got this."

"Wait," HWM protested, reaching out to catch Rhonda as she slid sideways along the bar. "I told you, I'm a structural engineer. This is my event. I guarantee a victory here!"

"But I can't eat any wings, or I'll explode, and if you get Three-Mile-Island Wings within ten feet of Rhonda with that much liquor in her system, she'll blow the roof off this whole place."

HWM looked over at the opposing team and grinned. "Look, the little one with the pigtails is their cup stacker. There's no way I don't crush her. But they're going to send the boyfriend in to eat wings, and he looks hungry. He also looks like he can put away some food. I'll give it my best effort, but I don't know if I can beat him. Why not take the one guaranteed win, and just throw the wing-eating event altogether?"

HWM wasn't wrong. Boyfriend was *thick*. Like linebacker thick, with no neck and sausage fingers that spoke of a high pain tolerance and probably an unholy ability to stuff food down his gullet. He was easily the size of two of me, and one and a half HWMs. We weren't beating him in an eating contest, no matter who faced him. So we were going to win one and lose one, leaving Rhonda, who could barely stand, much less focus her vision to throw a ping pong ball into a cup of beer, to save the last vestiges of our cash, or at least distract everyone enough for HWM to pull the car up to the door so we could run out on the tab.

"Fine," I said finally, gesturing for HWM to step forward. "Go ahead, but I am warning you, if you lose this event, whatever chance you might have had of getting to see how much of this—" here I gestured to my body "—is me and how much of this is underwire and chicken cutlets is completely out the window."

HWM gave me one of those long looks that started at my feet and did little circles around every part of my anatomy he found interesting before he finally stopped at my face. "Don't worry," he said with a grin partially obscured by that goddamned caterpillar on his upper lip. "I got this."

"You better!" Rhonda yelled, lunging forward and grabbing hold of my right boob. "Or you ain't getting any of this!"

That's my girl. Keeping it classy.

CHAPTER 19

T he Cup Stack was the first challenge, so HWM was our lead
batter. Now the Cup Stack is not any kind of real challenging
event under normal circumstances. You take a dozen plastic
cups, and you stack them up into three pyramids, two of three cups and
one in the middle of six cups. This is not anything that requires a structural engineer. Even trying to do it fast ain't what one would call taxing.
Until there's a crowd of rowdy drunks hollering and spilling beer down
your back and bumping into you while you try to stack up a dozen cups
that looks like thirty on account of all the cups of whatever you've done
emptied yourself over the course of whatever activities you've engaged in
that led to you stacking plastic cups for the salvation (or maybe resurrec-
tion) of your honor and dignity. Or for the chance to touch a naked
woman. Because that's what was on the line for HWM when he stepped
up to the table.

PH (Pigtail Hussy) stepped up to the table next to him and raised her
hands over her head, eliciting a huge roar from the gathered crowd. I
don't think it was completely because they all knew and adored her but
because she flashed a healthy amount of underboob when she jumped up
and down with her hands over her head, so I felt like there was some
audience manipulation going on. Whatever, we had a ringer.

"Okay, are our stackers ready?" the bartender asked through a megaphone. I wasn't sure if it was an upgrade that this bartender had a mega-

phone behind the bar instead of a shotgun, but it was probably less likely to result in bloodshed. It depended on how close he got to my ear with that thing, though. PH and HWM both nodded, PH with a bright grin on her face, and HWM with a resolute expression. I was glad to see he was taking this seriously, because I really wanted to bang him, and if he could pull this off, and we could find a twenty-four-hour drugstore so I could find some shaving cream and a safety razor, his odds were pretty good.

"GO!" the bartender yelled, and my eyes rolled back in my head. Not from anything good, either, but because he was standing right next to me with that damned megaphone, and I'm pretty sure he ruptured an eardrum. He got what was coming to him, though. Rhonda was standing beside me, so she caught the sonic blast right in her other ear, scaring the bejesus out of her and causing her to jump, fling both hands up in the air, and yell, "I'm not armed, Officer, that's just my boner!"

Now while I was contemplating what the absolute hell she was saying about a boner, I also watched in slow-motion as the strawberry margarita she'd been drinking flew straight up out of her hand, flipped over about eight feet in the air, and came crashing back down, straight on top of the bartender's head. He was instantly covered in cheap tequila and slushy mix, and I laughed so hard I spritzed a little. I was definitely going to need to throw those panties away before HWM came in contact with them.

The strawberry-flavored bartender glared at Rhonda, but I just held up one finger at him. And not that finger, either. I said, "That's what you get for yelling in a drunk woman's ear. Now go wipe the margarita mix out of your ears and play nice."

There aren't many advantages in this world to being a middle-aged woman, but developing a "mom voice" is one of them. The "mom voice" is that voice you slip into when you need to let whoever you're talking to understand in no uncertain terms that the time for screwing around is over and that you are to be listened to and obeyed without any further debate, discussion, cajoling, whining, begging, or bitching. It works about twenty percent of the time on my own children, but is over seventy-five percent effective on people who originated in wombs other than my own. Since I did not birth the bartender, he took in my "mom voice," shut his mouth, and got his happy ass back behind the bar.

I turned my attention back to the cup stack table, where I had missed the event entirely while dealing with the bartender. It doesn't take very long to make three stacks with plastic cups and then take them back down again into one stack of cups, even if you are drunk. But apparently we won, because HWM had his hands up in the air, and PH was getting consoled by OH and HB (Original Hussy and Hussy's Boyfriend). I ran over and threw my arms around his neck, pressing my lips to his cheek and my everything else to his everything else.

"I'm gonna assume you won?" I whispered in his ear.

"You didn't watch?"

"Rhonda dumped a margarita on the bartender, and I had to do damage control."

"I've known you for less than four hours, and I understand that sentence completely. Yes, I won."

"Excellent." I nuzzled his cheek, feeling a pretty healthy segment of his something else pulsing against my hip. "If we can get out of this competition without going to jail, I'll give you a reward later." Although, by the way things felt, it was definitely going to be him that was giving me a prize. Either he had a television remote in his pocket, or he was *very* happy to see me. I was going to be so pissed if he had a remote in his pocket.

"Next up, the Three-Mile Challenge!" The voice that came through the megaphone this time was female, and only about half as loud, and when I looked around, I saw that a different bartender had taken over announcing duties. Probably a good call.

I sauntered over to the new field of battle, where two plates of a dozen wings sat on opposite sides of a regular dining table. There was a bone plate on either side of the wing plates, so you could pitch for bones righty or lefty, and an extra-large side of ranch sat in front of each chair. I could smell the sauce from ten feet away, and that was not a compliment. The wings were a shade of orange that did not occur in healthy nature, and sure as hell was not a color that should be associated with anything that a human being put in their stomach. It was a terrifying mix of nuclear yellow, red, and brown the color of dried blood that made me rethink every dietary decision I'd made that calendar year. I was *not* eating that shit.

"The rules are simple," the bartender called out. "The first person to eat all the wings on their plate without puking wins! You cannot give any wings away. Each wing will be inspected by our judge Bitsy—" A smiling young woman with hair the pink of cotton candy waved to the crowd. "Any wing deemed not sufficiently stripped of meat will be returned to your plate to be finished off. You cannot drink anything but water or beer from our sponsor Keystone Light." That's when I swore I wasn't going to eat any of those wings *or* drink any of the provided beer. "Finally, you must keep the wings down for five minutes after you eat your last wing. No puking, no running to the bathroom, no sticking your head under a faucet, no milk. If you can't keep the wings down for five minutes, you forfeit. Understood?"

It took me a second to realize she was waiting for some kind of acknowledgement from me, because I'd tuned her out after the first time she mentioned puking. I don't have a weak stomach. I went to college and gave birth twice: I've seen some shit. But I was pretty gloriously drunk, and there was a lot of fried food in my stomach so I didn't need to spend a whole lot of time dwelling on regurgitation, not if I didn't want to experience it first-hand. I'd already peed my pants (just a little, but it was still peeing), I did not need to vomit before I even went down on HWM. I nodded, and the bartender gave me what I guess she thought was an encouraging smile.

"Go!" she yelled just as loud as the first idiot, but since she was twenty feet away, and she pointed the megaphone up toward the ceiling instead of at my ear, it wasn't nearly as jarring. I turned to see HB grab a drumstick in both hands, jam them both into his mouth at the same time, and pull out nothing but stripped chicken wing bone. He dumped the bones on an empty plate and grabbed up a pair of flappers, not even bothering to chew before he swallowed down that mouthful of meat. Guess I knew what initiation was like in his frat. Another pair of wings vanished into his reddening maw, and another set of bones came out clean enough for an archaeology exhibit.

HB was starting to look a little like a chipmunk by this point, because apparently his gag reflex kicked in somewhere around Wing Number Three. His cheeks were puffed out with unmasticated meat, and there was a little tendril of chicken skin dangling from his lips. Sauce covered his face in a wide streak that literally stretched from earlobe to earlobe, making him look like Hooters hired a new mascot and he was cosplaying the Heath Ledger Joker. He dropped two more sets of bones on his plate to be inspected by a concerned-looking Bitsy, who gave him a big smile and a thumbs-up. HB returned the thumbs-up with a sickly expression and a sweaty brow, and I watched him strain to chew and swallow all the meat in his mouth. He obviously wasn't used to handling a load of that magnitude.

After downing what looked like a pint of water, HB looked at me for the first time and noticed the untouched plate in front of me. "Why aren't you eating?"

"Oh, I already ate. But you go ahead."

"You have to eat the wings, or you lose the challenge."

"No, sweetie, *you* have to eat the wings. If I eat the wings faster than you, I win. If you eat the wings faster than me, you win. But if neither of us eat the wings, then we draw, and we're still up by a point. So you *have* to win. I don't."

It took him a moment to process that, a moment in which I remembered that in my college days his particular fraternity was not considered one of the academic powerhouses, even among the Greeks at my school. Then he realized that I was right, that I didn't have to eat the wings, but he did, and he dove right back in at the same pace he started with.

And that was his undoing, right there. If he'd realized that he had an easy win and didn't need to hurry, he probably would have been just fine. He could have eaten his wings one at a time, licked his fingers clean, drunk plenty of water, picked up the win for his team, and put our fate in the hands of my best friend, who was currently lying face down on the bar with the bartender firing shots of ginger ale into her mouth every few seconds.

But no. He was brought down by the same thing that has proven to be the undoing of millions of men throughout time immemorial. He was laid low by his masculine ego. He grabbed another pair of wings and sucked the meat right off the bone, smirking at me as he did so. He dunked the next pair in ranch all the way up to his fingertips and sucked those clean, too. He was at least swallowing as he went now, instead of having his cheeks all distended from the volume of meat he was taking between his lips. Eight wings down, four to go, and he was a little slower reaching for the next one. No longer double-dipping, he actually bit into this wing instead of just slurping it clean.

I saw a little sliver of hesitation, just a hint of fear in his eyes to go along with the tears from the hot sauce. And I pounced. "What's the matter, stud? Too hot for you? Can't handle it anymore? You can forfeit if you like. I'm sure your girlfriend won't mind you forcing her to pick up our bar tab. It's not like we've been drinking top-shelf liquor for the past five hours or anything." He didn't need to know that what passes for top shelf in that place was a lot closer to the shit booze I let my daughter drink than actual expensive alcohol.

He glared at me and shoved that wing in his mouth all the way to the hilt, sucking the meat off the bone like he was sucking a golf ball through a garden hose. I was pretty impressed by his technique. Maybe he was a theatre major. He cleaned the bone, then snatched up another and shoved it in his mouth, smearing more sauce all along his face as he did. It was a really good thing he didn't have facial hair, otherwise he was never getting the smell of Texas Pete out. Wing Number Ten came out clean, but he had to double-pump on Wing Eleven to get the last shreds of meat. He looked down at his plate, with one lonely flapper lying there staring up at him, and turned his gaze back to me.

Staring me straight in the eye, he picked the wing up, slid it between his lips, and let the orange flesh stick slide past his teeth. That's when I sprang my trap. Just as I saw his cheeks go flat from him sucking the meat off the bone, I covered my mouth and began to dry heave. I convulsed and twitched like I was either having a seizure or dancing to dubstep, the whole while with my hand clasped firmly over my mouth and making belching noises like I was about to puke up everything I'd eaten in a week.

HB saw me fake-puking, and with a mouthful of fiery wing, went into his own convulsions trying to keep everything in his stomach where it was supposed to be. The problem was, he was really trying to not puke. And failing. After I made one big convulsing leap like a salmon swimming upstream to spawn, he grabbed a nearby pitcher, poured a gallon of water out onto the floor and onto Bitsy, and hurled up a dozen of the hottest wings in Orlando right there into the pitcher. He stood up from the table and ran to the bathroom, his pitcher full of puke held tightly in both hands.

I looked around, took a sip of water from the glass so kindly provided for me, and turned to Bitsy. "I believe that's a forfeit, right?"

Bitsy looked at my untouched plate of wings, looked at the empty plate HPB (Hussy's Pukey Boyfriend) left behind, and grinned at me. She walked over, grabbed my left wrist in her right hand, and raised it high above her head. "Ladies and Gentlemen, your Three-Mile-Island Challenge Winner!"

I had just won a wing-eating contest against a twenty-something frat boy without ever taking a bite. This was truly one of the crowning achievements of my forties. I looked over at Original Hussy, now abandoned by all her friends who really didn't want to get stuck paying for part of our tab, and said, "I think that gives us two wins to your zero. Pretty sure we win."

She nodded, and she looked so heartbroken that I took pity on her. I walked over and gave her a hug and whispered in her ear, "Don't sweat it, honey. My date paid our tab while I was embarrassing your boyfriend. You only have to make him pay for all y'all's drinks."

She looked at me, eyes shining with relief. "Thank you! I didn't know how I was going to come up with enough cash to pay for everything she drank." I didn't have to look to know she was pointing at Rhonda, but when I did turn, I saw my best friend laying face-up on the bar, snoring like a lawn tractor.

"Yeah," I said. "She can be an expensive habit, but she's worth it. Now you have a good night, honey. And don't be too hard on your beefcake. He tried, but he got matched up against a woman who's been playing bar games for free drinks since before y'all were born. He never had a chance." With that, I sauntered over to the bar to collect my unconscious friend and my very conscious HWM and venture out into the Florida night in search of male grooming equipment and condoms.

CHAPTER 20

I woke up in the morning with a sore back, a mouth that felt like a cat took a crap in it, a pounding headache, and a desperate need to pee. So, pretty much like every other morning after I've been out with Rhonda. What wasn't the norm for a night on the town was the hairy arm draped across my chest. I turned to my left to see who the arm belonged to, and saw a pretty cute guy with no shirt snoring away in the hotel bed beside me. This was definitely *not* how most of my bar hops with Rhonda ended up. This also was not my hotel room, and I was one hundred percent not wearing any underwear. Point in my favor was that even with his face smooshed into the pillow, I could see that I was going to have to rename Harrison Wainwright Mustache, because there was not even a hint of a caterpillar on his upper lip. Mission accomplished, apparently.

I slid out from under his arm, using stealth that I had not employed since my days as a Chi Ho (and trust me, once I heard the nickname, I decided I would *earn* the nickname), and stood up. My back cracked in all the usual spots, my knees popped like a small-caliber pistol, and there was some soreness in my thighs and calves that was well out of the ordinary for a normal morning. Seemed like shaving that goddamn mustache wasn't the only mission I accomplished last night.

I found my bra draped over a lamp and my dress by the door to the hotel room, but my panties were nowhere to be found. I slipped into the bathroom to dress. And pee. I took care of the latter first, and while sitting on the thinking throne, pressed my head to the cool marble sink in a futile effort to get the drum and bugle corps to stop tromping all over my frontal lobe. Then I remembered that I'd ditched my underpants at the CVS when we stopped for condoms. Peeing your pants in a bar is uncomfortable in the best of situations, but I figured it was better to go commando than wear pee panties. Business attended to and the morning's first mystery solved, I looked in the mirror and jerked back in horror at the sight before me.

What had been classy, (okay, mostly classy) if heavy, makeup when we headed out to the bar last night had turned into some kind of hellish clown paint after a night of drinking, sweating, and some other activities that caused sweating and left me with one hamstring that might turn out to be pulled. I immediately started the cold water running and looked around for some kind of makeup remover, astringent cleanser, facial scrub, or anything a reasonable human being might have in their hotel room.

But I wasn't in a reasonable human being's hotel bathroom. I was in a man's hotel bathroom. A *single* man's hotel bathroom. So it was cheap hotel soap and a scratchy washcloth. I splashed water on my face and scrubbed like I was trying to get the bar stamp off my hand before my mom saw it. I had a lot more success with my makeup than I ever did getting those stamps to go away, and a few minutes later, I was clean, if a little red-faced from scrubbing. The application of a little moisturizer courtesy of the cheap-ass bottle of lotion on the hotel sink made me feel almost human, despite the drowned chihuahua look to my hair. At least I still looked pretty hot in last night's dress, and if my forty-plus years on this planet have taught me anything, it's that men often don't even make it to the part where they're supposed to look at your face.

I opened the door, and there stood HWM (which still worked on account of him now being Harrison Without Mustache as opposed to Harrison Wainwright Mustache. I probably could have gone with HWWM, for Harrison Wainwright Without Mustache, but that seemed a little much) in all his glory. And by all his glory, I mean *all* his glory. He had apparently missed the memo about putting on underwear before confronting his hookup in the morning, because there was not a single stitch of clothing on that man.

There also wasn't very much body hair. Like, suspiciously little body hair. Sure, there was a tuft here and there, and he still had a healthy garden around Little HWM, but even that looked freshly-trimmed. "Harrison," I asked. "Did we *shave* you last night?"

He looked a little chagrined, which I think is the appropriate response to admitting that you allowed a woman you met in a bar to shave not only your mustache but your chest, legs, upper arms, and...well, trim the hedges, as it were. "Yeah, we did. It started with my mustache, because that was a condition of our..."

"Connection?" I supplied. I can turn anything into a euphemism for either sex or genitalia. It's a gift.

"Connection," Harrison agreed. "But you really enjoyed using the clippers. Like, you *really* enjoyed using the clippers. So you asked me if you could shave anything else. I wasn't going to let you, but you promised to make it worth my while if I let you shave me bare and slather lotion all over my body, then you took your dress off, and..."

"I was persuasive," I said, nodding as the images started flowing back into my memory. I had indeed shaved Harrison pretty much everywhere, including his butt, and I had indeed made it worth his while. And then once I'd made it worth his while, I made it worth *my* while. Then I made it worth his while again. And I had the vaguest recollection of waking up in the middle of the night and making it worth my while one more time, but that was fuzzy enough that it might have been a dream. But looking at the bite marks on his thighs...probably not a dream.

"So when I heard water running, I thought maybe you were taking a shower, and I thought maybe you wanted company, but now I see you're dressed, and..." At this point Harrison seemed to realize that I was fully dressed except for my shoes, and he was just standing there swinging in the breeze, even more naked than usual because he was almost hairless enough to be a pro wrestler or an underwear model. And he could definitely fill out a pair of Calvin Kleins, based on what I was seeing.

"Yeah, not so much on the group shower, Harrison," I said, leaning forward to give him a lingering, but ultimately chaste, kiss. "I've got to find Rhonda and then go find the Russian mob bastards who stole my identity."

"Russian mob?" Harrison asked, stepping back to let me out of the bathroom. He stepped forward and just started peeing like we were an old married couple instead of two people who had just met the night before. I mean, we had been pretty intimate and really flexible together, but I wanted to preserve just the tiniest bit of mystery. Like, at least pee with the door closed until the fourth date.

"Well, I don't *know* that they're with the Russian mob. That's only one possibility. It could also be a Colombian drug cartel, or a cabal of hackers, or—"

"I thought you said all they did with your credit card was order lunch delivered," Harrison said, stepping out of the bathroom. At least he washed his hands.

"Well, they did, but—will you put that thing away? How do you concentrate with it just swinging around like that? Isn't it distracting?"

"Not really," he said, fondling himself and making his penis spin around like a helicopter rotor. "Why? Is it distracting you?"

"Well, it sure as hell is now!" I said, snatching up a pair of boxer briefs and throwing them at him.

He laughed and started to dress. "Are your boobs distracting?" he asked.

"Huh?"

"You asked if it was distracting, having it swing around down there all the time. Well, the same could be said for your boobs. Are they a distraction?"

"Constantly. Especially in a bra like this. I can't reach across my body for anything without bumping into them, I can't lean forward to reach the salt without sticking them into my plate, and every time I get naked, I find enough crumbs in my cleavage to bake a cake. Boobs are phenomenally distracting, and not just to men."

"Oh," he said, as if a whole world of understanding had just been opened up to him. "Well, penises aren't. We just kinda shove it down a pants leg and forget about it until it's needed. At least, after high school, we do. Before that there's no point trying to put it down anywhere, because a stiff breeze and it's right back up again. It's pretty much a constant boner for at least five years there."

"Sounds like heaven," came a new voice from behind me. I screamed and whirled around just in time to see Rhonda roll off the sofa and land face-first on the floor. She shot up to her feet and whirled around, holding her hands together with her index fingers extended like a gun barrel. "What? What is it? Where are they? I'll get 'em!"

"You'll get who?" I asked.

"Whoever made you scream," she replied, then looked at her hands. "Wait, I don't have a gun. That's probably good, because I don't know how to shoot a gun." She focused back on me. "Who made you scream?"

"You did!" I yelled. "What the hell were you doing on the couch?"

"Well, I *was* sleeping until you and Mr. Helicopter here started talking about dicks. It's really rude, you know, to talk about dicks with someone who isn't getting any Vitamin D in her diet."

"Rhonda," I said, keeping my voice low and steady. "Were you on that couch all night?"

"Probably," she said. "Last thing I remember is trying to talk your boy toy into letting me put Nair on his taint. Then everything fades to black. I didn't even get to see him naked. Until just now, that is."

I turned to HWM, who took an involuntary step back. "Did you screw me with my best friend passed out on the couch not ten feet away?"

"Well..."

"Harrison..."

"Not the first time," he said, then gave me one of those lopsided grins men give you when they think they're being clever. They're never really being clever. "The first time you screwed me."

Nope. Not clever. "How in the world could you let me do that?"

"If you had seen you last night, the more reasonable question would be how in the world could I have stopped you," Harrison replied. "You were a woman on a mission. Once my mustache was gone, and by the way, I'm going to have to vacuum out my rental car now because there is facial hair all over the dashboard, you would not be denied. I *was* going to get more parts of me shaved, and we *were* going to have, I think your exact words were 'wild monkey sex,' and nothing I could do was going to stop either of those things from happening. So I just lay back and thought of England."

"Oh, bullshit," I said.

"Yeah, you're right. I was absolutely a willing and active participant. Until Rhonda started talking about my taint, and that was the bridge too far."

"Well, it's good to know you have limits," I said. I turned to Rhonda. "And you remember nothing after the aforementioned taint discussion?"

"That's my story, and I'm sticking to it. I would not even mention it if I did remember waking up at five this morning to see you riding ol' Harrison like he was Hornicus Prime and we were back in that Charleston dive bar."

I flushed as red as my dress, and Harrison asked, "Hornicus Prime..."

"It's a long story, and it ends with me in jail. Now, I had a lot of fun last night, and if you're ever in North Carolina, let's get together for drinks—"

"And amateur rodeo hour!" Rhonda added.

"North Carolina? What part? I live in Stallings, right outside of—"

"Oh, we know *exactly* where Stallings is, don't we Lexi?" Rhonda had a Cheshire Cat grin so wide the ends almost wrapped around her head and met in the back. She snatched up Harrison's phone from the table and tapped on it for a second. "Here's Lexi's number. We live in Monroe. Call us next week. If we don't get offed by the mob hunting down identity thieves, I'm sure Lexi would *love* to see you again. Come visit sometime. I've got a pool. Bring a friend. Hell, bring a couple of friends."

"Come on, Rhonda," I said, shoving her toward the door and looking around frantically for my other shoe. Deciding to just forget about the shoe and get the hell out of there before Rhonda managed the impossible and made this morning after even more awkward, I gave Harrison another peck on the cheek and said, "Call me."

Then I bustled my best friend and my hangover and my sore thighs out into the Florida sun to hunt down the men who stole my identity and wasted a perfectly good felony on crappy sub sandwiches. I'd gotten laid; now it was time to get my revenge.

CHAPTER 21

B efore we took the law into our own hands, we decided to give the appropriate authorities one more chance to root out the evil in their neighborhood and hunt down these malicious malingerers. I don't really know what a malingerer is, but it sounds like something that someone would do maliciously. We pulled up in front of the headquarters of the Orlando Police Department after a brief layover in our hotel for a pair of much-needed showers, a change of clothes, and a complete pair of shoes. I was dressed for a sober discussion with the authorities in a pair of black capris, my favorite white sandals, and a red top that hopefully masked the red in my eyes.

Rhonda, however, looked like a spokesmodel for Harlots R' Us in a hot pink halter top that wasn't halting a damn thing, a pair of black yoga pants that didn't even leave imagination to the imagination, and a pair of hot pink peep toe slingback wedges that made her tower over me even more than normal. I glared up at her as we walked in the front door of the police station.

"You know we're talking to the cops about my case, not auditioning for a *Desperate Housewives* revival, right?" I asked as I yanked open the door.

"I know that I like a man in uniform," Rhonda replied. "Especially one who brings his own handcuffs." She gave me a saucy grin and swished into the station. I stood there, door in hand and mouth open, wondering how she could swish without bringing her entire Tower of Slutty tumbling down. My best friend never ceases to amaze me.

"Can I help you?" the female officer behind the reception desk asked us, her tone making it very clear that she thought we, or at least Rhonda, should be brought in wearing a pair of very uncomfortable bracelets. She was young, but life or the job had done a number on her, because her face had that perpetually pinched look that one usually only finds on ancient spinster librarians or professional lemon tasters.

Rhonda opened her mouth, but I slid in front of her before she responded. Officer Unfriendly had given her way too much of an opening, and I knew my friend. There was exactly zero chance she wasn't going to respond with some smartassed remark that would almost certainly be hilarious but would one hundred percent not get us any help with my case. "I'd like to report a crime," I said, trying to look businesslike and not at all hungover.

"Well, it's not an ensemble *I'd* choose, but I don't think it rises to the level of criminal," Officer Unfriendly but Hilarious said, looking straight at Rhonda's not-halter top.

I laughed and said, "I agree. It's not *quite* a crime against fashion. But it's also not why I'm here. I need to talk to a detective in your Cyber Crimes Division."

The officer, whose name was Gilread according to her nametag, instantly grew serious and picked up the phone on her desk. "I'll get one of the detectives out here to speak with you. Can you give me an idea of what kind of crime you're reporting? Child pornography? Cyber-bullying? Cyber-stalking?"

"Identity theft," I said, feeling for the first time all trip that maybe my twenty-six-dollar violation was not the worst crime committed against humanity in the past ninety-six hours.

"Your identity was stolen?" Officer Gilread asked, putting down her phone and picking up a pen.

"Yes." I decided to keep my answers short so that we could hurry up and get to the detective part of this. Officer Gilread seemed very competent, but I felt like my case really needed a detective's touch.

"Did they access any of your financial information?"

"Umm..." This was going to take more explanation than I really wanted to go through more than once. "Yes."

"Okay. Have you cancelled any affected credit cards and changed any passwords that may have been compromised?" It sounded like she was reading off a list, and when I leaned over a little, sure enough there was a printed sheet of paper taped to her desk that said "Identity Theft" across the top. Well, at least they had a system. Maybe they could catch these bastards after all.

"Yes, I did all that before I left home to come down here," I said.

At this, Officer Gilread vanished, and the stern countenance of Officer Unfriendly returned. I had aroused suspicion. Dammit. Now I was never going to talk to a detective and get justice for my wallet and revenge for the impugning of my taste in sub sandwiches. "Where are you from?" she asked.

"Monroe, North Carolina," I replied.

Officer Gilread's shoulders slumped, and she looked up at me with an expression that was part pity, part incredulity, and somehow all "Bless Your Heart."

Now, if you aren't from the South, or haven't spent at least the better part of multiple decades there, you may be unaware of the actual meaning of the phrase "Bless Your Heart." The veil of secrecy around this phrase has been lifted somewhat in recent years by popular culture, but there are still multiple layers of nuance wrapped around the phrase that can only be understood when the blessing has been wielded against you like a weapon on multiple occasions.

To start, there are certain circumstances where the phrase "Bless Your/Their Heart/Hearts" is sincere, which only lends further confusion to the whole situation. The sincere blessing is only used in times of illness or tragedy, typically when the blesser is speaking to an unrelated third party who has brought them news of some terrible happenstance that has befallen a neighbor, member of the church, in-law, cousin, or coworker.

For example, "Did you hear about June GoForth? Her husband was caught with the lead mechanic from Bernard's Auto Body and Bait Shop getting his chassis greased after hours."

An appropriate response would be, "Bless her heart, I always thought that husband of hers coordinated his neckties with his pocket squares a little too well to be straight."

Or in another instance, "Did you hear about Esther Monsand? She fell asleep at the wheel driving home from Bible study the other night and crashed her new car into Terrence Higgenbottom's azaleas. When the police got her out of the car, Tommy Hightower's sister's boy said she smelled like a distillery."

It's totally reasonable and sincere to reply with, "Bless her heart, I knew she was in for trouble when she married that Presbyterian. A good Baptist girl like that does not have the tolerance for extra-denominational Bible study."

But the vast majority of the time the words are uttered, it is with a level of sarcasm that can only be mastered by a people who refer to the deadliest war in American history as "the Recent Unpleasantness." Most of the time when someone with a twang in their voice and a twinkle in their eye looks at you and says, "bless your heart," it really means some flavor of insincere response along a short continuum between "oh, you sweet summer child, you are hapless but adorable" and "Jesus Christ on a cracker, did your parents have any children that lived, you moron?"

The look coming from Officer Gilread in that moment was laced with a lot more "are you out of your goddamned mind?" than "I'm so sorry that you've had to go through life dragging the anchor of stupidity along behind you like Christ himself lugging his cross up to Calvary," so I knew whatever came out of her mouth next was not going to be anything I wanted to hear.

"I know," I said, holding up a hand. "I know that the crime was committed against someone in another state. I know that even though the perp is here—" I may have been inordinately proud of myself for working in that little bit of cop-speak that I'd picked up in my recent time in the Big House. Or maybe I learned it watching *Law & Order: Criminal Intent*. One of those. "That the jurisdictional issues are a little confusing. I understand that since this is a clear case of interstate wire fraud, this falls more within the purview of the FBI, but who really wants to involve them?" I leaned forward, giving Officer Gilread a conspiratorial wink. I mean, I intended it to be conspiratorial, but from the confused look on her face, Officer Gilread couldn't tell if I was flirting with her or had something in my eye.

"So if you can just direct us to a detective, we'd like to get going on our plan to help your department bring down what must be a massive credit card...number...selling ring!" I admit, I lost a little steam there near the end when I couldn't figure out what to call a bunch of jerks who steal credit card numbers, but I felt like I finished pretty strong when I remembered that bunches of thieves are called "rings." Like a murder of crows, I guess? Or a pride of lions. A ring of thieves. Sure, that makes as much sense as anything.

Officer Gilread straightened up, pushed back from the front of her desk, giving herself a little more distance from the two crazy women standing in front of her, and said, "How much was stolen?" The look on her face told me she expected the number to be insignificant, inconsequential, irrelevant. And maybe it was. It was only twenty-six dollars. But it was *my* twenty-six dollars, dammit! And it was twenty-six dollars that had gotten me sent to jail, nearly into two different bar fights, and laid by a stranger. Although, I guess after you've shaved somebody's...everything, you're not really strangers anymore.

I stood up straight, stuck out my chin, and said, "Twenty-six dollars." No more information than they ask for. That's the secret to dealing with the cops. Wait, isn't that for the bad guys? Now I was wracking my brain trying to figure out what TV show that little nugget of wisdom came from, so I could remember if the hero was a cop or a criminal. It's so hard to tell these days.

Officer Gilread gave me what I guess would be described as a "level" look. You know them, the kind of "do you think I'm a complete idiot" look that your trig teacher gave you when you tried to use the dead grandmother excuse for not having your homework. For the sixth time that semester. "Your identity was stolen, and they took twenty-six dollars?"

"That's correct," I said, keeping my answers short. I still didn't know what show it was from, but it seemed like good advice in general—don't volunteer too much information to the people with the guns.

"And you live in North Carolina?"

"Yes, ma'am."

"So you drove...eight hours to come down here and file a police report?"

"Oh, no, sweetie," Rhonda said, shouldering me aside and leaning her elbows, among other things, on the desk. Officer Gilread scooted back a little, like Rhonda made her nervous. I understood completely. Rhonda can be a little much for some people. "We didn't just drive down here all willy-nilly. First we tried to report it to our local constabulary, but since the theft originated down here, they didn't care. Then we spoke to the FBI, but because it was just a little piece of money, they didn't care. Now we're talking to you, woman to woman, searching for justice in an unjust world. Are you going to tell me that you, a woman yourself, don't care about my friend's plight? About the violation she has endured at the hands of these nefarious perpetrators? About the—"

"Okay," Officer Gilread said, holding up both hands as if to ward off a rampaging Rhonda. "I'll get a detective to talk with you about your case. I think I know just the guy." She stood up, and as she walked through a glass door into the squadron teeming with cops, she looked back at us with what could only be described as...glee? I suddenly had a very bad feeling about whoever she was bringing back from the other side of that door.

CHAPTER 22

T he detective that Officer Gilread came back with looked like something straight out of Central Casting, if every casting agent in the world was stuck in 1977 and on a spectacular amount of cocaine. He was a skinny man with thinning brown hair that he wore long, in a Beatles-style shaggy bowl cut, and despite being rail-thin in the face, neck, and arms, he still managed to have a pot belly stretching out the front of his pale blue short-sleeved dress shirt that made him look like he was trying to smuggle a volleyball across the border. I almost reached out for it and asked when he was due, it was such a perfect little round tummy.

A girl I used to work with looked like that when she got pregnant, like somebody glued a grape to a Q-Tip. She was a size zero when she got knocked up and made it all the way up to a six before she squeezed out her kid in a heated swimming pool with some hippie woman playing catch with her placenta right out in her backyard in front of God, the UPS driver, and everybody. There were pictures. It was…messy. I was real glad I hadn't volunteered the use of my pool for the birth, because they must have replaced a couple of filters after that mess.

But I managed not to reach out and pat the detective's little belly, mostly because I didn't want to get within leaping distance of whatever he called the thing on his face. Because it wasn't a beard, and it wasn't a mustache. It was some kind of strange patchy growth that looked like brown-and-white fungus trying to creep across the surface of a piece of white bread, but not making too much headway. I was almost certain none of the hair on his face was sentient, but it had not been the kind of week that led me to take any extra chances.

"Hey there, ladies," he said, with a smile that made me squirm a little down below. Not like that! No, more like he made me feel like my bowels were a little watery, and I made a promise to myself not to trust a fart for the next couple hours, because I was running real low on underpants for this trip, and I could not survive a shart. "I'm Detective Baniff. But you can call me Rob."

Rhonda stepped forward and stuck out her hand, suddenly all professional. "Rhonda Mabry," she said, shaking his hand. "We're here to report a cybercrime."

Detective Baniff looked at Officer Gilread with confusion written all over his face. "I...don't really do cyber—"

"Trust me, Detective," Gilread said, a knowing smile on her lips. "This is exactly the kind of case the captain said we should hand straight to you."

Baniff's face fell, and I realized what was going on. This guy was in deep shit with his boss, so he's getting all the assholes and morons. We used to do that at my work, too. Anytime one of the salespeople was being an asshole, they would find themselves flooded with all the nuisance calls, all the time-consuming calls looking for a two-dollar part, and every obscure question about the specs of one model or another. After a few days of this, most of them came to their senses and apologized to whoever had called a Code Green on them. We called it a Code Green because the first person we unleashed it on was named Green. It wasn't a terribly original workplace.

I stepped up and held out my own hand. "Hi there," I said, putting on what I hoped was a reassuring smile. "I'm Alexis Lieberman, and I'm a victim of identity theft. We have evidence that the culprits are here in Orlando, and if I was a victim, it's highly likely that there are a lot more. You could be bringing down an entire international crime syndicate, and it all starts right here, with a couple of housewives from North Carolina."

"Well, house*women*," Rhonda said. "I haven't been anyone's wife in years, house or otherwise. Desperate, maybe, but not a housewife." She gave her chest a little shimmy that both grabbed Baniff's attention and demonstrated several laws of fluid dynamics all at once. "Can you help us, sir? Please?"

That "please" was accompanied not only by a little squeezing of her elbows together to perk the girls up even more, but also a world-class eyelash batting. I mean, if those fake lashes had come to life and flapped away like little butterflies, it wouldn't have surprised me, the way she fluttered those things.

But it worked. Something worked, anyway, because a smarmy smile stretched all the way across Baniff's face, showing brilliantly white capped teeth with a tiny little speck of something right between the two fronts. Poppyseed or something. Either way, it was damned distracting, and what the detective was saying didn't register with me until he cleared his throat and I noticed he was standing there holding the glass door into the bullpen open for me. Rhonda was already through, of course, standing on her impossible shoes making her ass look like something you could bounce a quarter off of and get a nickel's change.

I hurried through the door and followed the suddenly gallant Detective Baniff through the bullpen and into a room labeled "Interview 3."

Interrogation rooms in real life look just like the ones on TV, except this one had four chairs. I guess so you could have Good Cop, Bad Cop, Criminal, and Lawyer (aka Higher-Paid Criminal). Rhonda and I sat on one side of the table, and my best friend immediately leaned waaayyyy forward onto the scuffed tabletop. I swear, when we got back home, I was going to make her register those things with the Sheriff's Department. If she was going to wield her cleavage as a weapon, the least she could do was get a permit for it.

Detective Baniff sat down directly across from Rhonda, looking in her eyes with a herculean effort, and giving her the kind of smile that men think make women immediately moist in our nether regions, but really just kinda make us feel like we need a shower. Alone. In very hot water. "Now, Miss Liebowitz—"

"Lieberman," I said with a little wave, trying to direct his attention to me, the actual victim of a crime. Although I didn't really want too much of the skeevy detective's attention on me, I figured if we were going to get to the bottom of this caper, I was going to have to deal with him.

Baniff looked startled, like he just realized he was the one who farted during the teleconference. "Huh?"

Sparkling conversationalist, this one. "My name is Lieberman, with one 'n.' My identity was stolen and used by criminals here in the Orlando area to order food. I've driven all the way down here from North Carolina to seek justice. Can you help me?" I tried to put a little whimper in my voice at the end, to make it seem like I was the poor, maligned victim, but let's be real. I'd already spent ten times what they stole on this wild goose chase to find the bastards who violated my identity, and I was starting to feel like if I could get home without any further time locked up, chained up, or in any way associated with any mechanical farm animals named Hornicus Prime, I should just take the win and forget this whole trip ever happened. Except for maybe giving Harrison Wainwright Moustacheless a call in a couple weeks after all the scratches on his back had time to heal.

"Oh." Baniff seemed disappointed somehow, as if he really wanted Rhonda to be the damsel in distress. Or maybe he was just hoping he could find an excuse to pat her down. He pulled a small notebook from his shirt pocket, a pen from the honest-to-god pocket protector he had in the same pocket, and flipped the notebook open to a blank page. "Well, how about you tell me exactly what happened, to the best of your recollection?"

I did. It didn't take nearly as long to recount when I wasn't explaining to Rhonda just exactly how devastated I felt, or the degree to which my privacy had been violated. Sticking to a "just the facts" presentation made the whole thing, and my subsequent Road Trip for Justice (TM pending) seem a little silly. I could tell from the expression on his face that Baniff agreed.

He flipped the notebook closed. "Well, I have to say that I am impressed with your...tenacity. Not many people would drive, what, five hundred miles?"

"Roughly," I said, my voice flat as my hopes for glorious redemption when my Quest for Sub Money (not as good trademark also pending) resulted in the destruction and apprehension of an international money-laundering operation that used delivery orders to hide their underhanded activities. Although what kind of underhanded activities you can activate for twenty-six dollars was beyond me. You can't even get drunk enough to spank a stranger in a Dave & Buster's for twenty-six bucks. Not that we'd let a little thing like sobriety stop us from making a spectacle of ourselves.

Baniff went on, and I could almost hear the gurgle as my hopes for satisfaction swirled down the drain. "So you drove five hundred miles to get back, what, twenty bucks?"

"Twenty-six," Rhonda said, raising a finger to Detective Douchecanoe. "Don't act like this is some little petty theft, Detective. We have reason to believe that this crime is connected to a massive international criminal organization."

Baniff's eyes widened, and he straightened up in his chair, suddenly very interested in the words coming out of Rhonda's mouth and not just in watching her breathing. "What kind of reason?" he asked.

"Huh?" Apparently Baniff's verbal constipation was contagious, because now I was responding in grunts.

"What reason do you have to believe that your very small identity theft is the tip of some giant iceberg of international crime ravaging the Happiest Place on Earth?"

I saw his eyes flick up to a corner of the room and suddenly understood what was going on. I turned toward the big mirror set into the wall to my left, and said, "Do you want to come in here now, or do we have to continue this farce?"

Now Baniff looked confused. "Who are you talking to?"

I pointed to the corner of the room where his eye had gone There was a small surveillance camera mounted near the ceiling. Oddly enough, there was no little red light to indicate the camera was on. "Whoever is watching us through that camera," I said. I pointed to the mirror. "Do you have a bunch of your buddies on the other side of the two-way glass snickering at the crazy woman who got her identity stolen and came all the way to Florida looking for justice? Come on, Rhonda, we're obviously not going to get any help here. This dick just wants to stare at your boobs. He doesn't give a damn about busting up an international crime syndicate."

I stood up, slung my bag over my shoulder, and strode to the door. But before I could reach for the knob, it turned and the door opened to reveal a pair of familiar figures standing in the hallway glowering at me. I took a step back into the room, wondering how in the hell my world had gotten completely turned upside down over a couple of sub sandwiches.

Agents Kaplan and Burns, the two FBI agents who had come to my house to threaten me with shipment off to Gitmo if I didn't stop looking into this crime (okay, they never *said* anything about sending me to Gitmo, but it was definitely implied, an implication made all the stronger for their appearance outside an interrogation room five hundred miles from where I last saw them), stepped into the room and stood behind a very confused looking Detective Baniff.

Kaplan broke the uneasy silence, looking down at Baniff. "Could we have the room, Detective? We need to speak with Ms. Lieberman and Ms. Mabry privately."

Baniff stood up and headed for the door. "Of course, anything we can do to help. I'll just—"

"Just pretend we're not here," Agent Burns said. "And by that, I mean stay out of the observation room and leave the mics and cameras off."

A chastened Detective Baniff left, more slinking than strutting now, and the two agents sat down across the table from us. Kaplan leaned forward, putting his elbows on the table and unconsciously mimicking Rhonda's posture, albeit to much less effect. "Now," he said, "What the actual fuck are you doing here, and what will it take to get you to leave?"

CHAPTER 23

I was more than a little taken aback by Agent Kaplan's abrupt shift in demeanor. One minute he's stern but official and uptight, you know, how you *expect* an FBI agent to act. He even had the kinda crappy suit that they reference in movies and thriller novels. You know the ones, where the protagonist is either a retired or disgraced agent that they have to bring back into the fold to solve the case only he can solve. And it's always a "he." They're never pulling the scary middle-aged woman out of retirement to save the world. Probably because we're too busy actually saving the world every day, and we can't be bothered to judge every pecker-measuring contest the government gets themselves into.

But I digress. No, I really do. It's my thing, and being on basically a three-day bender-slash-chick flick with Rhonda does nothing to help me focus.

Agent Kaplan had been nothing but professional up 'til now, and to be honest, I missed that. I certainly liked his cold professionalism a lot more than I liked this prick looking over me with his testosterone poisoning the very air in the room. So I might not have responded to his intimidation efforts as well as I normally would have. I blame Rhonda for that, too.

"Am I under arrest?" I asked, meeting his glare with a steely gaze of my own. I have raised teenagers. There is no dirty look in the universe that has power over me any longer. Until you have seen the daggers a fifteen-year-old girl can fling with her eyes after you hold up a training bra and shout "Baby! Can you wear a 32A?" across an entire Walmart, you have not experienced the true magnitude of the phrase "if looks could kill." Agent Kaplan might have literally been able to shoot me, but he could not come close to beating my daughters in the dirty looks competition.

He leaned back, unsurprisingly surprised at my quick reversal of attitude. Agent Kaplan was obviously unmarried, because he seemed befuddled by my quick temperament shift. If he was wed to a woman anything like me (which is to say, brilliant, talented, and charming, of course) then my pivot wouldn't be surprising, it would have been just an expected tactic. "Um...no, you're not under arrest."

"Then I'm leaving," I said, standing up and letting the chair scrape across the tiles. The squeal of metal on cheap jail floor echoed off the bare walls, and I cringed a little.

Kaplan stared up at me, his mouth agape. "You can't leave." His voice was querulous, a confused little thing that was more asking me than telling me anything.

"You can't stop me," I said, straightening my spine and reaching deep into my bag of middle-aged White woman tricks and dragging out the mental blond wig and boob job that would turn me into Ultra-Karen, Revenger of Imagined Slights and Tormenter of Managers. "I know my rights, and if you aren't going to charge me, you have to let me go. So if you aren't arresting me, I'm leaving." I started moving toward the end of the table, and Kaplan stood up, his own chair almost toppling over in his haste.

"Wait," he said, holding his hands palms out in my direction. I looked down at where his hands were hovering a couple inches in front of my chest. He snatched the offending appendages back, giving me a guilty look even though he never touched me. "Sorry."

"Agent Kaplan," I said, leaning in to press my advantage as he backed up accordingly. I could see from his posture that this big burly federal agent was very unaccustomed to anyone, much less a woman, looming over him in any way. "I know there's a lot more going on than you can discuss with me, but I also know that you wouldn't be down here if there wasn't something behind my suspicions. They aren't going to send an FBI agent from North Carolina to Orlando just to hunt down a couple of middle-aged women. You're here for something real, and if you won't sit down and tell me what is going on, then I'm going to walk out that door and tell the media all about this whole thing. How the federal government has been conspiring with a secret ring of sex traffickers operating out of the back of a pizza shop—"

Kaplan held up a hand, palm out, and I was so stunned that I actually stopped talking. "You know we've literally debunked that *exact* bullshit rumor, right?"

"You *think* you've debunked it. Until I get it back all over the internet and make your cyber-life a living cyber-hell." I took a deep breath, ready to dive back in, but this time he froze me with one word.

"Okay."

If my mouth had feet, I would have face planted I stumbled so hard at his reply. "What?"

"Okay, I'll tell you everything. It's obviously the only way to keep you out of my hair. But not here. Too many ears. Come with me." He stood up, walked to the door, and left the room, his partner trailing behind silently. Rhonda and I watched in stunned silence, then scrambled to our feet when he turned back and motioned for us to follow.

We wound our way through the labyrinthine back halls of the precinct office, keeping tight to Kaplan's heels. This was very much a different way out than we took to get in, but as long as it got me closer to the truth, I didn't care if we walked all the way back to North Carolina.

Okay, that's a total exaggeration. With my shoes, and my knees, I wasn't even willing to walk all the way back to Jacksonville. I had an ancestor, Jeremiah Benedict Teagarde, who fought for the South in the Civil War and was a prisoner of war outside Baltimore. When the war ended, he walked all the way home from Maryland to the upstate of South Carolina just to be reunited with his family and his loyal dog, Rufus. He died of dysentery three miles from home, broken and dehydrated, with more blisters than feet by the time he coughed his last, dusty, desiccated breath out on the side of what would eventually become Highway 74.

I learned a few things from Great-Great-Great-Great-Uncle Jeremiah's journey and subsequent demise. First, I do not have the genetic basis upon which a Forrest Gump-like cross-country trek is built. Second, if I am ever taken prisoner by Yankees, I should be sure to drink plenty of water. And third, walking sucks and should be avoided under any and all circumstances. These truisms have stood me in good stead for all my forty-something years, not that I have ever been captured by Yankees or had any inclination to put on a red ball cap and run across the continent.

But I followed Agent Kaplan through the bowels of the Orlando Police

Department, hoping all the while that our march to justice wasn't all that long, or at least had plenty of bathroom breaks planned in, since that whole staying hydrated thing also meant that I had to pee at least once every hour. Fortunately for my ankles and my bladder, we burst out a side door into the brilliant Florida morning sun after what seemed like only two or three laps around the nearest football stadium. I swear on my living mother's grave that seven of those left turns were just to confuse us. He didn't really need to try all that hard; we were pretty easily confused on our best day.

I stood there at the top of a small set of brick steps, blinking to clear the dazzles from my vision. "Okay, Agent," I said. "Is this private enough?"

No response. I turned around to where Agent Kaplan should have been standing behind us, having been a proper gentleman and held the door open for Rhonda and I to pass through. Instead, I saw only a gray metal door, closed tight to the frame of the building. I reached for the knob, only to find that there wasn't one. Just a keyhole under a big sign, right at eye level, that proclaimed "AUTHORIZED PERSONNEL ONLY."

"Well, shit," I said, turning to Rhonda. "I think he ditched us."

"Ya think?" My best friend and co-conspirator asked as she leaned against the railing on the small landing. "What gave it away? The whole him not following us thing, or the him locking the door behind us and throwing away the knob, much less the key?"

"Well, you don't have to be a smartass about it," I grumbled, folding my arms across my chest. I have to admit, I was pretty dang disappointed. I thought we were getting somewhere. I thought we were getting to justice for my identity theft and the identities of all the women exploited by this band of criminal marauders since they began their reign of terror.

Okay, I watch too many movie trailers. Cut me some slack. Broadcast television sucks, and I can't keep track of all the streaming services I'm subscribed to, much less what's on them. So I watch trailers for movies I'll never watch. And that may have led to a certain level of hyperbole in my speech. Or maybe that's just me.

I looked at my smartassed friend, who stood there smirking at me. "What are you grinning about? You're in the same boat I am."

"Not exactly," she said, still smirking. She reached into her cleavage and pulled out a key card. "I bumped into an officer in the hall and lifted his ID badge. This should open every door in the place." She turned to the door, key card in hand, only to realize that there was nowhere to insert, swipe, or tap the key card. This door opened with a key. The old-fashioned kind, that end up living on a ring in your purse for three jobs after this one and you eventually find it and wonder what it's supposed to open, then you take an hour going around your house and trying to open every lock in there with this mystery key, only to finally remember that it's the key to your office from twelve years ago, and not only do you not work there anymore, but the entire building has been torn down because it was in Charlotte, and any building more than twenty-five years old in that city gets torn down and replaced with something equally architecturally milquetoast.

"So…" I started, but Rhonda held up a hand.

"Nope," she said, not looking at me, just holding up her hand and turning sideways to inch down the steps ahead of me. "We're never going to speak of this again. It was a great plan, and it was executed flawlessly; the building was just built incorrectly, and the architect's mistake screwed up my plan. That's my story, and I'm sticking to it."

And when Rhonda Mabry decides she's sticking to a story, she sticks to a story. I once watched her tell a highway patrolman that there was no way she was speeding on the interstate when every sign she passed told her the speed limit was eighty-five, and she was only doing eighty. The poor cop tried for fifteen minutes to explain to her that the speed limit on Interstate 85 was actually sixty miles per hour, and she was thus speeding like a bat out of hell. By the time she got out of the car, grabbed the cop by his arm and dragged him over to stand in front of the road sign to prove to him that the speed limit was eighty-five, he was so confused he didn't know whether to wind his ass or scratch his watch. I'm pretty sure he'd never called for an involuntary psych hold for a speeding ticket before, but he was seriously considering it that day.

And yes, she got off with a warning to watch her speed and a free DVD about the traffic laws of North Carolina. So when she said that an architect made a mistake in building the police headquarters in the early 1970s, and that's why her plan some nearly fifty years later all fell apart, that was just the law according to Rhonda, and I was just going to have to shut up and follow her in our bizarre walk of shame down the steps, through the employee parking lot, around the building, and to our car. It being Florida, by the time I got back to the car, I was glistening in places I was pretty sure weren't supposed to glisten, and I stood with the driver's door open for a minute as the air conditioning got some air moving inside the rolling metal toaster oven that our little Prius had turned into.

"Now what?" I asked over the roof of the car.

135

Rhonda leaned forward, then jerked her arm back as it made contact with the scalding roof of the car. I mean, even deep into the fall, the temperature in Orlando hovers between "lovely" and "sixth circle of Hell," so it's not a great idea to put your bare flesh in direct contact with any metal that's been in the sun for more than about eighteen seconds.

She stepped back from the griddle that was the roof of my car and glared at me. "We're gonna do what we came here to do. We're gonna hunt those bastards down ourselves, and we're gonna make them pay for their crimes."

Yeah, so that worked out well. Totally.

CHAPTER 24

Another hour in the ridiculous Florida heat found us sticky, sweaty, and thoroughly unsatisfied sitting in the front seat of my car staring at a building. It felt a lot like my senior prom, except it was daylight, I wasn't smothered in crinoline with a run in my hose, and I knew where both my shoes were. Also, Aaron Perkins wasn't leaning back against the passenger seat panting like he'd just run the Boston Marathon despite only engaging in strenuous cardio activity for about three minutes.

"Thinking about prom again?" Rhonda asked. I swear to God that woman is worse than Alexa about knowing exactly what is going on inside my head at every minute. Every time I see her, I expect ads for wrinkle cream and discount shoes to be scrolling across her face.

"How do you do that?" I asked.

"That's what you've said every time I've seen you with that sour expression on your face for the past ten years. Babe, your senior prom was in another *century*. Let it go. Be like Elsa."

"Did you just make a *Frozen* reference to me?"

"Did you get the reference? Then it must have been a good one."

"How have you even seen that movie? My girls were barely old enough to watch it, and you don't even have kids."

"No, but I have a reindeer fetish and a crush on Anna Kendrick."

I took a second to process that, then decided that I didn't want to process too deeply. "Well, who doesn't have a crush on Anna Kendrick? She's adorable. But yes, to answer your first question," I said, which felt a *lot* safer than going any further down the road of Rhonda's reindeer fetish. Or any of Rhonda's fetishes, frankly. I looked in her "toy box" once and spent three hours on Google just trying to figure out what everything was. I ended up taking a picture of one thing in there and emailing Adam & Eve tech support, only to find out that it was an eggbeater that had ended up in the wrong box.

I somehow wrangled my train of thought back onto the tracks and said, "Yes, I was thinking about prom. No, it wasn't a satisfying mental image. So yes, we should get out of this toaster oven of a car and go see what we can find out from the security guard." I opened my door, and a blast of warm, moist air enveloped me.

The South is great for a lot of things. Seriously, it is. There's great fried food, awesome beaches, easily hikeable mountains, lovely people, and Cheerwine. But what people who don't live in the South have trouble understanding, in addition to the many, *many* bizarre cultural mores that exist about when you can and cannot wear white shoes, is that year-round temperate weather comes with a price. And that price is humidity.

Heat is easy. I can handle heat standing on my head. And have, for one spectacularly awful summer camp where I tried to learn cheerleading and gymnastics. If I'd understood at fifteen that I could get the same attention by unbuttoning an extra button on my sweater that I got jumping around in thousand-degree heat, I would have just gone to school topless and saved myself the effort. But heat is not the challenge of living in the South.

It's the goddamned humidity. Imagine walking out of your home in the morning, freshly showered, powdered, shaved, and coiffed, only to be smacked in the face with a soaking wet warm washcloth. That's southern humidity. It's like stepping out of a normal environment suited for human life into a hellscape of boob sweat, butt crack sweat, sweat between your toes, and the absolute hairdo-wilting saturation of every square inch of air surrounding you. If you don't look like someone dumped a bucket of water on you between the time you step out your back door and the time you slide behind the wheel of your car, then congratulations, you are one of the three people in the world who actually keeps your car in the garage, rather than filling the space with unused lawn implements, forgotten

Christmas decorations, and half-completed "projects" that you know will never actually get finished.

Southern humidity is bad. North Carolina humidity is sometimes downright awful. But *Florida* humidity? That's some impressive shit right there. I hadn't even turned around to push the car door closed before I felt a drop of sweat start rolling down the center of my spine. I wasn't sweating when I was in the car. I hadn't done anything except stand up out of the vehicle. There was no exertion of any kind involved, and yet I broke a sweat just by standing up. That one little droplet was going to drive me nuts until it reached its final destination, I could tell. It was almost like the little bastard had a mind of its own.

It started in the perfect spot between my shoulder blades, where I couldn't have reached it if I tried, and would have just looked silly and possibly dislocated my shoulder had I tried. So I didn't. I just let the little guy run free, right down the center of my spine, tickling the tiny hairs on my back the whole way down. That one water droplet did a better job of exploring my flesh in one trip down to my ass than Aaron Perkins did in three months of "dating." The quotation marks are to really hammer home the point that we never went anywhere, just took his cousin's station wagon out to the field behind his house and fooled around for a few hours before he drove me home, usually missing a sock or some other less visible but more difficult to explain article of clothing. Let's just say that my senior year of high school made me very happy that I did my own laundry and that my mother didn't pay too close attention to how much underwear I was buying. Or from where.

As I walked, I wiggled my back trying to rub the sweat droplet off against the back of my shirt, but it would not be denied. That little bead of perspiration made it all the way from the top of my shoulders down my back, over the curve of my butt, and down into the tiniest of gaps between my underpants and the top of my butt, then it plunged headlong into the crack of my ass, leaving me to once again draw parallels between this trip to Florida and my senior prom. I only hoped that some portion of this journey would be more satisfying than the dance, which was so lame that I actually drank the punch. And not the spiked one. Just regular punch.

Of course, the cute little twenty-something guy in the guard shack got to watch me do my twitchy walk up to his door, where I knocked and leaned against the door frame in what I hoped was a seductive and not at all awkward pose. Yeah, I knew it was totally awkward, but I can dream, right?

The guard was a trim young man with short dark hair, blue eyes, and a jawline to die for. He was short, just a few inches taller than me, with the arms of someone who works out, but not incessantly. He looked me up and down, a puzzled expression on his face. "Can I help you, ma'am?"

Oof. I got ma'amed. That one still stings, even with a daughter in college. In my head, I still look like I should get carded buying booze, but unfortunately my body and my head are very different places, and it's been a long time since anyone asked to look at my ID because they thought I was too young to do anything. More often nowadays, they're asking to see my AARP card. I'd hoped at least showing off a little cleavage would help, but then I remembered I was in Florida, where the average age of the citizen is eighty, but the average age of the citizen's plastic surgery is only about six. Months, that is.

I straightened up a little, which had the dual effect of bringing my eyes almost directly in line with the guard's, and also pushed my boobs out a little in hopes that he would look at them instead of my crow's feet. "I need some help, and I think you might be just the man to provide it." I reached out to run a finger along his forearm in what I hoped was a seductive fashion.

He didn't seem the least bit seduced, but he didn't run screaming, so I took the win and plowed right ahead. "I need to see your security footage from three days ago. I believe a serious crime was committed here in your development, and I think you may hold critical evidence to bring the perpetrators to justice." If I couldn't seduce him with sex appeal, maybe I could appeal to his latent desire to be a hero, which is what all security guards want. They all either want to be a hero and then get to join the FBI, or they're serial killers. One of those. At least that's what prime time television has taught me.

The guard stepped back far enough for me to read his nametag, which proclaimed him "Jonathan," and shook his head. "Oh, I'm sorry, ma'am. Our residents really value their privacy, and I am under strict orders not to share any security footage with anyone unless my supervisor is present and the person requesting to see the tapes has a badge and a warrant."

"Well, I don't have a warrant, but you're welcome to search me and find out whether or not I have a badge hidden somewhere about my person," I cooed, leaning forward again. I was standing in the door of his little guard shack, so it's not like he had anywhere to go. He could either shove his way past me, or he could take one more step back, hit his chair with the back of his legs, and plop down onto his butt with my chest in his face.

Being a polite young man, he didn't knock me flat on my ass escaping from the crazy woman who wanted to see his surveillance video, so he plopped down on his ass staring right into the straining button on my overburdened top. I told Rhonda that shirt didn't fit right, but she insisted I pack it, saying it was flattering to my everything.

Jonathan the Guard stared up at me like a deer caught in headlights. Get it? Headlights? Like boobs? Lord, everybody's a damn critic. Anyway, Jonathan the wee little guard looked around frantically for a way out of this situation, but apparently he had no experience being cornered by a cougar in his security hut, so he was stuck. "I'm really sorry, ma'am, but I'll lose my job if I show you the video. I'd like to help you, really I would, but I just can't."

I leaned forward, putting both hands on the arms of his chair, pinning him even more tightly in place. I put my lips to his ear, letting my breath tickle the hairs on the side of his neck as I asked, "Are you *sure* I can't persuade you?"

The air was thick with innuendo, but any hopes I had for sashaying my way into young Jonathan's pants and video archives shattered when he held up his left hand, very carefully keeping it away from any of my zones, erogenous or otherwise. "I'm sorry. I'm married."

"Nobody's perfect," I replied, laying it on even thicker. By this point I knew I'd met my match, but with Rhonda watching, I felt like I needed to make every effort before admitting defeat. I could just see her walking up to the little dark-haired boy toy, flouncing twice and batting her eyelashes at him before his will crumbled completely and she got what we needed.

"No, I'm not perfect," Jonathan said, leaning as far back in his chair as he could with me pressing down on the arms. "But I am gay. So please. Just stop. I can't show you the footage, and you can't seduce me. So why don't you just go on your merry way and let me get back to my *Glee* rewatch?"

I nodded, beaten. I stood up, straightened my clothes, and patted him on one cheek. "You're a good man, Guard Jonathan. I almost feel bad about this." Then I turned and walked out of the guard shack.

Rhonda leaned on the fender of our car, having pulled a spare shirt out of our luggage to keep from scorching her butt cheeks. She gave me a cocky grin as I slunk back to her side. "No luck, huh?"

"Nope," I replied, holding my best dejected expression.

"Well, sister, you just wait right here and let me show you how it's done." Then she strutted over to the cabin to turn her considerable charms loose on what might be the most resistant victim she'd ever encountered. I gave her almost fifty-fifty odds. Almost.

CHAPTER 25

"That was totally not fair," Rhonda said as we turned out of the housing development's entrance. "You knew he was gay!"

"Yeah, but you've always said you could make any man do whatever you want. Now I know that's all BS." I was chuckling on the outside but rolling on the floor laughing my ass off on the inside. Watching Rhonda crash and burn with the cute security guard was worth almost everything I'd gone through on this trip. It didn't quite cover the night in jail, but everything else we'd dealt with since leaving home was now officially worth it.

"I assumed it was implied that I was talking about straight men. My charms are less effective on men with better manicures than me."

"He did have nice nails, didn't he?" I had noticed his lovely cuticles and almost asked where he went, but then remembered I was not only several states away from my manicurist (and calling the nice Korean lady at the Walmart by my house *my* manicurist is a stretch worthy of my yoga instructor), but I was also on a mission of justice, so I regrettably wouldn't have time to stop for a mani/pedi. And I needed one in the worst way. My toenails were looking more like a sloth's claws than human feet lately.

"So while you were yukking it up at my futile efforts to seduce a gay man, did you happen to come up with any bright ideas for how we're going to find your identity thieves? Since Captain Cuticles over there won't let us see the security video, what's Plan B?"

"I think I'm past the point in my life where I need to worry about birth control, but I appreciate your concern." After our second daughter, Kristen, was born, both Peter and I went under the knife to make sure Mother Nature didn't have any more surprises for us. I thought it was only fair if he was going to get snipped, that I get snipped as well, then I learned that like everything, the process was way more involved for a woman than a man. Peter had to lie on the couch with a bag of frozen peas on his junk for a couple of days, which wasn't much of a burden since he got snipped on a Friday during football season, so it wasn't like he was going to leave the couch for the next forty-eight hours anyway. I couldn't lift anything heavier than a gallon of milk for two weeks, and it was most of a month before I felt normal again.

"I'm not talking about you and Harrison Wainwright Mustacheless," Rhonda replied. "But I am proud of you for at least thinking about safe sex sometime within seventy-two hours of having sex. I suppose that's a small victory that we'll just move on from. No, I mean what's your next brilliant plan for uncovering the identities of the perps?"

"Oh, yeah, that." I handed her my phone. "Go to the ChowSprint app, then repeat the last order on my account."

"This is a weird time to be hungry. I mean, I get it, stakeouts are boring, but we aren't even parked."

"The last order was the one the bad guys placed on my credit card. If we order their favorite, albeit godawful, subs to be delivered, then we can set up our observation post somewhere in sight of the guard hut and watch as our identity thieves show up to get their food."

"Won't they know they didn't order anything?"

"If you got a notification that food you liked just randomly got delivered, would you open the door and eat it, or would you stare at it through the peephole in fear?" I asked.

Rhonda conceded my point and started tapping on my screen, holding the phone up to my face to unlock it. I'd seen articles about people getting murdered and the killers using their dead faces to unlock their phones, then stealing the dead person's money, and thought briefly about turning off the facial recognition on my phone, then I realized that I was pretty unlikely to be murdered for the contents of my bank account, and if anyone unlocked my phone and started poking around in my bank accounts, they'd probably steal money from someone else and deposit it into my accounts out of pity. I'm not saying I was broke, but I'd put every drop of gas for this trip on a credit card, and if the thieves had tried to order more than two lunches, they would have been sorely disappointed.

I circled the block, which as more like taking some bizarre trip through random residential neighborhoods then parking my car in front of a gas station in view of the guard shack, and settled in to get comfortable, and Rhonda finished ordering and passed my phone back to me. "Done," she said.

"That took a lot more tapping on my screen than I expected it to," I replied.

"I had to wait until you stopped to get the address of this place."

"Why? You're having the subs delivered across the street."

"I'm having *their* subs delivered across the street. I'm having *our* subs delivered to your passenger window."

"Good call. I'm getting a bit peckish." It had been a morning. Between dealing with the police, then the FBI, then Jonathan the Guard, it was well past my normal lunchtime, and I was starting to get hungry. That would soon lead to me getting grumpy, then downright hangry. And nobody wants to be in a car with me when I'm hangry. It's bad enough that my younger daughter Kristen carries granola bars in her purse for trips with me, because she knows I'd rather go into a murderous hunger rage than stop in the middle of a road trip.

"Yeah, I can hear your tummy growling over the radio," Rhonda said, and I flipped her the bird. We sat there staring out the windshield, occasionally fiddling with the radio, me wishing I'd kept the satellite radio hooked up after the free trial ran out, and Rhonda griping that all music today sucked. Basically proving that we were middle-aged and nowhere even close to cool. If we ever were.

Rhonda's phone dinged twice in rapid succession, and she looked at the screen. "Excellent. Rafael is approaching with both orders. I hope he delivers ours first, so we have our food before we have to pay attention to what's going on across the street. Did you bring binoculars?"

I'm sure my confusion showed on my face as I said, "Huh? Why would I have brought binoculars?"

"What kind of stakeout did you think we were going on that you wouldn't bring binoculars?" Rhonda shot back.

"Well, I didn't know we were going on a stakeout when we left home three days ago! I don't even own binoculars. Do you?"

"Hell yes I do," she said grinning like a cat coughing up feathers. "Henry Fields, the guy who bought the Masterson's place three doors down from me? He likes to sunbathe nude, and he thinks just because his back yard had an eight-foot privacy fence, that nobody can see him running around bare-assed."

"But the Peeping Tammy with the attic converted into her home gym can just sit at her window and gaze at his assets while she—"

"We don't need to discuss what I do when I gaze at Henry's assets," Rhonda cut me off. I was going to say she exercised while looking at him, but apparently that wasn't the only thing she was doing in her home gym. And I thought she kept those things on the shelf by the yoga mats to massage sore muscles.

"Wasn't thinking that, but now I can't think about anything else. So thanks for that," I said, watching as a black coupe pulled into a parking spot a few yards down from us. A tall Black man got out of the car and reached back inside to grab a large carryout bag. I beeped the Prius's horn at him, which was way less rude than it would have been in a bigger vehicle. In my car, it was the automotive equivalent of politely clearing one's throat. A little *beep* rather than a full-fledged *HOOOOOOONNNNNKKKK*. Which of course meant he didn't notice and stood in front of the store looking around before shrugging his shoulders and heading toward the pet shop we were parked in front of.

Rhonda hopped out of the car and waved, yelling, "Yoo-hoo! Mr. Food Delivery Man! Rafael! Over here!"

The guy walked over, looking totally befuddled at delivering food to a car rather than a building, but once Rhonda convinced him that the food was in fact hers, he handed her the bag and walked back to his car, shaking his head. I feel for delivery drivers nowadays. Most of them started their gigs to pick up some extra cash on the side. Then the apocalypse happened, their business exploded, and now, a couple years of pandemic later, those drivers all have the thousand-yard stare of people who have *seen* some shit.

I can only imagine the kind of sights that have greeted them the past two years. I mean, people are crazy, and Americans are crazier than most. But Americans who have been told they have to stay home with the families they've spent their entire adult lives trying to be around as little as possible? You trap them at home for an extended period of time, and I'm surprised we're not completely living in a *Mad Max* movie by now.

"Okay," Rhonda said, sliding into the passenger seat and laying a bag of delicious-smelling subs on the dash. "Now let's see who shows up across the street. Too bad we don't have binoculars."

"I didn't know!" I protested.

"It's fine. I tipped Rafael an extra twenty bucks to take pictures of the guys who picked up the food. He'll tell them he has to document delivery because there's been a rash of false credit card orders lately."

"That's a little on the nose, don't you think?" I asked.

"I had to improvise," Rhonda replied. "It's not my best work, but he took the twenty bucks, so let's see if he texts me a picture like he's supposed to."

"You gave a strange delivery driver your phone number?" I asked.

"You give strange delivery drivers your home address and phone number every time you order something to eat," Rhonda replied. "You are not living out the best practices of cyber security here, darling. Besides, he was *cute*."

"Was he cuter than Henry?" I teased.

"I don't know. But if I get to see him naked, I'll give you my honest comparison."

I was a little worried, because I knew that she would do exactly that. Not only her honest comparison, but her very detailed comparison, and I wasn't sure I wanted to know that much about either the delivery guy in Orlando or my neighbor back home in Monroe. Actually, I was a little curious about Henry. He seemed pretty shy, so if he was packing a killer body under the shapeless clothes he usually wore, it might be worth going over to Rhonda's to work out sometime.

"Let's hold off on the play-by-play," I said. "Looks like Raphael is handing the food to...Jonathan the Guard. Shit." Sure enough, Rafael handed the bag to the adorable little guy in the security shack, took a picture of him holding the bag, and headed back to his car. A few seconds after he got behind the wheel, Rhonda's phone *dinged* with a new text.

"Good picture," Rhonda said. "He really captured the blue in Jonathan's eyes. Are you sure he's gay?"

"Gay *and* married," I replied. "Two strikes and you're out."

"That's so not how baseball works."

"That's not the game you want to play with the gay guard," I said.

"Valid point. Now what?"

"Now we sit here and see who comes to get the sandwiches, then we try to follow them back to their house, or get a picture, or a license plate number, or anything that won't make this trip a horrible waste of time and money." I was starting to feel the last few days morphing into this massive ball of bullshit that I was going to have one hell of a time explaining to my girls. I guess the old excuse of "Your Aunt Rhonda made me do it" was always a possibility.

"I mean, you got laid, so it wasn't a total wasted trip, even if we don't get your fifteen dollars back."

"Twenty-six dollars," I said absently. "But I did get laid. You're right."

"I know. I was there, remember?"

"Trying really hard to forget that part."

"What about your night in jail? Trying to forget that part, too?"

"Yeah, when I think back fondly about this trip, none of my involvement with any law enforcement officer is going to be something I choose to recall. I'll remember hanging out with my best friend, having fun at Bar Olympics kicking the shit out of a couple of upstarts who thought they could hang with the old women, and getting laid. The rest I shall consign to the mists of memory, and let them be swept away like any evidence of my middle school hairstyles."

"Except Hornicus Prime," Rhonda said. "Can't forget ol' Hornicus. He was too damn funny to forget."

Yeah, she was right. No matter where I went from this point in my life, Hornicus Prime was something I'd never forget. Then something caught my eye, and I saw something else I'd never forget. There was a middle-aged man with a receding hairline wearing a burgundy track suit getting out of an SUV, walking up to the guard shack and taking the sandwiches from Jonathan. This was it. Our mission was about to be accomplished. We were going to take down...a bad Tony Soprano cosplayer?

"That's the guy?" Rhonda asked.

"I...guess. Doesn't look like a criminal mastermind, does he?"

"No, but he definitely looks like the kind of monster who would order extra mayo on a hoagie. He's gotta be our guy."

"Now what?" I asked.

"Now we catch the bastard, deliver him to the Orlando PD, and go celebrate. Easy-peasy, nice and sleazy."

"Pretty sure that's not how that saying goes."

"It is now," Rhonda replied. "Now come on, let's get over there and bring this bastard to justice!"

If only it were that easy. If only anything were *ever* that easy.

CHAPTER 26

N ow that we knew what kind of car the villains drove, it was pretty much child's play to circle the development a little until we found an entrance that didn't have a guard sitting there interrogating everyone who came in. I turned into the neighborhood, and we cruised slowly down the quiet streets, looking for an oversized pickup truck with chrome everything, fog lights hanging off every surface, and what must have been the last extant set of spinner hubcaps in the civilized world. If Orlando even counts as part of the civilized world.

We almost missed it, too. Well, I completely missed it, because it wasn't on my side of the street, and Rhonda almost missed it because the garage door was just starting to move when we crept by scanning for Tony Soprano sightings. She slapped me on the leg frantically, and I almost swerved into a brick-clad mailbox in surprise.

"What?!?" I yelped. "Why are you hitting me?"

"I just needed to get your attention. I think that's our guy!"

I looked over, and it definitely looked like the same tracksuit. And it looked like the same jiggly middle-aged guy wearing it. His ass looked like a couple of Honeybaked hams wrestling in a velour sack, kinda like if Santa delivered groceries instead of toys, and at one house, the food became sentient and tried to wriggle out of the sack and eat everyone in the house before Santa, actually a psychotic mass murderer using disillusioned goth sentient foodstuffs as his weapons, because they felt like everyone had lied to them their entire young grocery lives and now they were getting their hair dyed black, painting their rooms black, tacking aluminum foil and construction paper over their windows, painting their fingernails black, and stealing their mother's Siouxsie and the Banshees CDs.

I may have had issues with my oldest daughter and her more Edward Scissorhands-esque goth phase. It may have left scars. I also may have developed a serious aversion to the smell of spray paint after learning exactly how high you can get in a medium-sized house when your kid spray paints her windows black. At least she taped the aluminum foil to the windows first, so it only took a few hours to clean when she finally decided to stop being a Robert Smith cosplayer professionally and reintroduce color into her wardrobe, furnishings, and life.

"Now what?" I asked. I didn't stop the car, just kept on cruising. If moseying through the neighborhood at seven miles per hour wasn't arousing suspicion, stopping right in front of the home of suspected international arms dealers, human traffickers, and quite possibly terrorists to point at their front door would certainly be at least a little out of the ordinary.

"What do you mean, now what?" Rhonda asked.

Now I pulled the car over. I waited until the target house was out of sight, then turned to my best friend and partner in (quite probably literally) crime. "I mean, what is the next step in your plan to bring these bastards to justice? We've figured out where they live. Now we just need to do whatever it is you think we should do next to expose them to the authorities, get them arrested, and set me on the road to recovering my stolen property."

Rhonda looked like the dog who'd just caught a car and now had no idea what to do with it. "What do you mean, my plan? I don't have a plan. Plans are your thing, not mine. I don't really do plans. I show up, things happen, and I react to them. Usually in hilarious fashion. That's my whole shtick. You're the planner. I'm just the little chaos devil that rides along on your shoulder."

I'm not sure that in all our years of friendship that Rhonda has ever spoken deeper, more meaningful, less helpful, truth. Because everything she said was true. Everything she said was also a giant pain in my ass, because it meant that she not only didn't have a plan, she had no intention of ever making a plan. Leaving the planning of whatever caper we were about to engage in up to me. Again. My immediate acceptance of this just kinda proved her point.

"Okay," I said, putting the car into drive. "You don't have a plan. I don't have a plan. But we have a location, and we know what at least one of our perps looks like."

"How do you know there's more than one?" Rhonda asked, turning around in her seat and craning her neck as if trying to see the house again.

"Well, there were two sandwiches on the order."

"Were they the same thing?"

"Yeah," I replied.

"Then maybe the guy's just fat and both sandwiches are for him."

I paused. This was something I hadn't considered. We had only seen one guy. Maybe it wasn't a vast conspiracy. Maybe it was just a sad over-weight man with horrific fashion sense sitting alone in his McHome in the middle of his McNeighborhood hacking middle-aged women's credit card information. That was truly a depressing possibility.

"Nah, there's gotta be somebody else," I said after a moment's contemplation.

"Why?"

"Because if not, then I'm going to feel sorry for the miserable, lonely existence of the man who stole my identity for the purposes of ordering shitty sub sandwiches, and I refuse to have any warm places in my heart for him."

"Okay," Rhonda said. "Decisive, intentional callousness. I can get behind that. I've worked customer service before, I know how to harden my heart against any shred of sympathy. So what's the plan?"

I made a random right turn, then another. One more would have me back on the street in front of my target's house. "I've got it," I announced.

"Okay, wanna share it with me?"

"You're going to think it's stupid."

"Almost certainly," Rhonda said. "But I've never seen an initial plan yet that couldn't be improved by some targeted mockery. So lay it on me."

"I'm going to walk up to the front door, ring the bell, and accuse whoever answers it of being a part of an international ring of identity thieves, money launderers, and human traffickers. Then I'll see what their response is," I said, making that last right turn and heading back to the house where we'd spotted Tony Tracksuit.

"Yeah…" Rhonda said. "I've got nothing. That idea is so bad I can't even ridicule it into shape. That's literally the worst idea I've ever heard."

"This from the woman who stole a stranger's belt in the middle of a restaurant and spanked him with it," I said.

"That was hilarious."

She had a point. It was pretty funny. And I did get laid, so it wasn't like the trip was a total loss. I did not have such high hopes for my plan, but it was the only one I had, so I was stuck with it. I pulled the car over to the curb in front of a neighboring house and opened the door.

"You coming?" I asked Rhonda, who still sat in the passenger seat.

"Oh, shit. You were serious." She scrambled out of her seatbelt and joined me on the sidewalk. "Okay, I'm ready. Are you the good cop or the bad cop?"

"I'm Stabler. You be Benson."

"Which one is the guy?"

"Stabler."

"Can I be Ice-T?" Rhonda asked.

"You are way too white and nowhere near cool enough to be Ice-T. You can be Richard Belzer if you want."

"I'll be the chick."

"Okay, then. Let's roll."

We hadn't made it four steps from my car when a black Suburban roared to a stop in front of us, two wheels up on the sidewalk, and two men in cheap suits jumped out, handcuffed us both, threw black bags over our heads, and shoved us into the back of the SUV.

"Just think of England!" Rhonda yelled.

I thumped into the cargo area of the Suburban and felt the doors slam, then the behemoth rumbled back onto the street and roared off with us blindfolded and tied up, and now, thinking of England. I'm pretty sure this was not the circumstances in which one is supposed to just lie back and think of England, but once Rhonda said it, my mind was full of bobbies, Corgis, castles, and gin, all things I associate with our Merry Old former colonizers.

I felt the road bumping under the Suburban's tires, and lay in the back of the vehicle, wondering if this is what bondage was all about. If so, I didn't see the appeal. That said, I think real bondage play involves a lot more consent than I was currently experiencing, so I made a mental note to ask Rhonda when we stopped. I don't know if she's into BDSM or not, but she's been my go-to person for any flavor of kink for well over a decade now, so any time I don't understand something sexual, or need help translating something one of my daughters said in a text, I call Rhonda. There's often very little difference in the lingo, but she seems to perfectly understand the tiny but important gap between normal communication and asking someone to toss your salad.

I have no idea how long we rode for, but some amount of time less than thirty minutes later, the SUV squealed to a stop, and I saw just the tiniest sliver of light come in from the gap around the bottom of my bag as the back doors opened. "Don't you go looking at my underwear!" I yelled through the fabric.

"Ma'am, you're wearing pants," came a deep voice, which would have been a lot more attractive if it hadn't started that sentence with "ma'am." Like most women living in the South, I have a fractious relationship with the word "ma'am." On the one hand, I don't want anyone under the age of twelve to speak to me without at least some attempt at respect, so I want to be referred to as "ma'am" by children. I'm also fine with telemarketers calling me "ma'am," if they have to call me anything at all. And I know they do, because they're just poor schmucks sitting in a room chained to a desk by some awful modern-day Simon Legree cracking a money whip over their heads and screeching at them to make their call quotas.

I worked in a call center for three hours right out of college, so I know a little bit of how awful those working conditions can be. I may have quit before lunch on my first day, but the experience left scars. I could feel little bits of my soul dripping out of my ear and coating the cheap Plantronics headset they gave me (and didn't sanitize after the last loser that wore it), and when it came time for a smoke break, I made sure not to leave my keys behind. The manager called me two hours later asking if I was in the bathroom and sick or something. I did not mention that if I am spending two hours in a bathroom that it will involve candles, wine, bubble bath, and pleasant company. I just told her that I remembered my grandmother's funeral was that afternoon and had to leave suddenly. I'm not the best at improvising excuses.

When Barb, which is the most middle-manager name for a woman I've ever heard, asked if I would be in the next day, I told her that there was an outbreak of dying grandmothers in my family, and I wouldn't be able to come back to work, ever. I needed to spend all the time possible with my remaining three grandmothers before they all dropped dead. Yes, I know in normal circumstances most people only have two grandmothers. I told you I wasn't good at improv.

So I don't mind being called "ma'am" by children or telemarketers, but I'm less thrilled about being called "ma'am" by burly, hopefully handsome, federal agents. Then it seems to imply an age that is past attractiveness and sensuality, and a life that's only remaining pleasures are knitting tea cozies and telling stories about grandchildren. Since I neither have nor am in any hurry to have any grandchildren, and I can't knit a stitch, I need to avoid grown men calling me "ma'am" whenever possible.

Rhonda, on the other hand, feels no such conflict. I heard her through the bag almost purring at one of our captors. "Baby, if you're going to call me ma'am, we need to establish a safe word, because Mistress Rhonda is starting to feel a serious need to lay a spanking down on somebody."

"Well, that's not exactly how these kinds of meetings usually begin, but never let it be said that I'm not open minded." The voice coming from behind me was familiar, but not so much that I actually recognized it. It was just someone that I'd heard their voice before, but nobody that I had ever actually *listened* to. Which meant it could have been anyone from my junior high gym teacher to my ex-husband. The list of men who have droned on at me about useless crap is long and varied.

Then we were walked into a building, one hand firmly gripping each of my upper arms, and I was plopped down into an uncomfortable chair without so much as a "watch your bum." The black bag was yanked from my head, and as I blinked against the hideous fluorescent lights, I recognized the source of the voice.

Standing in front of me was a very grumpy-looking, very sweaty, Agent Kaplan of the Federal Bureau of Investigation. The look on his face was somewhere between "I just stepped in dog poop" and "I want to commit multiple violent felonies upon you." Agent Grumpypants glared at the two of us and said, "Give me one good reason I shouldn't have you both arrested on federal obstruction of justice charges right now."

"Um...no matter what the TV show says, orange isn't the new anything, and jumpsuits aren't the least bit flattering to my figure?" Rhonda asked. I could tell from the look on Agent Scowly's face that we were no longer his favorite housewives.

CHAPTER 27

Agent Kaplan paced a furrow into the floor in front of our chairs, scowling and muttering under his breath. I caught phrases like "crazy-ass women," "meddling pains in my ass," and my favorite "goddamned civilians." I couldn't really argue with him—our actions from the moment we left my house...hell, from the moment we sat around my pool drinking every shelf in my liquor cabinet dry, were nothing short of insane. We'd been arrested, kidnapped, thrown out of places I never even wanted to go into, and that's all before we even got to Florida! The last time anyone took a vacation this insane, Chevy Chase was driving the car.

"Would you like to explain to us exactly what the hell is going on here?" Rhonda asked. I looked over at my bestie, who had certainly recovered her aplomb faster than I had. I was still sitting there, hands tied, my butt getting numb in a crappy steel folding chair, totally aplomb-less. But Rhonda looked like she was about one improperly rung up avocado away from going full Karen in Walmart on the agents' asses, and by the look in the eyes of the one standing nearest her, he knew the signs of an impending Karen-splosion and wanted to be anywhere but standing next to the epicenter.

I think I mixed my disastrous metaphors there, but you get the idea.

Agent Kaplan turned to her, his eyes wide that anyone, much less one of these crazy, pain in his ass civilians, would have the temerity to speak to him at all, much less in that "can I speak to your manager" tone. "What the *hell* did you say?"

Oh, that was not the right tone to take with Rhonda. Maybe Agent Asshat missed the memo, but Rhonda was the perfect shitstorm of indignant, entitled, privileged, over-educated, and hungover to completely *wreck* his day. Which she commenced to doing. Right then.

My best friend, the forty-something divorcee from suburban North Carolina with the expensive implants and even more expensive ass (hey, goat yoga is not cheap) stood up from her crappy folding chair and marched right over to the bulky FBI agent and planted her feet right in front of his face. "I *said* you need to explain what the hell is going on right now, before I call my attorney. And yes, he works in Florida, is on speed dial, and is not shy about hopping on his private jet to wherever he smells a dollar. And when I mention the federal government is stepping all over my civil rights, he will smell a lot of dollars."

Now let's be clear, the only attorneys Rhonda has on speed dial are her divorce lawyer and a hunky paralegal named Chad who she bangs once a month after her bonus spin class on Saturday afternoons. She no more has the ability to summon a high-priced lawyer out of thin air than I can poop marzipan. Which would be far less useful than summoning a lawyer at will, as superpowers go.

But Kaplan didn't know that, and Rhonda knew that, or was at least willing to bet our presence outside of Gitmo on it. He spluttered a little, and Rhonda cocked her hips to one side, hands firmly on them, and said, "Well? I'm *waiting*."

It worked. It actually worked. Agent Kaplan deflated like someone had put a nail in his tire, and he waved at her chair. "Okay, fine. Just...sit down and I'll explain everything."

Rhonda looked a little dumbstruck, like she wasn't used to her plan working. Or at least not working so quickly. She went back to her chair, a little wobbly with surprise, and sat down. Kaplan grabbed another chair, spun it around backward, and sat down with his chest against the back of the chair. I've never understood why guys do that. Is it so we'll look at their junk? Because that's not really the most flattering pose, nor is it what women are really looking at, men's fragile egos and absorption with that chunk of their anatomy aside. It really just makes a guy look like he's trying to be young and cool, which never does anything but make a guy look older and less cool.

"The house you were approaching is in fact the base to a group of men that we believe are conducting criminal activity over the internet. They almost certainly are the men that used your stolen credit card number, even though they weren't the ones who stole the information themselves."

"So they didn't steal my number, but they used my number to buy lunch?" I asked.

"Pretty much," Kaplan confirmed. "There are hackers that just run automated sequences all over the net looking for insecure, repeated passwords. Then they scrape those numbers and sell huge lots of them to guys like the ones in that house. Those guys in turn try those numbers in batches until they get one that isn't locked down yet, then they use it as much as they can until the card either gets cut off, or they max it out."

"They maxed out your credit card with delivery subs?" Rhonda asked, giving me that "bless your poverty-stricken heart" look.

"No," I replied. "I saw the charge and canceled the card before they could do anything else. Thank god for the automated email system on the delivery app."

"Oh," Rhonda said, looking relieved. "That's good. I'd hate to think you were so hard up for cash that a couple of subs would max out your card."

"As if," I scoffed. I didn't mention that while a couple of subs wouldn't max out *that* card, it certainly would bring a couple of others right up to the edge of that cliff. There was one in particular that I'd used to pay for some of Kristen's dental work that would melt down if I tried to buy a pack of gum with it.

"So why the big coverup?" I asked. "Why not just tell me that you were working on taking these guys down instead of making me think you didn't believe me?"

"I didn't know anything about this until I got a call from the Orlando field office telling me that a couple of insane women from my neck of the woods were down here harassing the local police and stirring up shit in the middle of an ongoing investigation. Then I had to fly down here, get read in on what turns out to be a two-year RICO investigation, and be informed in no uncertain terms that if the two of you aren't headed north out of the city in twenty-four hours, that it would be my ass explaining to the Director of the FBI why this multimillion-dollar investigation has been flushed down the toilet thanks to the interference of a couple of housewives."

"We aren't housewives," Rhonda said primly.

Kaplan's head whipped around so fast it had to hurt a little. "What?"

"Housewives implied we're married and jobless. We're neither. We're strong, independent, employed women who don't need to be told what to do by a man we're not getting any sex out of."

"Yeah, that's the kind of thing that led to our divorces the first time," I agreed.

Kaplan looked befuddled, like Rhonda mouthing off to him was something completely outside his realm of experience. I guess he was more accustomed to people just quivering at the sight of his cheap suit and badge, and then submitting to his manly will just because he was the big strong federal agent. He had never encountered anyone like Rhonda, who might be intimidated by the average professional kickboxer, but not much else. As for me, I've raised two daughters and shepherded both of them through puberty without murdering either of them. It left me pretty hard to shake, too.

"Okay, so you're not housewives," the agent said, desperately trying to wrangle this kidnapping back around to something resembling a situation he was in control of. "But you are impeding a federal investigation, which is potentially a felony. So unless you want me to charge the both of you—"

"Oh, bullshit," Rhonda said, freezing Kaplan in mid-pace. He turned to her, his mouth hanging open, but she just raised a hand to him. "No, don't speak. If you're just going to lie to me, then let's keep it to you telling me how great my ass looks in these pants, ignoring the fact that we both know full well that I look like someone is smuggling raw potatoes on each hip. Don't try to tell me that you're going to have us arrested for screwing up your little stakeout. If you could do that, you would have. But you threw black bags over our heads and tossed us in the back of your SUV. That's not what good guys do, Agent Kaplan. So you're obviously working without supervision on this, and you couldn't arrest us for jaywalking, much less anything to do with this investigation. Am I right?"

Kaplan's mouth worked for a minute, making him look like a fish gasping on a dock. A fish in a pin-striped suit, but a fish nonetheless. Finally, he sighed and let his head sag. "You're right. I can't arrest you. I can just ask you, very nicely and calmly, if you will please go home and leave this investigation in our hands. It's what we do. Please let us do it."

I gaped at the defeated FBI agent and my beaming friend. I felt like my brain had short-circuited, and Agent Kaplan looked like he felt the same way. I'd just watched my best friend, who could be described as flighty on her best day, completely take down a federal agent with nothing but her words and logic. These are not the weapons I am accustomed to Rhonda deploying. They're usually what I use to try and get us out of whatever she's gotten us into. This role reversal was perhaps the strangest thing I'd experienced on the entire trip. Well, that and Fornicus Prime. That was pretty freakin' weird.

"Okay," Rhonda said, standing up. "Would you like to take us back to our car now, or should we call an Uber to your secret government detention facility?"

Kaplan still hadn't looked up. "It's not a detention facility. It's an empty storage unit. One of our agents manages the place as a cover. So no, we would rather you not call an Uber here. I'll get Jerry to drive you back to your car."

"Thanks," Rhonda said, walking over to the big roll-up door. "We'll wait outside. It's a beautiful day."

"It's Florida," Kaplan said, still staring at the concrete floor as if he could find some meaning in his life written there. "Every day is beautiful." He said it with the same hollow tone as someone announcing that he'd just put his dog to sleep.

I followed Rhonda out into the blazing sun. It may have been beautiful, but it was also hotter than the surface of the sun. "Jesus," I said. "It's brutal out here."

"Yeah, but it doesn't smell like bacon."

I thought for a second, but didn't remember anything smelling like... then I got it. Bacon. Pig. Cop. FBI. Rhonda was being snarky. Okay, the world was back on its axis if Rhonda was being a smartass. "So now we just go home?" I asked.

"Oh hell no," Rhonda said. "We're going back there, and we're going make damn sure those guys are brought down."

"But you just said..."

"Honey, I have been lying to police since I was twelve years old and got busted shoplifting training bras. It's not second nature to me by now, it's *first* nature. I couldn't have told that flatfoot the truth if he'd put electric nipple clamps on me."

"If he'd put electric nipple clamps on you, we'd still be in there."

"Damn right we would," Rhonda said, rubbing a hand across one boob. "Think if I go back in there he'll give 'em a try?"

CHAPTER 28

J erry dropped us off at one of the guard-less entrances to the neighborhood, and as we walked back to where my car awaited our arrival, I broached what I thought might be a sensitive topic with Rhonda. "So, what's the plan? Do we just walk up to the front door and ask for my money back? Tell them the jig is up, that the coppers are onto them? Try to steal a Wi-Fi password and hack the hackers right back?"

Rhonda stopped dead in the middle of the deserted cookie-cutter street in front of the cookie-cutter houses with their cookie-cutter yards, and gaped at me. "Plan? *PLAN?!?* Why in the hell would I start making plans at this point in my life?" Then she turned on her towering heels and resumed her strut toward my car.

Right. Not a planner, remember? Half the time she didn't know what was for dinner before she put the last dish on the table. Eating at Rhonda's was always an adventure. You were as likely to end up with a quivering cylinder of burgundy cranberry sauce Jell-O and a side of pretzels as you were a pair of fresh Cornish hens stuffed with rosemary and braised with something French and expensive. You ran with Rhonda, there was a lot of "strap in and hold on" in your life.

"So...you're saying I should come up with a plan?" I asked, catching up to her. One thing about having a bestie with a stiletto fetish—she never gets that far ahead of me walking. Those shoes might make her ass look great, and they do, but they also make her wobble like a drunk on his fourth bottle of rotgut gin.

"If you think we need a plan, then you're going to need to be the one to formulate it, sweetens, because all I'm planning on doing is sitting in your car, watching the perps for some kind of opening, and then bringing them down hard."

"That was a lot of cop show clichés in one setting," I said. "What did you say? Preferably in words that don't sound like they're written for an episode of *SVU*."

"Oh, I have no idea what any of those things mean," Rhonda replied, walking around my car and leaning her arms on the roof of the Prius before yanking them back, wincing. She might be my best friend, but she literally never learns from any experience.

"Careful, the car's probably hot. It's warm out."

"It's Florida, smartass," Rhonda shot back. "It's always warm out."

I pressed the button on my key fob to unlock the doors. "I'd rather be the smartass talking about the heat than the dumbass burning myself on the roof of the car." I slid behind the wheel as Rhonda hopped into the passenger seat.

I stared at the perps' house, sitting there looking all innocuous, just like every other house on the street. *Just* like every other house we'd seen since we got into the neighborhood, actually. And when I say "just like" every other house, I mean exactly that. Every house on the street, and every house I could see off any neighboring street, was identical to the one next to it. And the one next to that, and the one next to that, and so on and so on. There were no variations in color, no s"all tweaks to the I, not even a wreath on a door anywhere. The only distinguishing features were the different cars in the driveways and a few scattered toys strewn across various lawns like shrapnel from a joy grenade, just blown all over the place.

There was one house that stood out, though. It had a door painted bright magenta, and about three dozen pink plastic flamingos intricately arranged in the yard with string running from each bird's legs to the one next to it. I got the feeling that if I could gain enough height, it might spell out something, like a giant "HELP ME" written on the beach in rocks in those castaway movies. I felt an instant affinity to the homeowner, like she was standing there, trying to hold back an inexorable tide of conformity and HOA bullshit with her bright pink door and her flamingo army. Deep in my soul I felt like she and I were kindred spirits, her on a quest for artistic integrity and creative freedom through expressive yard décor, and me on a valiant quest for justice, far from home and with hope dwindling. I drew strength and inspiration from this one lone rebel battling the forces of congruity in the universe. It was all I could do not to march right up to the front door of this woman I had cast in my head as the newest Susan B. Anthony, Maya Angelou, and Katy Perry all rolled into one and give her a huge hug, thanking her tearfully for all the inspiration she'd given me in my own physical and philosophical journey.

I didn't, of course. I'm not a complete weirdo. Okay, I'm mostly a complete weirdo who totally would have rushed up to a total stranger's door and ambush-hugged her. Except half a second before I jumped out of the car, overwhelmed with emotion and the strains of Lee Greenwood's "Proud to Be an American" swelling in the soundtrack in my head, the blazing pink door opened and a big burly farmhand-looking man in overalls and work boots stepped out carrying a lunchbox. He stopped just outside the front door, and a gorgeous young man who looked like he'd never even heard of body hair stepped up to the threshold, threw his arms around the burly man, laid a toe-curling kiss on him, then patted him on the cheek and sent him off to work, presumably second shift somewhere loud and sweaty. The exceptionally pretty young man closed the door, and the sound of my imaginary story dissolving into nothingness filled my ears with sadness and Lee Greenwood, which also sounds a lot like sadness.

"Well, I guess the owner could just be a couple of gay dudes in Florida, which kinda matches my decorating sense," I muttered under my breath.

"What's that, love?" Rhonda asked.

"Nothing," I said. "So, no plan?"

"Plan? Pumpkin Bread, I can't even remember which damn *house* we're supposed to be staking out!"

Oh yeah. Every house did look exactly like every other house, and enough of the yards were toy-free that we couldn't just pick the one that looked like it didn't have kids in it. Hell, for all we knew, the villains had strewn toys around their front yard to make it look like children lived there, just to make better camouflage. Shoulda tried flamingoes. Nobody would ever guess that a criminal mastermind lived in a herd of pink birds.

CHAPTER 29

"I gotta pee." I snapped awake, blinking away confusion in my sleep-crusted eyes. Where was I? Why was there a woman in bed with me? Wait, this wasn't a bed. Then it all came rushing back to me in a torrent of bad decisions and prayers that no photos from this trip ended up online.

I turned to Rhonda in the passenger seat, who was bouncing like an excited toddler, except the look on her face was anything but excited. She had the pained grimace of someone who'd been holding her bladder for a long time and was about to either need to find a bathroom or some convenient shrubbery, and fast.

"Why didn't you wake me up sooner?" I asked, smacking my lips together and looking around for a stick of gum or a mint. Hell, even one of Rhonda's ever-present mini-bottles would have been better than the litterbox taste in my mouth.

"You're cute when you sleep. You drool a little." She reached out with a napkin and dabbed the side of my mouth. I took the paper from her and wiped my face. I was back in the land of the living, but still a little fuzzy-headed. I decided to give myself a pass. It'd been a long few days, and we weren't finished with our adventure yet.

I opened the car door and stepped out, then leaned back in to say, "I'll hide behind that SUV and keep an eye on our bad guys. You go pee and come right back. I saw a 7-11 on the corner a couple blocks back. Bring a couple bottles of water, too." We were incredibly ill-prepared for a stake-out. We didn't have any beef jerky, Slim Jims, coffee, doughnuts, or even a Gatorade bottle to pee in. Not that we could have gotten much use out of that, but it seemed like it was part of every stakeout kit in the movies.

Rhonda slid over behind the wheel, which took some contorting since she's several inches taller than me and I didn't move the seat back for her before she starting trying to Gumby her way into position. Nevertheless, a few seconds later she was pulling away from the curb, the near-silent *whirrrrr* of my Prius disappearing quickly into the placid neighborhood sounds around me. I knelt by the bumper of a well-loved Subaru and stared at the bad guys' front door. At least, I was pretty sure the front door I was watching was the door I'd seen our criminal mastermind walk through a few hours earlier. I was still a little disoriented from my unin-tentional nap, and every house really did look exactly the same, except for the cars in the drive.

That's how we identified our perp—their car. More their lack of car, really. When we followed them back to their house, before I was abducted by the federal government, they parked their car in the garage and closed the big roll-up door. That's how we knew immediately they were crimi-nals. They're sitting there in a nice, if spectacularly dull, housing develop-ment, in their nice little cookie cutter house with a two-car garage, and they're parking their cars in it! Nobody parks cars in their garage. That's where you store the shit you aren't willing to throw out but know in your heart of hearts you're never going to touch again. That's the space you turn into a "man cave" when your husband whines about not being able to hear the game over you vacuuming one time too many and since the TV is bolted to the wall you can't throw it at him, so you banish him and his recliner to the garage, leaving you with a quieter, less stinky den. But it's not where you park your cars. Not unless you're some kind of neat freak or weirdo.

So when we cruised through the neighborhood after being released from federal custody, it was simple enough to find the right place. We just looked for the house with no cars in the driveway. Since we knew our villains parked in their garage, any house with a car out front was obvi-ously innocent. The only problem was that there were two houses on this block with empty driveways, so Rhonda kept watch on one while I watched the other. Until I fell asleep. But I was absolutely certain that the house I was watching was the one I'd watched a fat man in a track suit go into a few hours before.

Mostly certain. Kinda positive. Okay, I thought there was a better than even chance that I was watching the right house.

Up until the moment I felt a tap on my shoulder and heard a voice ask, "What are you doing staring at an empty house?"

Several things happened simultaneously. First, I realized that there was a "For Sale" sign lying on the lawn of the house I was watching. It looked like it may have been knocked flat, or just pulled up and tossed aside by kids, or something. But there was definitely a sign there. And there had definitely not been one in front of the house where our bad guys were. Second, I realized that the finger I felt on my shoulder was thick and meaty, like a sausage. Also the finger felt like the kind of finger I would expect Tracksuit Man to have. Third, that the gruff, New York-tinged, grumpier Joe Pesci-sounding voice coming from behind me was exactly the kind of voice I'd expect from Tracksuit Man. Fourth and perhaps most importantly, I realized something that I probably should have noticed right when I woke up, but I was distracted by Rhonda wiping drool off my chin. I had to pee.

I turned around, and sure enough, standing there staring down at me like I was some kind of crazy person, was Tracksuit Man. He looked less like Tony Soprano and more like a big balding teddy bear close up, but there was a slight bulge in the waistband of his tracksuit that made me think he was packing. I mean, there was a bulge a little lower in his tracksuit, too, but that one was such a slight bulge it made me think he wasn't packing much there, if you know what I mean.

I mean he had a little dick. It was a dick joke. Just to clarify.

I looked up at Tony Wee-Wee (Get it, "wee" because it's small? No? Everybody's a critic.) and said, "I'm investigating the home for a potential termite infestation."

It sucked, and I knew it sucked, but it was all I could come up with on short notice.

"You don't look like any exterminator I've ever seen," Tony said.

I looked down at my black capri pants, sandals, and cute red top and remembered that I was dressed way more for talking my way into a police station than anything that required actual work. Like exterminating. I mean, I have no idea what exterminators wear. Do they have uniforms or coveralls or something? Probably coveralls. That would be my luck: randomly deciding to impersonate a career that I could never in a million years look good in the uniform for. And with the exception of Danica Patrick, nobody looks good in coveralls. What? I'm from North Carolina. I know my race car drivers.

"I'm not an exterminator," I said, my mind racing. "I'm an...evaluator. We've already done a pest abatement treatment on their foundation and property line. I just need to keep an eye on the structure for a few days to make sure...that it worked."

"And you're doing that from across the street?" he asked. The look on his face said that he knew I was lying, just couldn't figure out how to call me on it.

"It's best to observe from a distance. That way I get...a holistic view of the environment and can see any deleterious effects our treatment may have on surrounding foliage." I was pretty proud of that one. I'd never managed to work "deleterious" into conversation before. It was on one of those Word-A-Day calendars on a co-worker's desk back before I left corporate for a slightly more fulfilling, significantly worse paying, and far more stressful career in education.

Don't ask. But if you or anyone close to you is interested in some great makeup, scent diffusers, household cleaning products, plastic storage containers, or shoddily manufactured leggings, I can hook you up.

"Somehow I don't believe you," Tony said with a grim look on his face. "You ain't a cop, because I can't see where you would even carry a badge in those pants. But you ain't no exterminator, neither. Why don't you come inside, and we can have a little chat about why you're really hiding behind my neighbor's car?"

I looked up to see him gesturing over one shoulder to the other house with no car in the driveway, and this one did not have a "For Sale" sign in, or on, the yard. It did have an open garage door, through which I could see the car Tony had arrived in before I fell asleep watching him do nothing. I stood up with what very little grace I could muster, wiped a little dirt off my knees, and waved at his house. "After you."

He looked surprised, like the last thing he expected me to do was go into the home of a strange man in the middle of an unfamiliar neighborhood with no backup and no plan for getting away.

Well, the joke was on him. He didn't know I didn't have a plan, which meant that he would assume I did have a plan, and he'd keep watching for some signs that my plan was going to come together, A-Team style, in a giant rush of charming grins, snappy dialogue, and thrilling action. I, on the other hand, would be wracking my brain trying to come up with said plan and giving not a single shit about charming grins, snappy dialogue, or thrilling action. Actually, I would prefer *not* to have any thrilling action, because that would probably mean that either I hadn't come up with a plan quickly enough, or my plan had unraveled faster than my New Year's resolution to stop eating sweets after dinner.

Tony let me into his garage and stopped at the door into the house, removing his shoes and placing them carefully on a rack provided for just that purpose. He stared at me until I did the same, then we went inside. Now, when I embarked upon this journey, I had no intention of walking barefoot into a gangster's house with no backup, no communication network, and no plan for getting out. But when I embarked upon this journey, I thought there was only about a thirty percent chance Rhonda and I would even make it to Florida. I'd traveled with her before, and while the amount of chaos in this trip was higher than normal, it wasn't by much.

I followed Tony into a big sunken living room with plush white carpet. I understood the shoe thing then. If I lived in a place with white carpet, I'd make guests leave their *feet* at the door, much less their shoes. Actually, I'd probably have a box of those crime scene booties beside the door for everyone to use rather than take their shoes off. Nothing kills a date faster than funky feet. Well, uncontrollable farting will do it, too.

There were two other men in the room, one a massive wall of humanity with crude tattoos and a face that even a mother would think twice about loving, and the other a pinched-faced little man with enough product in his slicked-back hair to qualify for an environmental threat. The mountain stood up when I came into the room, then reached down to the sofa and thunked the little guy on one shoulder.

"Stand up when a lady enters the room, you goon," Mount Fiji said with a glare. The little guy gave him the finger, but stood up just long enough to make it clear he was being perfunctory and petty, waved in my general direction, then sat back down. He was pretty engrossed in a wrestling match on TV, so I wasn't offended by his lack of manners. I also wasn't expecting much in the way of chivalry from gangsters, so I wasn't disappointed on that front.

Lying on the coffee table in front of Mutt & Jeff were the two most hideous half-eaten sub sandwiches I'd ever seen. Nestled in open white paper wrappings were a pair of identical foot-long subs that even without peeking under the hood I knew contained salami, pastrami, pepperoni, no lettuce, no tomato, extra oil and vinegar, extra mayo on garlic parmesan loaf. Those were the sandwiches. These were my guys.

I had 'em. Now what the hell was I going to do with them?

CHAPTER 30

T ony motioned for me to sit in an armchair perpendicular to the end of the sofa, putting me far closer to the mayonnaise-riddled monstrosity of blandness that was staring up at me from the table. The more I was in the room with those things, the more pissed off I was that they used my credit card number for *that*. I mean, they weren't going to be buying any new laptops or cruises or airline tickets, not with my credit. If they'd tried to order three subs, it probably would have been declined faster than my junior prom date's advances. But they could have at least ordered something with a little flavor. A little style. Some kind of panache. Those pitiful slabs of bland white bread with even blander mayo on it just lay there, staring up at me, panache-less.

I sat, giving the subs a dirty look so they knew that I knew what they were and how much trouble they'd caused and that I wasn't so much angry as I was disappointed in them. I have a teenaged daughter; I can absolutely convey that much meaning in a single glance. It's a superpower we are given the moment our oldest child enters puberty, and we retain it until their student loans are paid off. The way my older daughter was looking at grad school flyers last month, I was going to have my Super Glare until I was glaring at the inside of a casket.

Which might be sooner than I expected, if I didn't come up with some way to get out of the den of iniquity I suddenly found myself in. Get it?

Den of iniquity? Because we're in the living room. Which is called the den. And a lair is...never mind.

Tony sat in an armchair parallel to me and perpendicular to the other end of the sofa, then leaned forward with his elbows on his knees, steepling his fingers like my old undergrad psych professor used to do right before he told us some misogynistic Freudian bullshit about how all women wanted to sleep with their fathers. I always thought Dr. Needham was gross, with his scraggly chin beard and spotty mustache, but apparently his schtick worked with some girls, because he was fired in my junior year when three students and one grad assistant that he was having an affair with all got into a screaming match with his wife and girlfriend in the hall outside his office. Apparently his wife had come to campus to confront him about his girlfriend, who was there to yell at him about the graduate assistant he was banging, who was coming down the hall to bitch him out about the undergrads he was sleeping with, who were all there to "earn extra credit" but had to wait out in the hall while he had a "private meeting" with the department secretary. I didn't see the encounter, but I happened to walk down that hall three weeks later, and there was still a head-shaped hole in the sheetrock and a little smear of dried blood on the doorknob.

So Tony assuming the psych professor seduction pose threw me off my game a little as I wondered how many wives and girlfriends Tony had, and if serial infidelity was thing with all men, or just all men who put their elbows on their knees and steepled their fingers like that. I finally wrangled my attention back to the problem at hand when I noticed that no one was speaking, and hadn't been speaking for several seconds.

"I'm sorry, what?" I asked, giving Tony a look of abject cluelessness.

"I asked you why you were outside of my house staking out an empty building," Tony said, his voice lowering into that grumpy-growly "why aren't you hanging on my every word" tone that men get when their widdle egos are offended that you aren't already hanging on their every word.

"I told you," I said, then wracked my brain for what exactly I had told him. "I was evaluating the property from a distance to ensure that our exterminators had properly treated the edges of the lot and the exterior foundation." That sounded sufficiently building-persony that I hoped he'd let me go. Or at least decide that he needed the coffee table to torture me on so he'd get those subs out of sight.

"I don't believe you," Tony said. "What about you boys?" he asked the goons. "Do you believe her?"

The two lumps of humanity looked back and forth from me to Tony to each other, back to me, then finally back to Tony before giving a noncommittal shrug. They had no idea whether or not they believed me. It struck me at that moment that finding good henchmen must have both been immensely aided and immensely complicated by the internet. Seems like in the old days of crime, finding a henchman was probably a word-of-mouth thing, or maybe an apprenticeship system, with henchman dads bringing their henchman sons and daughters into the family business. But now, it's not only easier to just go online and find a henchman with the specific skills for a job, but it's also more complicated, because you're more likely to be betrayed by a henchman you don't have an emotional connection with than one you do. Unless the emotion connecting you is hatred, I guess. That would probably lend itself more to betrayal than any other emotion. Well, hatred and horniness, I suppose. I have done a lot of stupid things in the name of getting an itch scratched, and Rhonda was the queen of bad decision-making due to horniness, so the idea of her betraying a crime boss for a guy that could find the clitoris without needing a flashing neon sign and a GPS was not much of a stretch.

The boys didn't seem to have an opinion one way or the other on my trustworthiness, so I decided to just ride this bullshit train until it completely derailed. I stood up and looked around the room, plastering my brightest fake smile across my face and looking around. "You know, since I'm here, I could provide one of our free in-home consultations. Just look around and make sure you don't have any little creepy-crawlies hiding in your walls, chewing on the...boards and things that hold the house up."

I was afraid that my ignorance of construction terminology may have done me in there, but Tony looked so surprised at me taking control of our meeting that he didn't say anything. So I just breezed right past him into the nearby dining room and bent over at the waist, ostensibly to examine the baseboards, but mostly to give them something to think about that wasn't how abjectly stupid my story was. I heard a low whistle, followed by a meaty *"thwack"* as one goon slapped the other goon on the arm.

"Be respectful, dude," Goon 1 whispered.

"Sorry," Goon 2 whispered back. They weren't very good at whispering, so it was a good thing this bunch did all their stealing over the inter-

JOHN G. HARTNESS

net, because they weren't going to do much sneaking into anywhere to rob it. Their sneaking would also be impeded by the fact that they were flipping *giants*. But that's beside the point. Their inattention had bought me a few seconds, so I kept up a steady stream of prattling nonsense about good bones in the house, and lovely flooring choices as I meandered through the dining room and into the kitchen.

I had the back door in my sights and was beelining for it when Tony stepped around a little chunk of wall from the hallway in front of me and cut me off. "Going somewhere?" he asked, his grin as oily as his hair.

"Into the back yard to check for termite hills," I said, smoothing my expression into what I hoped was one of vacuous banality. I'm not totally sure what banality is, but I'm equally mostly kinda sure that I want my banality to appear vacuous at every opportunity.

Tony wasn't buying it. "I think you should check something in the garage," he said, his voice low and ominous. He tilted his head down at me and gave me a disapproving look.

"Garages aren't usually a problem in modern construction," I said. I'd decided on a cover story, so I was playing it to the hilt. "Not enough wood. It's outside and the foundation where we worry. I'll just do a quick walk around the back yard and then I'll work up an estimate for you on a whole-house treatment and maintenance program. Our annual follow-ups are very reasonable, I think you'll find."

I reached for the doorknob, turned it, and pulled the kitchen door toward me. Another few inches and I'd be home free. Well, home free if no one tried to chase me, since I was about to be running barefoot through an unfamiliar Stepford neighborhood in the middle of a Florida summer. I was not looking forward to putting my little tootsies on that asphalt but I thought that would be better than anything that would happen to me if I *didn't* run.

Spoiler alert: I was right. Burning my feet would have been immeasurably better.

But that wasn't to be, because just before I got the door open wide enough to slip through, a meaty palm slapped the door closed, and I turned to see a broad-faced sweaty man mere inches from me, grinning the kind of grin that someone only grins when they know things are about to go spectacularly badly for the person they're grinning at.

"Something about you doesn't add up. I think we need to go ask our questions in a more...personal setting." That grin didn't waver. Mine wavered. Mine wavered a lot. Like, a lot a lot.

"I think it's time for me to be getting back to the office. Lot of paperwork to write up before I can head home for the day. You know, miles to go before I sleep, and all that." I pulled on the doorknob, but I was not moving that door. Not with several hundred pounds of track suited fluffiness leaning against it.

"I don't think I was asking what you thought," Tony said, and the grin fell away from his face. Then the lights went out as a black bag was placed over my head for the second time in one day. What is the deal with black bags lately? Is that just something people keep around their houses? I'd have to dig into the very bottom of the linen closet and hope I hadn't thrown out every piece of black bedding once my daughter finally allowed color back into her life and got over her goth phase. I don't just have black pillowcases or hoods lying around all the time.

Maybe it's something that comes in the Federal Agent/International Identity Thief Starter Kit. I made a mental note to ask Tony when we got where we were going, if there was any time before he got too far into my torture and I wasn't able to form a coherent thought anymore. *Oh shit.* That idea landed on me like a ton of bricks, about the same time I felt someone pick me up by my elbows and carry me into the garage. I was then shoved into the back of another SUV (after you've been shoved blindfolded into the cargo area of one Suburban, you can kinda tell what's going on the next time it happens, especially if there's only a few hours between kidnappings. There was plenty of room for me to stretch out, so I was either in an SUV or a pickup truck, and I felt carpet under me, so it was definitely an SUV. Also, I remembered seeing one in the garage when I went into the house.)

So I was bundled into the back of a Ford Expedition, blindfolded, my hands and feet were taped together, and we were off to see the Wizard. Or the interrogator. One of those. Oh please, let it be a wizard.

CHAPTER 31

I t wasn't a wizard. It wasn't a wizard, or a castle, or anything whimsical and fun, despite us being close enough to the Magic Kingdom to get splattered with puke off one of the rides. I rode in the back of the SUV for about half an hour, over several sets of railroad tracks, but I lost count after three and thus was going to be absolutely no use when I got on the phone with the FBI and couldn't tell them where I was being held captive because I had no idea if we ran over three sets of railroad tracks or five. But after some number of railroad tracks, I felt the vehicle lurch to a stop, then heard the cargo door open.

"Here's the deal," said a gruff voice. "I'm going to pull you out of there, help you stand up, and walk you into the building. I'm going to be gentle. But if you scream, or kick, or try to run away, I'm going to stop being gentle. You really don't want me to stop being gentle. Do you?"

"I don't know," I said, trying to sound seductive, which is a lot harder to accomplish than I expected while wearing a black pillowcase over your head. "If you stop being gentle, will you spank me?"

It seemed like the kind of thing Black Widow would say, and I had these hopes of head butting my invisible captor in the nose, bloodying it and blurring his vision, then running away, stealing a gun, and blasting them all to bits. Never mind that I was not wearing shoes conducive to running, or that I hate guns, or that I had never head butted anyone in my life. I have watched a tremendous number of police procedural TV shows, so I was pretty sure I had my plan of action down cold.

"No, I won't spank you," Gruff Voice said. "I'm not into chicks, so you're outta luck here. Why do you think they have me carry the hostages around? Because I don't want to bang any of them, so they never escape."

"So what, you guys never kidnap any guys? That seems kinda sexist."

"I'm ace, lady. I'm not into dudes, either."

An asexual hired goon. That made a lot of sense, actually, especially if kidnapping and guarding people were things you needed a goon to do on the regular. Finding someone who wouldn't be swayed by the advances of either gender was a damned good idea. It totally screwed my escape plans, but I still had to respect that kind of out-of-the-box thinking. It showed some real vision on the part of management.

"Then how about you just let me go and I won't tell any of the rest of your crew?" I asked, putting a hard edge into my voice.

"Tell them what?" he replied. "That I'm ace? They know. Nobody cares. Jeez, lady, where are you from? West Virginia?"

"North Carolina, thank you very much," I replied.

"I didn't think North Carolina was so prejudiced. Live and learn, I guess."

I felt a need to defend my state's integrity, then remembered the massive Confederate flag flying just off I-40 and decided there probably wasn't that much integrity to defend. "Well, *I* don't have anything against asexual people—"

He cut me off. "Is this where you tell me one of your best friends is ace?"

"Um, no. I don't actually know anyone who is asexual. Not that I know of."

"Well, you probably do," he said. "Maybe you need to do a little work on your personal inventory and see if maybe there's a reason none of them have felt comfortable talking to you about it."

I was getting schooled on diversity and inclusion by a mobster in the parking lot of wherever it was they planned to torture me for information I couldn't provide because I didn't have it in the first place. This was going to be a very long afternoon, I thought. "Can we just get to the torture?" I asked. "I don't mind a little introspection and self-examination, but I usually prefer to do it without my hands tied together."

A big hand gripped my bicep and led me forward a few steps, then I heard the squeal of a rusty hinge as he opened the door. Good. Now I knew I'd hear it if anyone else came in. Of course, as soon as we were inside, my escort pulled the pillowcase off my head, so I didn't have to rely only on hearing to tell me who was in the room.

And the room was already teeming with activity. It was a big space, warehouse-sized, and there were at least a dozen men and a handful of women working there. Besides my escort Gigantor, there were people packing boxes with stuffed animals, people packing stuffed animals with plastic baggies full of some unknown substance, and a line of people in nothing but their underpants and heavy-duty respirators packing white powder into plastic baggies.

"You guys are drug dealers?" I asked, honestly surprised.

"We prefer to say that we are in the import/export business," Gigantor said.

"But that's heroin you're putting up those bear's butts, right?"

"And some coke. Sometimes pills, but we aren't doing another shipment of that until next week. I think this load is mostly coke. A few bears full of acid, too, but not a lot."

"No marijuana?" I asked.

"Nah. Weed takes up too much space and smells up the joint."

"Pun intended."

"Oh, one hundred percent intended. Besides, the government's getting into the weed business in most states. Makes it hard for an honest man to make a good living when the legal stuff is so easy to get."

"What is an 'honest living' for a drug dealer?" I asked.

"Um, selling drugs. Duh."

I'm not sure Gigantor had any real idea of what an honest living was, based on his reply. But I guess that's one way people end up as drug dealers. Maybe. Apparently no longer interested in discussing his life choices with me, he took my arm again and led me over to an empty corner of the warehouse where another mountain of humanity, the man I would come to decide was named Gregdre, stood. I didn't know at the time that this was the beginning of a brief but intense relationship between me and the man who looked remarkably like someone who eats bowling balls for breakfast and flosses their teeth with power lines.

Gigantor maneuvered me in front of a chair and stared at me until I sat down, then he picked up a roll of duct tape from a nearby table and knelt in front of me.

"Would you mind making sure that you tape me over my pant legs?" I asked. Gigantor look up at me in confusion, so I decided that I was going to have to explain, regardless of how embarrassing it was. "Okay, there was this one time that my husband, ex-husband now, to be clear, decided to try to spice things up a little. To say it wasn't exciting in my bedroom while I was married to him would be a dramatic understatement. So we decided to experiment a little with tying each other up. Except we didn't have any soft rope, just this spool of that yellow shit that people use to winch a boat up onto the trailer, and tie up to a dock. And that was *not* going around my wrists and ankles, no sir. And Peckerwood refused to let me use any of his neckties, despite the fact that with two daughters, he'd been getting at least six neckties every year for a decade, every one of them uglier than the one before. You know, the last year we were together, I overheard the girls comparing their choices to see who was giving him the uglier tie!

"I decided that if he wasn't willing to use those nice soft silk neckties on me, that I sure as hell was not going to let him stretch out any of my scarves or put runs in my hose with his bony-ass wrists, so I grabbed a roll of that stuff out from under the kitchen sink, made a couple loops around his wrists and ankles, then kinda twisted it into a rope and looped it around the feet of the bed. Yeah, we discovered about halfway through the tying-up process that since we had a modern sleigh bed, there weren't any bedposts to tie anybody to, so I had to go all the way off the mattress and wrap the end of the tape around the leg of the bed. It wasn't ideal, but by the time we'd realized our problem, Peter was already pretty wound up, and he wouldn't shut up about how kinky this was and how hot I looked in the lingerie he bought me, so I didn't have the heart to call the whole thing off.

"Anyhow, I taped him to the bed and had my way with him, and no more than five minutes later, as I was climbing off him thoroughly unused, unfulfilled, and unsatisfied, I found out why the websites say to smear Vaseline on any skin you're going to put tape on. Because not only did that duct tape rip out every bit of hair around his ankles and wrists, it took a couple layers of skin with it. Which woulda been funny if Peter hadn't tried to jump to his feet with one wrist still tied to the bed. That dumbass got hung up on his own bondage fantasy; it snatched him backward, he lost his footing, fell flat on his ass, and smacked his head on the corner of the nightstand. Not only did it bust him open worse than a pro wrestler in the 80s, he also knocked my alarm clock off onto the floor and broke it." I took a breath, about to sum up my request, but Gregdre ripped a hunk of duct tape off and slapped it over my mouth.

"Does she ever shut up?" Gregdre asked Gigantor.

"Not for one second the whole way over here. I've never wished for a cargo truck so much in my life," Gigantor replied with a chuckle.

Gregdre reached out and slapped his buddy on the shoulder and turned to me. "Now I need to make something really clear here. I'm about to send everybody out of the building for the day, then you and me are going to have a little chat. If you decide, against all indications that it is possible for you to do so, that now is a good moment to play The Quiet Game and not talk to me, then I am going to hurt you. A lot. I won't enjoy it, but I sure as hell will be having a better time than you. Now you sit right there, not moving a goddamned muscle, while I send the rest of the boys home, or Ethan here is going to shoot you in the foot. Do you understand me?"

I nodded, then looked at Gigantor/Ethan and nodded at him, too. Gregdre turned and started shooing all the other people out of the building, and Ethan/Gigantor knelt beside me, set a pair of jumper cables down conspicuously in my line of sight, and started zip-tying my legs and feet to the chair. Oh. So the duct tape was just for my mouth. I guess I could have done without telling them my own personal *49 Shades of Grey* story. Only 49 shades because like so many things in my marriage to Peckerwood, it didn't finish the job.

And that's how I ended up tied to a chair in a mostly abandoned warehouse when Rhonda drove my car through the door and came to my rescue. Now if only she'd brought someone along to rescue *her*.

CHAPTER 32

To recap: I was in Orlando, tied to a chair by a mountain of a man who had expressed his willingness and perhaps even desire to torture me, while my best friend and co-conspirator in so many of the greatest mistakes of my adulthood (except picking my ex-husband; I screwed that one up before I met Rhonda, so she's off the hook for the pinnacle of my poor decision-making) drove my car through a giant roll-up door to rescue me from my torturers, who were criminals of some flavor I had yet to really understand, but since they had me tied to a metal chair with my feet in water and jumper cables heading toward parts of my body that I do *not* want alligator clamps used on (Not judging or kink-shaming. If you want to hook jumper cables up to your nipples and try to jump-start your erogenous zones in a whole new way, I'm not gonna tell you how to live your life. But it's not what *I* want out of a date, first or otherwise.), I assumed this was probably not their first criminal activity.

A lot of things happened at once when Rhonda drove through the garage door. First, Gregdre dropped the jumper cables into the bucket of water that also held my feet, providing me with more than a little bit of a tingle. In fact, the lightning running up my legs made it very hard to hold both my seat and my bladder, so I sprang to my feet, the same feet that were still tied to the legs of the chair, and promptly toppled over on my side, which hurt like a son of a bitch, but it did get my feet out of the electrified washtub and the water within.

You know how they tell you that when you fall, you shouldn't try to catch yourself with your hands, because you'll break your arms? Well, apparently, you're supposed to kinda roll sideways and let yourself fall on your shoulder and hip. Lemme tell you something, that is nowhere near as simple and easy as they make it sound, not even for a woman who has been known to carry more than a little padding on both her hips and waist. I slapped down on the concrete and it sounded like somebody tossed a ham off the garage roof to *splat* on the hood of a minivan. If that sounds oddly specific, it's because I know exactly what that sounds like, thanks to my younger daughter, her best friend, a stolen Honeybaked spiral-cut ham, and the roof of my old minivan. As she put it, it was a physics experiment. As I put it, she tossed a goddamn slab of pork off the roof of the garage onto my car, denting my hood and ruining a perfectly good, if overpriced, chunk of meat.

So that's what I sounded like when I slammed to the concrete, with an accompanying clatter of the chair I was still fastened to. I was connected to the chair at my ankles, wrists, and elbows, which basically meant that my hands were completely useless, and it was going to be very difficult to right myself. And Gregdre had his hands full as Rhonda drove my car all through the big warehouse, sideswiping pallets of TVs, laptops, iPads, and other expensive stuff that doesn't do well with a car hitting it, even a little bitty thing like a Prius. I wriggled around and humped the air enough to spin myself over onto one side and twist so I could at least see the rest of the room.

Gregdre was running after Rhonda, waving a surprisingly small pistol through the air. I expected a dude his size to have a gun that matched, but apparently Gregdre was either supremely confident in his masculinity and felt like he had nothing to prove, or...nope, that's about all I can think of now—Gregdre having a big enough dick that he didn't need another big gun. Gigantor was standing stock-still in the middle of the floor, his head whipping from side to side as he looked from Rhonda to me and back again. After a couple of cycles of this, he came over to me and righted my chair.

"You okay?" he asked.

I didn't reply, just raised an eyebrow at him. He stood there staring at me for several long seconds before he said, "Oh!" And took the duct tape off my mouth. "Sorry. You okay?"

"No, I am not okay!" I shouted. I'm not usually a shouter. A screamer, sometimes, but not a shouter. But I felt the circumstances warranted it in this case. "I am tied to a chair in a warehouse with my feet soaking wet, my best friend is driving my car around the inside of a warehouse being pursued by a mobster, and as soon as your buddy catches her, it's almost certainly back to the being electrocuted and tortured for me. So no, Gigantor, I am not okay!"

"Ethan," he said after a second of staring at the crazy lady before him.

"What?" I, the aforementioned crazy lady, asked.

"My name isn't Gigantor. It's Ethan. I don't like being made fun of about my size. It's hurtful." He looked so pitiful that for about an eighth of a second, I almost cared. Then I tried to lift my hand to pat his hand in a comforting fashion, only to be forcibly reminded that my hand was still *tied to a chair*.

"I am so sorry, Ethan," I replied, my voice dripping honey. Then it turned hard as I glared at him. "I am so sorry that I am hurting the *feelings* of one of the men who brought me here to be tortured and probably murdered! And probably raped, too, huh? That part of your plan? Tie me up, have your way with me, and then cut my throat. Toss me in the swamp for the gators. I've seen the movies. I know how y'all do things down here in the 'Glades."

"Uh...we're not in the Everglades. And, no! I'm not gonna rape you. I told you about that. And I'm not going to kill you, either. I couldn't. You remind me..." His voice trailed off, and he wouldn't meet my eyes. I knew what this was. This was some kind of reverse Stockholm syndrome, where Gigantor...Ethan, I mean, was falling in love with me after the deep psychological trauma we had suffered together. I'm not really sure exactly what it was about seeing *me* tied up and tortured that gave Ethan PTSD, but if I could work this into some kind of a sexy spy thing, I was going to go for it. Eat your heart out, Scarlett Johansen.

"You remind me of who, Ethan?" I purred, my voice low and sultry and with even more Southern accent than normal. Which is saying something. "Was she someone special to you?" I really leaned on the sibilance of the "someone special" until I almost sounded like the snake from *Jungle Book*. The cartoon one, not the weird live-action thing they did a few years back. That was just *odd*.

Ethan seemed a little uncomfortable, and I wondered if I had bad breath. I couldn't think of anything I'd eaten that would have given me halitosis, but we'd consumed a biblical amount of alcohol in the past few days, and I just woke up and hadn't had a chance to grab a mint, much less brush and floss, so there was a better than even chance that my breath could not only peel paint but could also give someone a contact high.

But no. Ethan wasn't freaked out because I had bad breath. Oh no. Nothing that flattering. "You remind me of Mrs. Perfitch, my first-grade teacher. She was smart and funny, like you. And you're about the same age as she was when I had her for school. You're about fifty, right?"

And that's where Gigantor *fucked up*. He not only guessed a Southern woman's age, but he committed the one truly unpardonable sin—he guessed too high. While I will admit that my age could certainly be described as "about" fifty, I am not yet at the half-century mark, not for a couple of years, and I did not appreciate the implication that I might be *over* fifty, and thus look older than I actually am. That, and reminding someone of their elementary school teacher is not the kind of hot, memorable, independent image that I attempt to portray. No, telling me I remind him of his first-grade teacher means that somewhere in the recesses of his mind, Ethan had a mental image of me in a Laura Ashley jumper, with my hair in a bun and bifocals.

We are going to completely ignore the fact that I did get my first pair of progressives last year and they are fantastic, because the stereotype of a grandmatronly-looking woman with a pinched expression and bifocals sliding down her pointy nose as she looks disapprovingly down upon her charges is not one of the many, *many* stereotypes about women, Southerners, and divorcees that I promulgate on the regular. So when Ethan thought I was *fifty*, a whole two years older than I actually am, I saw red.

I saw red like I hadn't seen since I found my husband's (now ex-husband's) "special" selfies that he had taken and sent to the new receptionist at his office. The same receptionist that I later found blowing my husband (now *very* much an ex-husband) in the parking garage of his building when I brought his favorite carrot cake to surprise him for his birthday. He was surprised, all right. The last time she spent a weekend with him, my daughter Kirsten told me his car still smelled like cream cheese icing.

I don't know if my rage gave me super-strength, or if I'd finally stretched the zip ties around my ankles past their point of survival, but I felt them both part as I stared at Ethan in sudden, unadulterated fury. The zip ties snapped, and I sprang to my feet, lunging right at Gigantor's face. Gigantor now, because any bit of good will he might have earned by sharing his given name with me evaporated with his overestimation of my antiquity.

Unfortunately, I was still tied to the chair by both wrists and both elbows, so when I stood up, the chair was still attached to me, forcing me to lunge bent double at the waist. So it wasn't so much of a "lunge" as it was a "lurch." Maybe even a "stumble," if we're being particularly ungenerous in our evaluation. Either way, my head slammed into Gigantor's belly, and the air rushed out of him in a loud sigh. I always thought people went "oof" or "whoosh" or something like that when they got the wind knocked out of them, but he just went "uhhh," and tumbled over backward.

My balance is not all that great at the best of times, and with both my feet asleep from being tied to a chair, this was most certainly not the best of times. I followed right after the collapsing Gigantor, landing atop him in a tangled heap of man, woman, and chair. Unfortunately for Ethan, he managed to take one big step back before he fell. I did not, and I'm considerably shorter than Ethan, so when I fell on top of him, my forehead impacted him in an altogether unintended, but extremely debilitating, place.

Yeah, I tripped over my own two feet, and when I fell down, I head butted poor Gigantor right in the nuts.

CHAPTER 33

If there was a bright side to landing with my forehead in the groin of an organized crime torturer/kidnapper/goon, it's that the shock of landing put the last bit of strain on the rest of my zip ties that the poor things could handle, and they snapped like tiny little cables trying to hold up a suspension bridge in the middle of a superhero fight. Or like zip ties trying to hold a tomato plant up when it gets weighed down with more 'maters than any sane family could consume in a month, regardless of the fact that you know damn well you're going to have the same amount of fruit popping up on every one of six plants within a week and every person you are related to, are friendly with, and realistically everyone who comes within a mile of your house for the next month is going home with a Walmart bag full of juicy red deliciousness.

Damn, now I want a tomato sandwich. Nothing better on a hot summer day than a freshly sliced tomato, with a little bit of salt and pepper on it, plopped onto two pieces of white bread slathered in mayonnaise (The only acceptable time to eat mayo is on a 'mater sandwich, and then only between Memorial Day and Labor Day. Think of mayonnaise as the white shoes of condiments.) and cut diagonally across and dripping down your chin with every bite.

Hmmm…let's not focus on things dripping down my chin while I've got my face buried in the crotch of a man who kidnapped me, tied me to a chair, and turned a torturer loose on me. At least not if he's not cute. And

Gigantor wasn't my type. Maybe if he had a mustache. Or no eyebrows. If this trip had taught me anything, and it's highly unlikely that it did, it's that I am pretty flexible on what styles and types of facial hair I can tolerate on a man.

But I felt Ethan stir beneath my skull, rolling over to one side and shoving both hands down into his crotch. As Ethan lay there writing in pain and swearing in a couple of languages I had no familiarity with, I pushed myself up from the concrete and looked toward the squeal of tires to see if Rhonda was still driving my car around inside the warehouse.

Spoiler—she was. I saw her chase Gregdre all the way to one end of the warehouse with my car, then spin that little electric hot rod around on a dime and rush back to the other end, cutting Gregdre off before he could make his exit through the destroyed roll-up door Rhonda drove through. She seemed to have things pretty well under control, until she made one more lap down and back, only this time to find Tony Soprano stepping through the hole where the door used to be with a pistol in his hand.

Several things happened in quick succession, each one making our situation more dire than the last. First, I saw Rhonda's eyes go wide as Tony raised the gun in her direction. Then Gregdre dove to the side behind a pallet of TVs, taking himself out of both the line of fire and the game of car-and-mouse they'd been playing. Finally, and perhaps most disastrous, although not for me, per se, Rhonda and Tony Soprano both learned the horrible secret of my yearly safety inspection.

You see, brakes are expensive. They're important, but really expensive. And if you are really familiar with how a car behaves, and you generally drive like you're a hundred and ten years old, you can put off getting the brakes completely redone in a car for a long time. I've had new pads put on half a dozen times, had the rotors turned two or three times, and generally told my mechanic that "I'll just baby her" until I can afford to get the brakes totally redone. And it works for me, because I know how much space I need to give myself before I stop, and I slow down way ahead of stops and turns, and all the little tips and tricks to keep from dying in a car with crappy brakes. The other thing that works for me is that one of the mechanics at the shop down the street from my house used to date my oldest daughter and is always trying to get me to give him her new number, so he does my "inspection" each year without ever looking at any of the safety equipment on my car. Like...the brakes.

All those tips and tricks Rhonda knew absolutely nothing about, and she slammed on the brakes while my little car rushed toward Tony Soprano with the deafening…well, with pretty much silence, since it's an electric car.

Tony, for his part, was pretty cool as his death rushed at him with the squeal of abused brakes and the whisper of an electric motor. He raised his pistol, leveled it at the windshield of the oncoming car, and fired three shots at Rhonda's face. Well, I kinda assume he aimed at her face. I was all the way across the room and couldn't see *what* he was aiming at, but if he was trying to shoot out the radiator, he was in for a bad time. I'm pretty sure that will only stop a car in a few feet if it's in a movie. And if it has better brakes than mine.

I saw a bullet spiderweb the windshield, then saw another ricochet off the roof, then Tony learned in the hardest way possible that once Rhonda locks in a course of action, or a course of navigation, that nothing will deter her. Not gangsters, not bullets, and certainly not something as inconsequential as running over a gangster who is shooting at you. She stayed on the brakes, of course. She wasn't trying to *murder* anyone. But those brakes weren't stopping that car in that amount of space, not after getting heated up on several laps around the warehouse chasing Gregdre.

Rhonda did turn the wheel hard to the side, so she didn't run Tony completely over. She did slam the right rear fender of my car into the gangster with a sickening *crunch* and a Jersey-accented scream from Tony. He went down in a heap, his gun went flying across the room, and my car finally slid to a halt a few feet from where the boss gangster lay clutching his left knee and screaming.

I looked at Gigantor, who was still clutching his yams and whimpering. I couldn't see Gregdre where he hid behind the stolen merchandise, and Tony was out of the fight. So I walked over to the writhing boss, looked down at him, and held out a hand, palm up.

"You gonna help me up?" he groaned. "I think my leg's broke."

"I don't give a shit," I said, my voice hard. This had started off as a lark, but after getting arrested, renditioned, kidnapped, and (almost) tortured, some of the gild had rubbed off this particular lily. I waggled my hand at Tony. "You owe me money. I came a long way to get it, and I'm not leaving without it. Now you've seen what my partner and I are capable of, do you really want to experience it again?" I was channeling my inner Liam Neeson in *Taken*, but might have come across a little more Bea Arthur in *Golden Girls*. Whatever, she was terrifying, too.

"I don't know you, bitch. I don't owe you—ow!" That last bit was because I kicked him in his hurt knee. The way his lower leg moved in a different direction than the upper made me think he might be right, that his leg might be broken. Oh well.

"You did not just call me a bitch," I said, glaring at him. "I will accept a lot of things. I am a redneck, I am a bit of a cougar, I've even been referred to as a MILF without being offended or bothered by it. But *bitch*? No, sir. I did not drive five hundred miles from North Carolina, deal with police in two states, the FBI, and now you assholes, just to have some carpetbagging Yankee greaseball call me a bitch because I want what was taken from me. Now, you *will* give me my money, and you *will* do it with respect, or I *will* tell Rhonda that since the windshield's already busted, she might as well go full demolition derby on your ass. I don't know what kind of damage a Prius can do to the human body, but I'm going to bet it's significant. So why don't you save me the time, Rhonda the therapist bills, and yourself a world of hurt, and hand over the twenty-six dollars you and your idiot friends stole from me."

Tony stopped rolling around moaning long enough to stare at me in what was either honest confusion or the best feigned confusion I've ever seen, and I have teenaged daughters. I have seen some spectacular feigned ignorance in my day. Hell, I see it on Rhonda's face every time I ask her what happened to all my liquor.

"What the actual fuck are you talking about?" Tony asked.

"You and your goon squad here ordered ChowSprint on my account, had the most whiteboy subs I've ever seen in my life delivered, with extra mayo just in case there weren't enough boring, tasteless stereotypes involved, and stole twenty-six dollars from me. I'm here to get it back."

Now Tony wasn't even holding his leg. He was just laying flat on his back staring up at me in complete shock. "All of this is over twenty bucks?"

"Twenty-six," I replied. "Thirty with tip. By the way, your boys should tip better. Delivery drivers working during a pandemic have it hard enough, no need to make them starve for your hoagies."

"You drove all the way down here from...where?"

"North Carolina."

"You drove all the way to Orlando from North Carolina, tracked us down, ordered more subs to lure Ethan into picking them up and leading you back to our house—that was you that sent the subs this afternoon, right?"

I just nodded. May as well let him run with his monologue. He had everything pretty well figured out. I was content to let him talk, as long as it got me my money.

"Then you let us think you knew something about our operation, so we brought you here, where your crazy friend busted down my door, hit me with a car, and almost killed me. For twenty dollars?"

"Twenty-*six*," I repeated. After all this, he was not going to short me on my six bucks. I was willing to haunt Tony's life like that little kid from *Better off Dead* if that's what it took.

"Twenty-six," Tony said. "But that's it? You aren't working for the cops, or the Mexicans, or the Russians, or the bikers, or the Bloods?"

"I just came here for my twenty-six dollars, and to let you know that somebody's on to you and you need to stop whatever you're doing, because if a housewife from North Carolina can hunt you down, then the cops are probably watching you right now. Which reminds me..." I looked around, then leaned out the busted roll-up door looking for black SUVs. "I'm a little surprised they aren't here yet. This afternoon, they didn't even let me get to your front door before they whisked me away in a black Suburban."

"Well, that's gonna end up being too bad for you, sweetheart," Tony said, hauling himself up to one leg. "Because if the cops ain't here, that means we can just get the door put back up as soon as we take care of the two of you. Barry! Get out here and slap this bitch around until she tells us everybody she told about us, then shoot her and her friend and haul the bodies out into the swamp. I gotta get Ethan to drive me to the hospital."

"I told you not to call me a bitch, fatass," I said, stepping closer to Tony.

"What are you gonna do about it, *bitch*?"

"Not much," I said. "Just this." Then I kicked him in the shin. The broken one. He fell back onto the concrete and resuming his swearing and writhing. I walked over to the passenger door of my car and opened it. "Hey sweetie," I said to Rhonda. "Nice driving."

Rhonda was behind the wheel hyperventilating a little. "He shot at me," she finally managed to get out.

"Did he hit you?" I asked.

"No."

"Okay, then. You wanna drive home, or should I?" I'm not usually quite this blasé about someone shooting at my best friend. Well, I assume I'm not. This is the first time I've ever actually known about anyone shooting at Rhonda, and certainly the first time it had ever happened in my presence, so while I assume I wouldn't be blasé about it, I don't really have any direct experience.

"I think you might need a new windshield," Rhonda said, pointing to the starred mess in front of her face. If you just listened to the sound of her voice, you might assume that Rhonda was also very blasé, but since I could see the way her eyes darted from side to side and hear that she was on the very jagged edge of hyperventilating, I was pretty sure she was in shock, not actually calm.

But she was right about the windshield. There may have only been one small actual bullet hole, but the safety glass did its job and just cracked the whole damn thing all to shit. No way I could drive my car until it got fixed. "Okay," I said. "Hand me your cell phone. I'll call AAA and get them to tow us to someplace that can replace the glass. Do you have any cash?"

She laughed, a sharp little barking thing. "Ask your gangster friends where they keep their money."

"Ooh! Good point." I went back to Tony. "Give me your money," I said.

"Screw you—" He cut off whatever else he was about to say when I raised my foot over his broken leg. I was starting to get the hang of this whole "being the heavy" thing. Tony handed me his wallet. I peeked inside, saw several lovely portraits of Benjamin Franklin, my favorite dead president (yes, I know he wasn't a president, but the saying isn't "dead founding fathers," it's "dead presidents"), and headed back to the car.

"Okay, got some cash. Gimme your phone," I said to Rhonda.

"I'm afraid I can't do that," she replied.

"Why not?"

She just pointed out the driver's side window. I looked up over the top of the car and saw Gregdre standing there, gun in his hand. He didn't have the gun pointed at Rhonda, exactly, but this definitely felt like one of those situations where just its presence told me everything I needed to know about how this was going to go.

"Is that how it's going to be, Gregdre?" I asked. "I thought we had a bond developing. I thought our connection was real, something that could last beyond this initial meeting and might develop into a solid friendship eventually."

Gregdre's face softened, and the gun's barrel drifted further away from Rhonda's head. "Really?"

Rhonda let out a snort, and Gregdre's attention swung back to her just

189

in time for the driver's door to swing open and slam into his knees. Gregdre staggered back, and I leapt forward, sliding across the hood of the Prius and swinging my feet around mid-slide to slam into his chest and knock the goon to the ground.

I mean, that's what happened in the movie in my head. In the movie I actually had to live through, I thumped my ass onto the hood of the car, promptly got stuck trying to slide across because my ass was all sweaty from being tied to a metal folding chair and threatened with torture, then barely managed to hop off and try to tackle Gregdre, who took one step to the left and watched as I crashed to the ground beside him.

Maybe I didn't have the whole "being the heavy" thing down as well as I'd hoped.

CHAPTER 34

S o there I was, lying face down on the cold concrete floor of a gangsters' warehouse in Orlando, Florida, with one of said gangsters staring down at me and stifling his giggles at the sight of my middle-aged ass sprawled on the floor after trying to tackle him. He was at least rubbing one knee, though, so Rhonda smacking him in the knee with the car door had *some* effect.

"Get out of the car," Gregdre said to Rhonda. He looked down at me. "Get up."

"Wanna give a girl a hand?" I said. "My feet are still a little asleep from y'all tying me up."

As goons go, Gregdre was certainly among the most chivalrous I'd ever met. Since I'd only ever met three men who I think could rightly be called "goons," and all of them were in the building with me at the moment, my sample size was pretty small, but I felt confident in my assessment of Gregdre as the kinder, gentler of the goons I knew. So it didn't surprise me at all when he took his gun off Rhonda and reached down to give me a hand up.

I am not nearly as chivalrous or kind as Gregdre, and being the kind, chivalrous sort, he apparently expected everyone to operate with a certain code of honor, which did not seem to include an expectation of reaching down to help some up off the ground only to have that person sink her teeth deep into your wrist while grabbing a handful of your testicles and latching on like her very life depended on it. Which, given the fact that even a chivalrous criminal probably has his limits, and those limits are typically reached well before someone grabs said criminal by the balls and squeezes like she's making fresh OJ, it probably did.

"OOOOOOOWWWWWW!" Gregdre howled, trying to simultaneously shove my head off his wrist and step backward to free himself from the death grip I had on his sack. Unfortunately for Gregdre, this caused me to lose my balance and tip forward, leaving all my body weight supported by my teeth and his balls. He dragged me back for a few steps before pain exploded on the side of my face and I gasped, letting go of the wrist in my mouth.

Gregdre remembered that he had a gun in his other hand and smacked me in the cheek with it, knocking me loose from his left arm. But that slung me sideways, and as I twisted around, trying to keep my face out of the line of his handgun, I also torqued even harder on his testicles, dragging Gregdre to the ground with me. I let go of his balls to scramble up his toppled redwood of a body like a spider monkey, trying like hell to get hold of the gun before he used it for its intended purpose and put a couple of brand-new holes in me.

Gregdre struggled, but he was at a serious disadvantage. He was bigger, stronger, and younger, as well as better trained, more experienced, and more violent in general. But all of those things were no match for my years of chasing two active girls around our house and yard, jumping on and off of every piece of lawn furniture in games of "hot lava," fending off multiple attackers in tickle fights, and juggling the multiple simultaneous activities required to tend and clothe a pair of teenagers. I learned years ago the kind of single-minded doggedness that is required to thread the maelstrom of a mall Christmas Village with one child who loves Santa and another that is terrified of the giant in red velvet without losing sight of my wandering husband and his wandering eyes.

He didn't have a chance. As soon as I let go of his nuts, I immediately jumped up his body and pressed my left elbow into his throat. I slammed my right knee into his crotch, because once you find a chink in the armor, you exploit it. I mean, really, if you're a guy, and you're a criminal, doesn't it stand to reason that getting in fights is part of your normal routine? And if that's the case, why wouldn't you wear a cup as part of your everyday routine? Are they that uncomfortable? I mean, we were in Florida of all godforsaken places, and it was so hot that I was really tempted to strip down and wrestle Gregdre in my underwear, more for temperature management than any fun reasons to be in my underwear, but still, if I had nuts, I'd want to protect them.

Gregdre hadn't thought of that. Maybe it was part of the Bad Guy Code that you don't hit other Bad Guys in the balls. But since I'm not a guy of any sort, and not typically a Bad Girl, I wasn't briefed on the societal norms for villains.

So I planted a knee solidly in Gregdre's balls, and Rhonda started the car up again, and as I stood up to kick Gregdre's gun away from him, I heard a sound that was only familiar because of the number of times I've rewatched every season on *Justified*—a cocking pistol.

Oh, come on, tell me you don't want to be the meat in a Walter Coggins/Timothy Olyphant sandwich and I will call you a liar right here in front of God and everybody. Anyway, my lust for drawling actors notwithstanding, I turned to see Tony Soprano leaning up against a pallet of what looked like laptop boxes and holding a gun. This one looked smaller than the one he'd shot at Rhonda with so I assumed it was his backup piece. Or that it was the same gun, it hadn't slid as far away from him as I thought, and I had no concept of what size really was in all the excitement. I mean, I'd spent the first year of our marriage thinking Peckerwood was well-endowed. Then I went to a bachelor party for this girl from work, and this fella came out dancing in nothing but a sequined thong and a fuzzy bear head, and I learned that his endowment was more "well, I reckon that's all there is" as opposed to actually being "well-endowed."

Either way, Tony had a gun, and it was pointing right at my face. He was several yards away, but I wasn't going to risk my life on him not being able to hit the broad side of a barn. I raised my hands and saw out of the corner of my eye Rhonda do the same thing.

"Now you," he said, looking at Rhonda. "Get out of the car."

She turned to slide out from behind the wheel, then turned back in as the car started to roll forward. She put the car in park, then got out. I thought that would have been a perfect opportunity for her to hit the gas and try to run him over again, but I wasn't the one who'd already been shot at through the windshield once today, so I was trying not to judge. Besides, given how well my attempts at Jason Bourne-ing my way out of this mess had gone, it was starting to look like there was a lot to be said for a well-thought-out surrender.

Tony waved her over to stand next to me, then he took one step in our direction before remembering that he probably had a broken leg and decided to lean on the pallet instead. "Okay," Tony said. "Let me get this straight. You think my boys hacked your credit card and used it to buy lunch. So you drove to Florida from North Carolina to hunt down a band of evil lunch thieves and get your twenty dollars back."

"Twenty-six dollars," I corrected. "But basically, yes."

"And since that time you've destroyed my warehouse, exposed my operation to the police, brought the FBI's attention down on me and my boys, and stolen my wallet. Is that basically it?"

"I mean, I don't want your wallet," I said, tossing it back to him. "I just needed some cash to pay the tow truck because you shot out my windshield." I folded up the cash I'd taken and stuffed it into my bra. It was going to get sweaty, but I've never had a tow truck driver, mechanic, pizza boy, valet, or any other male object to sweaty money if it's boob sweat. I figure they'd think differently if I pulled it out of the back of my pants, or my sock, but maybe not. I'm not gonna rain on anybody's kink parade.

Tony caught the wallet in midair and slipped it into his pocket. "Thanks. I'll get the cash back later."

"And how do you plan to do that?" I asked, giving him my very best "where do you think you're going wearing that skirt, young lady" look.

Tony looked confused. Maybe his mother had never been very judgmental about his wardrobe choices, or maybe the looks just mean different things when you're raising boys, but he seemed to be not the least bit intimidated by my arched eyebrow. "I'm going to take it off your body after I shoot you and before the boys dump your bodies in the swamp. That's how."

"Oh." I didn't have a really good response to that. I've never had anyone tell me that they're planning to kill me before, so I wasn't sure what the expected response was. I didn't have a gun of my own, so I couldn't threaten him back. I was pretty sure he saw enough of my "fight" with Gregdre that he wouldn't be intimidated anyway. "Well," I said, wracking my brain for a reason he shouldn't kill us. "How about you don't do that?"

"Don't do what? Don't take my money off your dead body? Why do you care?"

"No, let's back up a little further and skip the part where you shoot me."

"Us. Don't shoot *us*," Rhonda chimed in.

I nodded. "Us. Let's skip the part where you shoot either of us."

"And why exactly would I *not* shoot you both?" Tony asked.

"Probably because murder is the kind of thing you try not to do with a bunch of witnesses," I said, pointing over his shoulder.

Now, usually, in the movies at least, the bad guy says something snarky like "you expect me to believe that?" and refuses to turn around, leaving the good guys' rescuers to step up and clobber him in the back of the head. But Tony continued to defy expectations and turned to look where I was pointing.

"Well, shit," he said upon seeing Agent Kaplan and a dozen men in tactical gear with assault rifles lined up outside the gaping hole that used to have a door in it. Tony set his pistol down on top of the pallet of laptops and slowly sank to his knees with his hands on his head, trying hard not to jostle his broken leg any more than he had to.

Kaplan led the cavalry in through the destroyed door, and his men fanned out just like they were in a movie, or a video game, covering all the bad guys and sweeping the warehouse to make sure it was clear. They even really yelled "Clear!" every once in a while, like the cops on TV. Then he walked over to us, holstering his gun.

"I'm not sure if I should arrest you, shoot you, or thank you," he said, looking from Rhonda to me and back again.

"How did you find us?" I asked.

"I didn't. I followed her," Kaplan said, pointing at Rhonda. "She wasn't exactly inconspicuous."

I turned to my bestie. "And how did you find me?" I asked.

"I tracked you. Duh."

"When did you put a tracker on me?"

"Remember last Christmas, when we went to the ice-skating thing down in Charlotte, and you put your phone in my Find My Phone app so if we got separated, we could find each other? And I told you it was dumb because why wouldn't we just call one another?"

"Yeah, I remember."

"Well, it wasn't all that dumb, I guess."

"I guess not." Wow. Saved by the cell instead of the bell. There was no way I was gonna tell my daughters about that part. The last thing I needed was another reason for them to tell me I needed to be more tech-savvy.

I turned to Agent Kaplan. "So if you're not going to shoot us or arrest us, can we go? I really need to pee, and I do not trust the cleanliness of a gangster's warehouse bathroom."

EPILOGUE

I ended up peeing in the gangster's warehouse anyway, because it took almost an hour for AAA to get there to fix my windshield. I thought about complaining, but decided that since the poor guy did come into a huge crime scene and replace the glass for less money than Tony had in his wallet, I let it go.

We answered a lot of questions, almost none of them to Agent Kaplan's satisfaction, and after several hours of "interviews," he sent us on our way with a stern warning to leave the apprehension of criminals to the people who are paid to apprehend criminals. I didn't remind him that I had tried every step of the way to get the authorities to handle this affront to my personal security, but they chose not to. I just slid in behind the wheel of my Prius, looked at the Florida sky through my brand-new windshield, and pointed the nose of my little car north.

"Well," I said to Rhonda as we pulled out of the industrial park where Tony and his goons had their warehouse. "I'd say that was a pretty successful trip. We got the bad guys, got my twenty-six dollars back, with a little interest, and even got a new windshield. What more could we have asked for?"

"I reckon if I'd been doing the asking, I would have requested that I be the one to get laid on this trip," Rhonda said. "All that driving around and staring death in the eye has got me hornier than a two-dicked tomcat."

I just grinned at her. "I already called in sick to work for tomorrow, and Peckerwood is going to take the girls to school. We can be in Charleston by eight tonight, and you can have your legs wrapped around a thousand pounds of Hornicus Prime by eight-thirty. What do you say, bestie?"

Rhonda looked at me with a grin that made the September sun look dim by comparison. "I say giddy up, cowgirl. Let's ride!"

So we did.

THE END...?

AUTHOR'S NOTE

So this is a book based on true events.

Loosely.

Like, those pants you wore right before you went in for gastric bypass surgery a couple years ago and now they're six sizes too big and your belt wraps around your waist twice to hold them up and you're bemoaning the fact that suspenders ever went out of style. That kind of loosely.

At the very beginning of the pandemic, my wife's Walmart.com account was hacked, and her debit card number was stolen. We know it was that site because we never used her debit card to buy anything else online. We know it wasn't stolen from a skimmer or unscrupulous cashier writing down the number, because my wife hadn't left the house in months before this (she was ahead of the curve on quarantining). And I did call Walmart corporate to report the breach in their security, and Wells Fargo to report the card number stolen, and the Charlotte-Mecklenburg Police Department, and the Orlando Police Department, and the Cybercrimes Division of the Federal Bureau of Investigation.

Leave me alone. It was the beginning of quarantine and I had some time on my hands while I tried to stop doom scrolling on social media.

Needless to say none of the thought the affront to my fiscal security was nearly the heinous offense that I did. I think the general consensus was "It was less than thirty dollars, get over it."

I didn't. I decided that I was going to get my twenty-six dollars and change back the old-fashioned way - by writing a book about the whole affair and selling at least enough copies of it to recoup my losses. That is the book you just finished. Or the book that you skipped the text of to read the Author's Note which is a little odd, but you do you, boo-boo.

This book was a lot of fun to write, and I hope you had fun reading it. I don't know if there will be more of Rhonda and Lexi, but I do have ideas, so if you want more, please be sure to tell all your friends, leave a review, and buy a thousand copies to send to everyone you know.

Okay, you don't really have to do that last bit, but I won't complain if you do. In the meantime, have a margarita of Rhonda!

JGH
2/20/23

ABOUT THE AUTHOR

John G. Hartness is a teller of tales, a righter of wrong, defender of ladies' virtues, and some people call him Maurice, for he speaks of the pompatus of love. He is also the award-winning author of the urban fantasy series *The Black Knight Chronicles*, the Bubba the Monster Hunter comedic horror series, the Quincy Harker, Demon Hunter dark fantasy series, and many other projects. He is also a cast member of the role-playing podcast *Authors & Dragons*, where a group of comedy, fantasy, and horror writers play *Dungeons & Dragons*. Very poorly.

In 2016, John teamed up with several other publishing industry professionals to create Falstaff Books, a small press dedicated to publishing the best of genre fiction's "misfit toys." Falstaff Books has since published over 250 titles with authors ranging from first-timers to NY Times bestsellers, with no signs of slowing down any time soon.

In his copious free time John enjoys long walks on the beach, rescuing kittens from trees and playing *Magic: the Gathering*. John's pronouns are he/him.

Social Media & Contact –
Find John or follow him here –
www.falstaffbooks.com
www.johnhartness.com
https://www.amazon.com/John-G-Hartness/e/B0043EUZHC
www.authorsanddragons.com
www.facebook.com/johnghartness
https://www.youtube.com/channel/UC56p-bUX1sveyLtc5n96d0Q
@johnhartness on Twitter
@falstaffbooks on Twitter
https://www.facebook.com/groups/johnhartnessbooks/

https://www.facebook.com/FalstaffRises/
https://www.facebook.com/authorsanddragons/
https://www.facebook.com/groups/falstaffmisfits/

STAY IN TOUCH!

If you enjoyed this book, please leave a review on Amazon, Goodreads, or wherever you like.

If you'd like to hear more about or from the author, please join my mailing list at https://www.subscribepage.com/g8d0a9.

You can get some free short stories just for signing up, and whenever a book gets 50 reviews, the author gets a unicorn. I need another unicorn. The ones I have are getting lonely. So please leave a review and get me another unicorn!

ALSO BY JOHN G. HARTNESS

THE BLACK KNIGHT CHRONICLES
The Black Knight Chronicles - Omnibus Edition

The Black Knight Chronicles Continues - Omnibus #2

All Knight Long - Black Knight Chronicles #7

BUBBA THE MONSTER HUNTER
Scattered, Smothered, & Chunked - Bubba the Monster Hunter Season One

Grits, Guns, & Glory - Bubba Season Two

Wine, Women, & Song - Bubba Season Three

Monsters, Magic, & Mayhem - Bubba Season Four

Born to Be Wild

Swamp Music

Houses of the Holy

Shinepunk: A Beauregard the Monster Hunter Collection

QUINCY HARKER, DEMON HUNTER
Year One: A Quincy Harker, Demon Hunter Collection

The Cambion Cycle - Quincy Harker, Year Two

Damnation - Quincy Harker Year Three

Salvation - Quincy Harker Year Four

Carl Perkins' Cadillac - A Quincy Harker, Demon Hunter Novel

Inflection Point

Conspiracy Theory

Histories: A Quincy Harker, Demon Hunter Collection

SHINGLES
Zombies Ate My Homework: Shingles Book 5

Slow Ride: Shingles Book 12

Carnival of Psychos: Shingles Book 19

Jingle My Balls: Shingles Book 24

Snatched: Grandma Annie and the Cooter of Doom: Shingles Book 29

OTHER WORK

The True Confessions of Fandingo the Fantastical (with EM Kaplan)

Queen of Kats

Fireheart

Amazing Grace: A Dead Old Ladies Detective Agency Mystery

From the Stone

The Chosen

Hazard Pay and Other Tales

FRIENDS OF FALSTAFF

Thank You to All our Falstaff Books Patrons, who get extra digital content each month! To be featured here and see what other great rewards we offer, go to www.patreon.com/falstaffbooks.

PATRONS

Dino Hicks
John Hooks
John Kilgallon
Larissa Lichty
Travis & Casey Schilling
Staci-Leigh Santore
Sheryl R. Hayes
Scott Norris
Samuel Montgomery-Blinn
Junkle

www.ingramcontent.com/pod-product-compliance
Lightning Source LLC
Chambersburg PA
CBHW030426120726
47903CB00003B/823